Popular
CLONE

Popular
CLONE

THE CLONE CHRONICLES #1

M.E. CASTLE

EGMONT
USA
New York

EGMONT

We bring stories to life

First published by Egmont USA, 2012
This paperback edition published by Egmont USA, 2013
443 Park Avenue South, Suite 806
New York, NY 10016

Copyright © Paper Lantern Lit, 2012

 paper lantern lit

5 7 9 8 6 4

www.egmontusa.com · www.theclonechronicles.com

THE LIBRARY OF CONGRESS HAS CATALOGED THE HARDCOVER EDITION AS FOLLOWS:

Castle, M. E.
Popular clone / M.E. Castle.
p. cm.
Summary: Twelve-year-old Fisher Bas, a science-loving bully magnet,
clones himself, only to discover that his double is infinitely cooler than himself.
ISBN 978-1-60684-232-4 (hardcover) -- ISBN 978-1-60684-301-7 (ebook)
[1. Cloning--Fiction. 2. Self-confidence--Fiction. 3. Bullies--Fiction.
4. Middle schools--Fiction. 5. Schools--Fiction.] I. Title.
PZ7.C2687337Po 2012
[Fic]--dc23
2011024410

Paperback ISBN 978-1-60684-414-4

Printed in the United States of America

For my father,
Who, right up to his final days,
Spent most of his time in his chair with a book.

≋ CHAPTER 1 ≋

For every action, there is an equal and opposite reaction. For every geek, freak, or nerd, there are three massive and ruthless meatheads. Ergo: the universe does not like geeks.
—Fisher Bas, Scientific Principles and Observations of the Natural World (unpublished)

Thwack, thwack, thwack, thwack. Fisher Bas dashed down the main hall of Wompalog Middle School, wishing he hadn't worn flip-flops. Walls of puke-green lockers blurred past him.

The predators were closing in, quickly. Brody, Willard, and Leroy. The Vikings. Fisher's archenemies.

Fisher knew he shouldn't have gone to the principal after the Vikings had put a live, very unhappy squirrel in his backpack just before biology lab. They didn't take kindly to being snitched on, and they definitely didn't take kindly to detention, and now Fisher was going to pay the price.

Sweat beaded on his forehead as Fisher analyzed possible escape routes. The Vikings were getting closer. The C wing bathroom was out. He had a far-too intimate relationship with the interior of the toilet bowls. The library was close, but usually when he tried that option they'd find him and play Study Hall, which involved hitting Fisher over the head with each of his textbooks.

The cafeteria contained its own terrors. Last time Fisher had hidden behind one of the hot-food stations, he'd seen a lunch lady flick her boogers into the sloppy joe meat.

Having no other choice, Fisher bolted along his original course like a spooked antelope. He dodged a fellow student walking down the hall in the costume of their school mascot, the Furious Badger.

"Nice speed!" the badger-costume-clad kid called after him, giving him a furry thumbs-up.

Fisher had no time to respond. He did some quick calculations in his head. *Assuming a straight-line course with minimal trajectory variance, with V_F = the Velocity of Fisher, and H being the Length of the Hallway, taking into account the Traffic Density of students as T, at current levels, T should provide a theoretical limit of $.73V_F$ until the plausible minimum value of T is reached in approximately . . .*

"Watch it, dude!" he heard, but it was too late—he was already careening off Trevor Weiss, a glasses-wearing neat freak from his debate class. The soup in Trevor's open thermos splattered across Fisher's white shirt, and Trevor's glasses fell straight into the thermos.

"Sorry, sorry!" Fisher half mumbled, half shouted as Trevor blindly tried to fish his glasses out of the soup.

Fisher swiped a finger across his shirt. Potato leek. Not bad, actually.

"Aw, come on, Fisher!" Trevor yelled after him. "That was my lunch, you—*ow*!" Brody, leading the Vikings, elbowed Trevor out of the way. Trevor crashed back into his locker, and what was left of the soup spilled all over his books.

"You can't run from us, Fisher!" bellowed Brody, gaining on him.

The books in Fisher's backpack shook up and down along with him, its straps digging into his shoulders with every step. The Vikings' voices and the sound of their echoing laughter were getting louder by now; the teachers were in their classrooms, getting ready for the period to start.

Nobody was going to help him.

Fisher bolted past the academic standings board, and the names all blurred together. If he'd paused to look, he would have spotted FISHER BAS, in proud, bold letters, at the top of the math and science rankings. He fell squarely into the middle of the group when it came to English, history, and language, though.

On the attendance awards board, his name was dead last.

Just as the Vikings rounded the corner behind him, the door to the teachers' lounge opened and out walked Mrs. Sneed, the vice principal. Her dark eyes swept the hall, and the Vikings skidded to a halt when they saw her.

3

"Something the matter, boys?" she asked. "What's the hurry?"

"Just eager to learn, ma'am!" said Brody, pasting an enormous smile on his face.

"G-Got to make sure we have time to study and review," said Willard, clasping his hands behind his back.

"We really value our altercation," Leroy said proudly.

"*Education*," muttered Brody.

Fisher used the distraction to slip into an empty classroom, slamming the door shut. He leaned back against the door, his breathing quick and shallow.

"Hey, Fisher! You're early today." Mr. Granger popped up suddenly from behind his desk, giving Fisher a shock. Fisher's favorite biology teacher was somewhere around forty-five, though his smallness often made him seem younger. He had narrow shoulders and tiny eyes, which were obscured by the wide, thick glasses that were constantly slipping off his nose. He didn't look like he weighed much over a hundred and ten pounds. He could probably be knocked over by a not-too-strong wind (maybe even the kind Gassy Greg was known for). Fisher and Mr. Granger regularly lunched together in his classroom.

"Vikings," Fisher panted. And then, suddenly, he heard them: their low, grunting voices were just on the other side of the door. Fisher made a beeline for the lab storage cabinet, shutting himself into it seconds before the classroom door was shoved wide open.

The acrid scents of a dozen bottled chemicals seeped into Fisher's nostrils—he hoped they'd disguise the smell of the potato leek soup still coating his clothes. Squeezed into the tiny cabinet, his breathing sounded like a revving engine. His back and arms started to ache after half a minute. He tried to force every muscle in his body to stand still, which just made him twitchier. Through a narrow slit between the cabinet doors, he saw the three very large, very ugly boys saunter in.

Brody Minas, whose forward-jutting forehead hooded his eyes like the headlights on a muscle car, was the leader. Willard Mason and Leroy Loring flanked him on either side. They were in that lumpy, awkward, in-between stage of growing up: large and powerful but still unbalanced in their newly big bodies, like toddlers who have just learned they could stand.

Fisher balled up his fists. He wished he could make the Vikings vanish into a cloud of disassociated molecules. He *had* done some work in his home lab on the Viking-atomizer project, but the particle stream hadn't been up to calibration.

The Vikings advanced on Mr. Granger, who backed away nervously. Brody was nearly as tall as Mr. Granger, and Willard was at least twice as heavy.

"Can . . . Can I help you boys with something?" Mr.

Granger asked, smiling halfheartedly while fidgeting with his clipboard.

"Oh, we were just lookin' for a good friend of ours, Missster Granger," said Brody, his smirk growing as he picked up a glass flask from one of the lab stations and tossed it at Willard, who caught it, but just barely. "You know Fisher, don't you?"

"I, uh." Granger looked back and forth between the flask and Brody. "Yes, Fisher is a student of mine. I'm afraid I haven't seen him all day."

Brody crossed his bulky arms. "Are you sure about that? 'Cause we're pretty sure we saw him slip into this room a second ago, didn't we, Willy?"

Willard put the flask back on the desk. "Yep, yep, Brody! That's t-true!" Willard followed with a mild hiccup. He always seemed to have the hiccups. Fisher guessed it was because Willard was secretly scared of Brody, too. That or he simply drank too much orange soda.

Fisher clamped his hand over his nose and mouth, suffocating a sneeze before it had a chance to come out.

Brody turned his attention back to Mr. Granger, who was attempting to stack some graded papers into a neat pile and mind his own business. "Mr. Granger, maybe with those big glasses of yours, you just didn't spot him. Maybe we should have a look around ourselves, just to make sure. We wouldn't want to miss our *good friend* Fisher." The way he said "good friend" turned Fisher's neck hairs into spikes.

The three boys split off and began looking under desks.

"He's *not here*, boys, I told you," said Granger, putting as much authority as he had into his voice. "Now, now, the period's already started. You don't want to be late for lunch. You should go and get something to eat before your next class." He turned nervously away from them, moving papers around his desk with no real purpose. Fisher tried to bunch himself up even smaller, and his left thigh pushed against his wristwatch.

"You look splendid today!" erupted from its tiny speakers. He had built-in a compliment generator to his watch, for when he talked to girls. For *if* he talked to them. Fisher inhaled sharply and held his breath.

"Did you say something?" asked a confused Brody. Mr. Granger, who had gone stiff as a scarecrow, cleared his throat.

"I, er, I said you boys look . . . splendid." He tried to tone his voice to match the watch, with little success. "Been, um, striking the weights? Pumping the, uh, gym? Hauling iron?" With each attempt to remember a workout-related expression he sounded more ridiculous, so he finally stopped trying and smiled weakly. Brody and Willard exchanged suspicious looks. Then they continued with their search.

"Well, well, well, what have we heeeere?" said Brody, coming across the glass tank where Mr. Granger kept Einstein and Heisenberg, his white mice. The tank was much bigger than necessary for the tiny animals. All that extra space was taken up by elaborate playthings Fisher had helped design. There was a little mouse washer, a tunnel that sprayed warm water followed by a segment that blew hot air down its length. Einy and Berg always emerged from their mouse wash all puffed up and slightly dizzy.

Fisher had also designed a running wheel that slowly wound up a little slingshot. One of the mice would run on the wheel while the other would get in the sling basket and be flung across the tank onto a little hill of cushions. There was even a tiny mouse telescope in the corner of the tank.

The mice were curled up napping when Leroy wrapped his bulky hand around one, and Willard snatched up the other. Fisher's eyes widened.

"These little guys look like fun," rumbled Brody in his uneven, still-changing voice.

Mr. Granger began stammering lightly, almost under his breath. "B-Be careful with the . . . Please don't . . . Watch out for their . . ."

"Maybe we can play catch with them!" said Leroy. "They'd abbreviate that, wouldn't they?"

"*Appreciate*, not abbreviate, sausage-brain," snapped

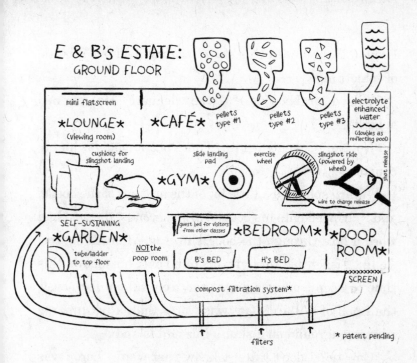

E & B's ESTATE:
GROUND FLOOR

mini flatscreen
LOUNGE
(viewing room)

CAFÉ pellets type #1 — pellets type #2 — pellets type #3 — electrolyte enhanced water (doubles as reflecting pool)

cushions for slingshot landing

slide landing pad — exercise wheel — slingshot ride (powered by wheel)

GYM

wire to charge release

shot release

SELF-SUSTAINING ***GARDEN***

tube/ladder to top floor

NOT the poop room

guest bed for visitors from other classes

BEDROOM — ***POOP ROOM***

B's BED — H's BED

xxxxxxxxxx SCREEN

compost filtration system*

filters

* patent pending

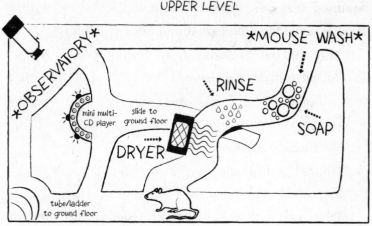

E & B's ESTATE:
UPPER LEVEL

OBSERVATORY — ***MOUSE WASH***

RINSE

mini multi-CD player

slide to ground floor

SOAP

DRYER

tube/ladder to ground floor

9

Brody. "Hey. What's this stuff?" Brody held out a bottle of something.

Willard grabbed it. "Mouse cleaner!" He grinned eagerly.

"No! No!" Granger cut in. "That's acetic acid! It's highly caustic!"

Willard splashed a little bit of the acid out of the bottle, and it dripped onto his boot. Within seconds, the acid had worn a hole through the boot, showing Willard's big toe. Again, Fisher had to clamp his hand over his mouth, this time to keep from gagging. Even from fifteen feet away, the smell of Willard's feet was worse than a trash barge running aground on a skunk-infested island.

"Caustic? I don't think I know that word," Leroy was saying.

"Caustic?" Brody stroked his whiskerless chin and squinted his eyes in mock thought. "Pretty sure that means—good for mouse-cleaning! Let's give it a try!"

Leroy started counting down from ten as Granger moved out of Fisher's vision, babbling and stammering protestations.

"Ten Missouri . . ."

"Not Missouri, Leroy. *Mississippi.*"

"What's the difference?"

"Just count, okay?"

Fisher imagined what his favorite comic book character

would do. Vic Daring, Space Scoundrel had been in spots like this before. Two issues ago, he'd smuggled himself inside an asteroid pirate's ship by hiding in an ore crate. Then, just as the pirate captain and his gang were about to execute the captured crown prince of Mars, Vic had burst out, subdued the pirates, and returned the captured prince. For a hefty cash reward, of course.

Fisher imagined himself springing from his hiding spot, asteroid-forged sword in hand. Brody, Willard, and Leroy would back away from him, trembling. *We can't all be brave enough to pick on tiny rodents,* he'd say. *Why don't you go find a species closer to your mental level. Like sea slugs.*

But instead, he did nothing. And Leroy kept counting.

"Five, four . . ."

"Please, boys, I'm telling you—he's *not here.*"

"Three, two . . ."

"Please!"

Just then, Brody put his hand up.

"Put 'em back," he said to Willard and Leroy. "He's not here."

Leroy tossed the mouse carelessly back into the cage. Einy was lucky enough to land on the slingshot, bouncing up and down a few times before going on his way. Willard put Berg back after giving him a few pats on the head that had the poor mouse walking in loops for a minute.

Fisher heard the classroom door open and shut. Then,

Graph of Viking Retaliations
in Relation to Trigger Behaviors

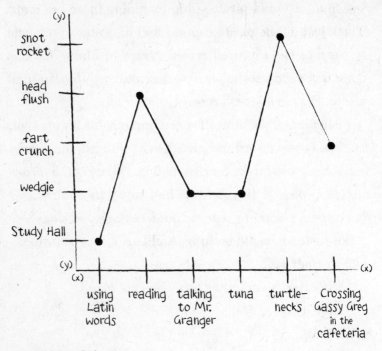

x=Trigger Behaviors
y=Viking Retaliations

after a minute, Mr. Granger's defeated voice. "It's okay, Fisher. You can come out now. They're gone."

Fisher crawled out, a little woozy from chemical fumes, and collapsed into the nearest chair. Mr. Granger sat down next to him, mopping his forehead with his necktie, which was decorated with carbon molecules.

"I should've stood up to them," Mr. Granger said as much to himself as to Fisher. He unpacked a small lunch and used a plastic cafeteria knife to divide a tuna sandwich evenly in two. Fisher took his half and sighed.

"It's all right, Mr. Granger. The Vikings are determined to make my life miserable. Nothing either of us says or does is going to change that."

Mr. Granger wilted in his chair like a piece of old lettuce. For a moment he and Fisher sat in silence, munching despondently on their tuna fish. Fisher polished off his sandwich without having tasted a single bite. He usually relished the fact that once a week or so that he got to escape from the biohazard of a cafeteria, but the Vikings had so spoiled his mood, he couldn't even enjoy Mr. Granger's company.

"How are your parents?" Mr. Granger ask break the silence. "Did your father's e harmonizing crickets ever turn

"Not really," Fisher sa

"And your mom?

"She's fine. T

in their own pr

all." Fisher sighe

Granger offered hi

"Hey!" Mr. Grang

"I know something tha

finally arrived from New York—the cross sections of the polygamous tube worm I was telling you about. You want to come by my house after school and see them?"

"I can't. Too much homework. Besides, I'm in the middle of a very important experiment. I'll tell you all about it once I've got the final kinks ironed out." Fisher sighed again. "Well, I'd better get ready for my next class. Thanks, Mr. Granger." Fisher got up and walked out, shoulders slumped, his stride small even by his subnormal standards.

Mr. Granger watched him leave and a dark look suddenly spread across his face. He stood over Einy and Berg's tank, petting the mice as he pondered. He had big plans for Fisher. It was all just a matter of timing.

"Holy polygamy!" he exclaimed. "That hurt!" He looked down to see that Heisenberg had bitten his hand.

≋ CHAPTER 2 ≋

Objects in motion remain in motion until stopped by friction—or by the metal toe of Willard's army boots.
—Fisher Bas, *Scientific Principles and Observations of the Natural World* (unpublished)

Fisher ran his hand through his springy hair as he walked through Wompalog's main entrance. Thick dust billowed out from his head, clogging his eyes, and making him sneeze. Between seventh and eighth period he had had to hide in a dusty maintenance closet in order to avoid the Vikings. The soup splash across his shirt had turned into a crust.

But now, finally, he was free.

The bus sat ahead, its open door gleaming in Fisher's vision like a stairway to the stars. But his attention was quickly taken by something even more beautiful.

Veronica Greenwich.

Fisher glanced around carefully to make sure nobody saw how he was looking at her. He had never told a soul about his feelings for her, and he didn't plan to admit it, ever. Her bright eyes radiated sweetness and intelligence. She was tall, towering over Fisher, with long, blond hair that she usually wore down and wrapped around her left shoulder. Although she didn't share Fisher's scientific mind, she was a gifted student of language and history.

Once, at the end of their fifth-grade year, she had touched his hand. At the annual academic awards, as she walked from the stage with her French prize and he was approaching to receive his science honors, her right hand had brushed his left. She probably hadn't done it intentionally, but she hadn't pulled away from him, either, which was a lot more than he had come to expect.

Just then, Veronica glanced up and made eye contact.

Fisher's insides turned to grape jelly. He wanted to look away, but he couldn't. He was frozen, paralyzed.

Veronica's mouth spread into a small smile. She lifted a hand . . . and *waved.*

Fisher's mind began to stutter like Willard. *Veronica waved. Veronica waved at* you. *What is the normal social response when a person waves? Think, Fisher, think. . . .*

Just when he remembered how to lift his hand in response, he saw the Vikings step out of the school's front doors. His ability to move instantly came back as the fight-or-flight instinct kicked in—although Fisher's instincts didn't really include the "fight-or-" part.

A decorative shrub arrangement stood a few feet from Fisher and without thinking, he dove in. Spindly branches raked his clothes and left long red lines down his arms.

He pushed his way as far in as he could, wedging himself among its thick leaves. He didn't know if Veronica had seen him. But right now his survival was at stake.

He could see the Vikings through a gap in the leaves. They were looking for him. Willard was plodding his way along the sidewalk, his heavy-lidded eyes moving back and forth. Leroy paced along one side of the bus, then the other, looking up into the windows, like a shark circling a boat, hoping for it to capsize. And Brody stood on the steps of the school, overseeing the expedition.

Fisher knew there was nothing to do but stay put. The leaves were itchy, but they kept him well hidden. He almost wished he had a shrub he could lug around wherever he went. *Mental note: research portable shrub concept.*

After a few minutes, Brody walked to the bus, shouting something Fisher couldn't hear, and Willard and Leroy followed him aboard.

Fisher pushed, twisted, and hopped his way out of the shrub just in time to watch the taillights of the school bus vanish around the far corner. Veronica was nowhere to be seen.

He took a deep breath, resigning himself to the long walk home.

It was a typical late September day in Palo Alto. The sun was beaming brightly, and palm trees swayed lazily

Possible designs for
PORTABLE SHRUB:
DESIGN A.S.A.P.!

spring-loaded
shrub in a box

insta-shrub
(just add water)

OR

shrub hat
(pull ripcord to
deploy downward)

shrub shoes
(button deploy)
added benefit: taller

Other options:
shrub in a cell phone?
shrub in a thermos
shrub in a ???
• *NEED BETTER IDEAS* •

on either side of the road. After about five minutes, a familiar hum and crackle filled the air. Fisher looked off to his right at the enormous concrete-and-steel complex that housed TechX Enterprises.

Somewhere inside those laboratories was the well-known Dr. Xander, more commonly known in popular media by the nickname Dr. X™.

Dr. Xander had been a mysterious figure ever since he arrived on the scene back when Fisher was just learning to walk. He had brought all sorts of inventions to public light, some more successful than others. Fisher himself had used Dr. X's Shakespearean-to-Modern English Instant Translator Earpiece. The Voice-Responsive Moving Propane Grill, by contrast, had rolled blazing into a few too many living rooms to catch on.

But these were only his little gizmos, the everyday products to keep his operation funded. Years earlier, he had successfully teleported a small car from one end of the city to the other. He claimed the technology was still a long way from being practical and widely useful, but no one had forgotten the moment that a green convertible had popped into being right before their eyes. Nor the day that a drill-headed machine the size of an office building had plunged beneath the ground at Dr. X's command and literally stopped an earthquake. And his bid to enclose all of Palo Alto in an immense dome to "optimize the imperfect weather in the region," had received sharply divided opinions.

What few announcements Dr. X had ever made to the public had all been made by video, with his face in complete darkness and his voice disguised. No one seemed to know what he looked like, or anything of his personal life.

People didn't know what to think of Dr. X. They adored his inventions and hailed his genius, but the fact that he never showed his face made them wonder. Was he trying to hide something? Or was he just . . . shy?

Many people were scared of Dr. X, but Fisher wanted to be just like him. As he passed the impenetrable walls of the TechX compound, he imagined a possible future Fisher: a dark, shadowy figure silently stalking the halls of an immense laboratory complex. The people would react to his name with awe. No—with *reverence*! They would whisper and wonder about him, about his amazing machines and miraculous discoveries. And he'd gaze at the masses from a tall tower, above and apart from it all.

Fisher's thoughts of future power and prestige distracted him so much that he almost walked right past his house without noticing. And not noticing Fisher's house is like failing to notice a two-hundred-man bagpipe parade.

The Bas's neighborhood was pleasant and well-groomed. The streets were lined with short trees, many with oranges or lemons hanging off them. Flowers of every color dotted the trim green lawns. No, the Bas house didn't stand out because it was more beautiful than the other houses.

It stood out because Mr. and Mrs. Bas were geniuses who had no reservations about using their genius anywhere and everywhere they could.

Fisher's parents had lent all of their scientific ingenuity to the construction of their home. Broad banks of solar panels extended out from all sides of the roof like an upside-down umbrella. Huge antennae bristled on the roof. One was for high-speed encoded transmissions between the house and the field labs where his parents worked. One was set up to communicate with the family's personal satellite. Another was a fully featured radio telescope that Fisher's father used for studying distant galaxies and celestial phenomena.

Above the roof hovered a cloud. Not a cloud hanging majestically in the stratosphere like good, polite clouds generally do, but a little cloud floating about twenty feet above the house, moving only very slightly in the wind. In the house there was a keypad with a series of controls and dials, like a thermostat. Fisher's parents could adjust the cloud's density with a slider, depending on how much shade was needed. A light drizzle was a button-press away, and a moderate downpour a quick knob-twist later.

Fisher walked through his front gate. This would not be so unusual except that he didn't walk through his front gate by opening it, walking in, and then closing it behind him, but by actually walking *through* it. To the casual observer, the iron gate appeared perfectly normal, but it was in fact composed of Mr. Bas's patented Liquid Door. When the gate detected a family member, it was programmed to drastically lower its density, allowing Fisher to walk right through it as if it were fog.

He passed his mother's garden. At its center was a cantaloupe the size of a small car. There had been a cantaloupe the size of a large one, but its rind was so thick that a cutting torch had been needed to slice it. For the smaller ones they just used a buzz saw.

As he began to cross the front yard, stepping-stones skimmed across the grass to place themselves beneath his feet.

Situated in the midst of everything else, the front door seemed a bit out of place. It was about six and a half feet tall and three feet wide, made of wood, and set into hinges that allowed it to swing open and closed when unlatched by a brass knob.

In other words, it was just a door—which, for the Bas home, was the strangest thing of all.

Fisher sighed to himself as he shoved open the door. As useful as all of the gadgets and thingamajigs both inside and outside the house could be, he often wished that he lived in a house that didn't have its own weather or throw

22

newspapers back at the paperboy if they landed in the wrong spot. He was getting tired of other kids pointing and laughing at it when they passed by.

He wished, in fact, that his family could just be *normal*.

"Hey, I'm home," he said as he walked into the front hall. After a few seconds, a tall figure wearing a full-face respirator, enormous goggles, and a pair of thick lab gloves walked over to meet him.

"Wrrcm hmmm, Fshuhh!" came the muffled reply. Then the gloved hands reached up to remove the mask, and Fisher's mother smiled down at him. The mask had left red welts on her forehead and cheeks. "Good day?"

Fisher was about to launch into a multi-point lecture detailing all the ways in which it had *not* been a good day at *all*, but before he could say anything, a crash sounded from another part of the house, followed by a man's voice saying "Ow, ow, ow, ow . . ."

"Oh dear." Fisher's mother sighed. "The hermit crabs must have staged another breakout." She ran up the stairs.

Fisher set down his backpack, took off his coat, and flung it into the air. Just then, the hall closet spat out a coat hanger on an extendable boom, caught the coat, and retracted, storing his coat neatly inside.

His mother came downstairs a few minutes later

followed by his father, who was holding an ice pack to his nose.

"I told you their aggression impulse was overengineered, but you didn't believe me," Fisher's dad said.

"Well, if your little cage was up to par they wouldn't be able to get out, now would they?" his mom replied, adjusting the ice pack.

"All right, next time *you're* on maintenance duty. I'll work on the enclosure if you try to make some crabs who don't act like they're James Bond."

"Of course, sweetie," said Mrs. Bas. They reached the bottom of the stairs. Mr. Bas glanced over his ice pack by tipping his head down, and noticed his son standing in the hallway for the first time.

"Hey, kiddo! Good day at school?"

"My day . . ." He looked from his mother to his father. Both were blinking at him expectantly: his mom with the mask slung around her neck, his father with the ice pack pressed to his nose. No. His parents wouldn't understand. "Normal day. Y'know. I'm going to get started on my work. Let me know when it's time for dinner." Fisher headed up the stairs as his parents resumed their discussion of the rogue crustaceans.

Fisher headed straight for his room and, for the first time all day, allowed himself to relax. Fiber-optic cabling and hydraulic tubes snaked along every wall, connecting banks of computers, massive microscopes, and chemical apparatus that would shame most universities.

Here, Fisher truly felt he had a place in the world. He wished more than anything that he felt even half as comfortable in a crowd of other twelve-year-olds as he did when surrounded by test tubes and bubbling solutions. If telling a joke or talking to a girl were as effortless as splicing bacterial DNA, Fisher would be the most popular boy in school.

He turned to his closet door and waved a hand in the air. The door got brighter as its metal surface slowly resolved itself into a mirror. Fisher looked himself up and down. He raised his arms up above his head so his sleeves fell to his elbows, wishing he had big muscles instead of scarecrow arms. Then he tried to pat down his light brown hair, which never could decide on a single direction to go in. The three oblong freckles on his nose completed the picture.

Pathetic. He was doomed forever to be a geek. He waved his arms rapidly in the air, causing the motion-detecting closet door to shift into a crazy carnival mirror. Fisher's image was distorted and warped, bending in all directions. Fisher walked toward it, striking funny poses and making faces. At *least* he didn't have a forehead as large as an eggplant . . . or a body stretched out like taffy . . . or squashed up like a bowling ball. . . .

Too late, he felt a cool object under his foot. A moment

later he was crashing to the ground as a steel test tube rolled away from him. "Oof," he grunted. He had landed among a pile of dirty socks, and his flailing legs had made the mirror fade away.

As Fisher stood up, he heard a soft, snuffling sound and light footsteps approaching him. A few seconds later, a pinkish, lightly fuzzy object glided into the room and came to an unsteady landing at Fisher's feet.

"Hiya, boy." Fisher reached down to scratch his pet pig, FP, under the chin. FP was an unusual pig. In fact, he was a Flying Pig. His parents had once gotten into a debate about adding on additional lab space to their house. Fisher's father had told his mother that he'd agree to expand the property "when pigs fly." His mother had taken this as a challenge and won her new lab expansion by biologically engineering little FP.

FP looked like any other pig, except he had light bones and weblike tissue stretching between his front hooves and the middle of his back. This allowed him to glide as gracefully as his pig body permitted—in other words, not gracefully at all. But he was adorable nonetheless.

"Miss me?" Fisher asked, patting FP on the head.

FP squealed enthusiastically. Fisher sighed. At least someone cared about him, even if the Vikings were intent on making sure that he graduated from the school system without a single human friend.

Fisher walked over to a tightly sealed, clear plastic cube in which dozens of tiny mosquitoes swarmed, bouncing off the walls like compressed gas molecules. He had been working for months on mosquitoes, trying to modify their genes so that they would bite only certain chosen people. Certain meathead bullies, to be precise. If it worked, Fisher would be able to walk straight through a swarm of them and emerge on the other side without a single mosquito bite. The Vikings, on the other hand . . . Fisher smiled, picturing them covered in murderously itchy red spots.

"Let's see how this batch came out, FP," he said. "If I can get these to work, I bet I finally find a place among my own species. No offense, boy."

He stuck his arm through a mesh-guarded port in the side of the tank, and left it there for thirty seconds. When he removed it, the smile on his face dropped away; his arm was covered in tiny red welts. "On second thought, maybe I should just go back to that dark, sinister tower idea."

FP made a whining sound, bumping Fisher's leg with his snout. Fisher sat down and set FP on his lap. "What do you think, little guy? Would I make a good villain?" A quick series of snuffles sounded like laughter. "What, not intimidating enough?" FP looked up at Fisher and dragged one hoof across Fisher's stomach, as if petting him. "Oh, I'm too nice, is that it?" FP made a satisfied-sounding snort and nuzzled back into Fisher's lap. "Well,

Recalculations for VTMs

P Generation

Fisher Biters ✕ Viking Biters

F₁ Generation
Hybrids

Fisher Biters (all)

F₂ Generation
Hybrids

Fisher Biters
(672)

Viking Biters
(224)

*still too
many of these

***New VTM Hybrids
show preference for:
• high testosterone
• muscle tone
• pepperoni smell

28

you just wait. Middle school is bound to turn me into an angry force of destruction. I'll be an evil mastermind by the time I get to eighth grade. You'll see."

The soft sound of FP's chuckling soothed him as he got back to work, determined to find a solution to the disaster his life had become.

≋ CHAPTER 3 ≋

It is surely a sin for one man to covet another man's wife. But it is a sin of far greater proportions (and fatal possibilities) to covet another man's wife's untested, artificial human growth hormone. Especially if we're talking about my mom.

—Fisher Bas, *Scientific Principles and Observations of the Natural World* (unpublished)

"Down, boy," Fisher said as he walked into the kitchen a few hours later. FP was doing his best to leap onto the counter, but kept landing with a thump back on the tiled floor.

The three freckles on Fisher's nose scrunched closer together as he tensed his face in pain, and scratched his new insect bites. It felt like he'd dipped his arm in a tankful of needles and salt water.

His father didn't even notice the boy—or the leaping pig—as he stood beside the oven and adjusted the controls on a screen with a full thermal map of the chicken roasting inside. His mother, meanwhile, was involved in an argument with the refrigerator over whether the white wine was chilled enough.

"Madam Bas," said the refrigerator in a high, droning voice, "need I remind you that I can detect temperature variation to a precision of one two-hundredth of a degree kelvin?" If the refrigerator had had arms, it would have been crossing them in front of its chest. Or, rather, its ice drawer.

"I'm well aware of your thermometric abilities," Fisher's mom said to the fridge, beginning to get annoyed, "since I invented them. Now, can you tell me how the wine *tastes*? Or would you prefer to leave that to someone who has *taste buds*?"

The refrigerator stuttered slightly, relented, and opened its door with a puff of air that sounded a bit like a reluctant sigh.

"Dinner's almost ready, Fisher," said his dad, turning off the oven. "Could you set the table, please?"

"Sure thing," said Fisher. He went to the touch screen on the table's side and slid the plates to their proper spots, following up with forks, knives, napkins, and glasses. When he had finished configuring the layout on the screen, he pressed a button and a little hatch popped open on the kitchen countertop. The requested items began surfacing, one by one.

What appeared to be extra legs on the dining room table were, in fact, arms. So with multiple joints bending and sliding smoothly, it reached toward the counter, took hold of each plate, glass, and piece of silverware and placed it softly on its appointed spot as everyone sat down to eat.

Except that without anyone noticing, FP had finally made it onto the counter. So when the table's arm stretched out to grab the third plate, it grabbed the flustered pig instead and placed him down in front of Mr. Bas. He looked startled for just a moment, but then nudged FP onto the floor with a shake of his head, and picked up his own plate.

"So really, Fisher, how was your day?" his mother pressed as she sliced herself a piece of chicken. Fisher shrugged.

"About normal, I guess. Treated like I have a contagious disease and generally shunned."

She frowned. "Fisher, I hope you know not to buy into what any of those boys say. People your age aren't usually as bright as you are, and sometimes other kids take that as a personal insult."

"I know," Fisher said, "but it's less than a month into the school year, and I just feel like everyone else knows where to go and what to say and I'm just wandering around trying not to get knocked over."

"Everyone has a tough time when they're twelve years old. Bullies are just the people who deal with that frustration by taking it out on those around them. In a few years, they'll look back and realize how childish they were being."

Fisher sighed and nodded, wondering if he could possibly last a few more years. This was why he didn't like to talk to his parents about school; they just didn't understand. They always told him that things would get better. But time was passing, nothing was getting better, and he was sick of waiting. Desperate to change the subject, he said, "So, what about your day at work, Mom?"

"Oh, we're starting to see some progress with the artificial protein chains. I made a few tweaks to the sequence, and things look much better."

Helen Bas was a world-renowned microbiologist, biochemist, and genetic engineer, and much of her work involved efforts to increase food production around the world. As she went on about her day, she took a sharp knife and thinly sliced a tomato the size of a basketball—one of the runts of the patch. The properly grown ones would have had to come in through the garage door. His mother had spent many years genetically developing giant vegetables and was largely responsible for helping significantly close the gap in world hunger.

"One of my biggest problems now is industrial espionage," she continued, passing a slice of tomato to Fisher that was as big as his dinner plate.

"What, like spies?" Fisher said.

"Exactly," Mrs. Bas said. Fisher choked on a tomato seed when she mentioned the spies. He coughed and the seed flew out of his mouth, landing in his father's wineglass. His father, absentminded as usual, didn't even notice as he took a sip.

"The formula I'm working on is very powerful," Mrs. Bas went on, "and it could be very dangerous. We need layers of security to catch agents from other companies trying to sneak into our lab."

For about a year, Fisher's mom had been working on a delicate and carefully guarded project. The government had approached her team with a revolutionary task: to develop a synthetic version of human growth hormone, the natural chemical that stimulates growth and healing in humans. This artificial version was intended to achieve the same effects as natural HGH, but at a much faster pace. His mother had named it AGH, for Accelerated Growth Hormone.

She'd been more high strung ever since the project had begun, but she was determined to see the project through. If the AGH was perfected, it could start a revolution in medical technology. Some diseases could be wiped out entirely, treatments for others drastically improved. Surgery recovery times and physical therapy could be advanced far beyond anything the medical world had ever seen. Fisher just hoped all of these long days and extra hours would get her the breakthrough she was looking for.

"Why would someone want to steal your work?" asked

Fisher, deliberately knocking over his glass. Intentional spills were actually encouraged by his parents to make sure the table was in proper working order. With a snap of plastic joints, the table arm zipped up, caught the glass before it hit, and righted it.

"The problem with AGH," she said, and the way she pronounced it made it sound momentarily as if she, too, had a tomato seed lodged in her throat, "is that it's a very powerful substance that can be used in many ways, some of which we can't even predict."

"You could alter a person physically to make him more powerful, or even grow an army from embryos in a matter of weeks," said his father. "Like every new technology, it can be used for good or evil purposes."

The way Fisher's dad said "evil purposes" gave Fisher a quick chill.

Walter Bas, Fisher's dad, divided his attention between particle physics and field biology. Years ago he won the Nobel Prize for his pioneering work on the biology of sea slugs. That particular species of slug was virtually extinct, because they'd become too lazy to choose mates. He had manipulated the slugs' DNA so that a single slug possessed both male and female parts and could reproduce all by itself.

Fisher was proud of his father, although he did wish that his last name had not become synonymous with the

Bas-Hermaphrodite-Sea-Slug Hypothesis.

It used to be great being the kid of two genius inventors. When he was little, all the neighborhood kids loved to come over and play tag around the cucumber forest, or try to beat the refrigerator at a game of chess. Then, a few years ago, it was as though a switch flipped in everyone else's head. Suddenly, people who were curious, who wanted to learn new things and explore the world, were nerds.

Fisher could never adjust. He loved discoveries and inventions and knowledge. He didn't understand what had happened to all the other curious, adventurous kids he used to play with.

"Wow," Fisher said, "that sounds—"

All of a sudden, he was cut off by the *breep, breep, breep* of the house alarm. Someone was on the perimeter fence!

Fisher's mom leapt from the table. "Intruder location!" she shouted.

A map popped up on the opposite wall showing a top-down view of the house, and a small dot appeared just to the side of the front gate, on the inside of the fence.

"Immobilize!" Mrs. Bas commanded as she darted from the room toward the front of the house, knocking over a chair in the process.

Security systems reared up from hidden spots in the front yard. With an airy *pomf!* they spat out enormous nets of artificial spider silk. Fisher's father had engineered them based on an Amazonian specimen he had collected.

"Target immobilized!" said the house in its perpetually upbeat, booming voice, as if an immobilized target was exactly what it had wanted for its birthday.

Fisher followed his parents to the front door. Outside, they heard hard breathing and what sounded like surprised shouting. They opened the door, walked out into the yard, and realized that it wasn't shouting.

It was squealing.

FP was struggling frantically with his little hooves, superglued to the fence by dozens of adhesive web strands. Fisher ran forward to help, getting his hands just as stuck in the sticky, tacky mess of spider strands. FP looked at him in panic and squeaked repeatedly.

"I'm sorry, boy," Fisher said, trying to wrench his pet away from the fence. "What were you doing out here, anyway?"

FP squeaked again, moving his forelegs the tiny amount that he could. "Were you trying to fly with the ducks again?" FP snorted guiltily, and Fisher sighed. "Well, at least you have goals."

Mrs. Bas let out a deep breath, the tension and fear slowly leaving her face as Mr. Bas put his arm around her shoulders.

"De-immobilize," she said to the house. A smaller apparatus popped out of the side of one of the net-guns, and sprayed pig and boy alike with a solvent that turned the webbing to a thin liquid instantly. FP squeaked in surprise as he dropped the few feet to the ground. He then gathered his bearings, shook off the liquid like a dog would, and trotted back toward the house with as much dignity as he could muster.

"Target de-immobilized!" said the house in the same cheery tone.

Fisher returned with his parents to the dinner table. He held FP on his lap this time, scratching his pet's ears and back as FP napped off the excitement of the evening.

"I'm sorry, Fisher," his mother said, smiling a bit sadly. "I may have overreacted a bit when I was programming the house's security settings. I'm just worried about what could happen if someone got a hold of my work. In the wrong hands . . ."

"In Dr. X's hands, you mean," said his father, furrowing his brow.

"He's made no secret of the fact that he wants to secure the formula for himself," she replied, taking a sip of water. "Our security has already caught three of his agents trying to break into the lab complex. He's a ruthless man, whoever he is, and he's willing to do anything to advance his own purposes."

Fisher hoped his parents wouldn't notice that he was blushing. His parents made no secret of the fact that they despised Dr. X. Fisher felt ashamed for thinking Dr. X was actually pretty cool.

"He may be secretive and a little odd," said his dad as FP twitched under Fisher's hand, dreaming about soaring through the sky. "But there are limits to what he can and will do. Remember everything he's done for our city! For our country—and for science at large! I know he's your fiercest rival, and he wants to beat your team to the discovery of functioning AGH, but I can't see him going so far as to actually rob us to get ahead."

"I hope you're right," his mom said, her voice full of doubt. A few seconds of silence followed, broken only by Fisher's chewing and the dreamy snuffling of the pig in his lap.

"Speaking of hostile invasions," his father said, his voice low and frustrated, "did you see the article in the paper yesterday about the new King of Hollywood franchise that's going to be opening up nearby? It's an outrage."

"An outrage? How come?" Fisher blurted, an excited edge to his voice. He loved the restaurant chain, and there hadn't been one in Palo Alto—until now!

"Because of *where* they're putting it," his father replied. "They bought out a plot on land that was supposed to be under the protection of the state government. They're going to be paving over acres of pristine peat marshland." Fisher's father was one of only a few dozen people who had ever used the word *pristine* to describe a peat marsh. "That is precious land among all of the development around here, and moreover, it is one of the few natural habitats left to the DBYBBD."

"The what?" said Fisher and his mother simultaneously.

"The double-billed yellow-bellied bilious duck," he said. Seeing his wife's and son's blank stares, he continued, "It's a very rare species of duck, and most of them have been pushed off the West Coast. If this land is taken away from them, I don't know if the species will be able to survive outside of captivity." He shook his head. "Once again consumer culture nudges a precious piece of the ecosystem toward its doom."

The news plunged both of his parents into gloomy meditation, and the Bas family spent the rest of dinner in comparative quiet. But however much Fisher might try and empathize with the plight of the—he had already forgotten the name of the duck—he couldn't help but be pleased by the news of a King of Hollywood opening right in the neighborhood. Their star-shaped spicy fries were the stuff of legend, and Fisher relished the thought of slipping out of school during lunch period, escaping the horrors of his cafeteria, and drowning his sorrows in spicy sauce.

Later that night as Fisher got ready for bed, he selected a small bottle from the hidden cabinet he had built behind his bookshelves.

Secret Ingredients
King of Hollywood
Special Sauce:

mayonnaise ✓✓
tobasco
ketchup (good possibility per 3-23 test)
~~clam juice~~
garlic?
hot peppers ·
~~orange soda~~
~~lemon juice~~
duck fat? (ew)
cheddar cheese
chicken stock
~~chicken liver~~ (blech!)
~~white asparagus~~
red Skittles (maybe)

"Mmm," he said as he swallowed the serum. "Doritos flavored."

By the time his mother came in to say good night, his skin had broken out in real but entirely cosmetic red dots.

"I think I'm sick, Mom. Maybe contagious. I should stay home tomorrow."

Mrs. Bas sighed, having seen things like this many times before. She knew Fisher dreaded going to school, and knew just as well that the only way it would get better was for him to buckle down and face it.

"Fisher, you've already been out as many sick days as the school allows. Even if *I* let you stay home, you'd get in trouble with them. I know you're having a hard time, but I promise you, it won't be like this forever. Now get some sleep." She kissed him on the forehead and walked out.

"There's always college," Fisher said, a little bit of hope remaining in his voice. "I know I could get into a science program if I applied now. If I went to Stanford, I wouldn't even have to leave home."

"Fisher, if you feel like you don't fit in now, just imagine how it would be if everyone around you was almost twice your age. College will come soon enough. Besides, tomorrow's Friday. Just one more day and then you'll have the whole weekend to relax. Sleep well, okay? I love you."

"Love you, too," Fisher said, and then rolled over next to FP, who was already snoring lightly—no doubt dreaming of open fields, fresh hay, and infinite snacks. Fisher closed his eyes and willed himself to sleep, savoring the precious hours of unconsciousness like the calm before a big, ugly, hormone-warped storm.

CHAPTER 4

Hot air is less dense than cold air and thus rises. Ergo: Gassy Greg's farts must be perfectly room temperature, as they hover and hover, and never disperse.
—Fisher Bas, *Scientific Principles and Observations of the Natural World* (unpublished)

Fisher leaned carefully over the tank in Mr. Granger's room, scattering food pellets for Einy and Berg. He wished that he were in Mr. Granger's position: home sick. Granger missed almost as many days as Fisher did.

Fisher leaned over the tank and picked up Einstein, holding him gently in one hand and looking into his beady, black eyes as his jittering jaws worked their way through a morsel.

"I don't understand people, Einy. In science, there are rules for everything. But people don't behave according to rules, do they? I have no idea what people are thinking, or what they might do next." The mouse continued to chew, twitching his nose and brushing Fisher's fingertips with his whiskers. "Sometimes I wish I wasn't so smart. If I were a dumb little thing like you, scurrying around a little box waiting to be fed, I bet I'd be pretty happy. You're happy, aren't you?" Einstein continued to twitch. "Well, enjoy it, Einy. And if you don't see me again, it'll be because I finally reach my pummelings-per-lifetime limit."

The bell rang sharply, and Fisher, realizing he would be late, slipped the mouse back into the tank and hurried off to debate class.

He opened the door as quietly as he could, but then tripped on someone's backpack, and all the debaters turned their eyes to him. So much for a stealthy entrance.

He slipped into a seat near the middle of the room, next to Amanda Cantrell. Her jade-green eyes blazed right through him when he sat down. Amanda was small, but intense and often intimidating. She captained both the debate and the girls' wrestling teams, and was a lot stronger than she looked.

"Where have you been? You missed the opening arguments," she said in a hissed whisper.

"I had to feed Mr. Granger's mice," said Fisher. "He's out sick today."

"Something you know all about," she said bitingly, then softened a bit. "I'm sorry, Fisher. We've just been getting our butts kicked so far."

"What's the topic?"

"The new King of Hollywood, and whether—"

"Whether it's infringing on the territory of a duck with fifty adjectives in its name?"

Amanda looked impressed. She even smiled, just a lit-tle. "Yep, that's it. We're on the side of the ducks." Fisher lent his attention to the current speaker, who was on the pro-restaurant team.

"As you can see clearly on this map of California marsh-land, there are several other spots around this and sur-rounding counties where the bili . . . the triple . . . the, uh, duck, regularly makes its home," said Trevor Weiss in a nasal voice. Today he was even more buttoned up than usual, and his stiff hairdo was dangerously approaching a pompadour. "Furthermore, as a source of sustenance to humans, especially kids such as ourselves, there can be no denying that the value of a King of Hollywood is immea-surable, and its excellent fry sauce even more so."

There were subdued exclamations of approval and scat-tered applause. The two sides went along more or less the same lines, the pro-duck arguments attempting to play on the students' natural feelings toward small, cute animals, and the pro-restaurant arguments appealing to their love of tasty fast food.

Amanda watched the arguments go back and forth like a hawk, keeping careful track of the debate and making furious scribbly notes with her pink pen. When she saw that the debate had reached a standstill, and neither side would alter its strategy, she chose her moment to strike.

Fisher accompanied her to the front of the room,

borrowing her pen to take down notes on her concluding argument. Amanda stepped confidently toward the microphone, and even though her head barely cleared the podium, somehow she seemed to fill the room with her presence.

"The team arguing in favor of the King of Hollywood has been happily sidestepping the issue of whether or not it can rightfully occupy the land in question," she began, and instantly a hush fell on the room. Fisher marveled at Amanda's ability to take control.

"Instead you've all chosen to reiterate again and again the benefits that the franchise will bring," she went on. "My teammates have been a *little* bit more on topic, but only insofar as playing on sympathy toward the little animals in the marsh, describing their feathers, their family habits, and their daily lives, which even I have to admit are beyond boring."

Corey Devonshire and Jenny Bits, who had both described the ducks' dietary habits at length, squirmed uncomfortably in their seats. Amanda narrowed her eyes right at them. Corey adjusted the collar on his polo shirt to break eye contact, and Jenny decided to carefully study the wall.

"The issue in question isn't restaurants, and it's not ducks. It's *land*," Amanda resumed, adjusting her pink headband and allowing herself a small, proud smile. "The land that we are *supposed* to be talking about was signed into protected status by the state legislature ten years ago. That status has not been revoked. It doesn't matter how good the restaurant is. It doesn't matter how many thousands of acres the ducks could still live on. The land, itself, was a part of a transaction that was not sanctioned by law. No commercial interest has any right to it. End of story."

She strode quickly back to her chair, and Fisher scurried off behind her. The pro-restaurant team looked at one another, and began chattering among themselves and scribbling notes, trying to rethink their tactics.

"Nice job, Amanda," said Theresa Keller, brushing her red bangs out of her eyes. The rest of the team complimented her. It was obvious she had won the debate for them.

"Good work!" said Fisher, handing her back her pen.

"Thanks. I just need to make a few posters to tell people about the protest I'm going to stage in the parking lot of the new King of Hollywood, and hopefully I'll get at least a decent crowd to—Ew, Fisher, what *is* this?" She was about to scribble a few notes when she let out an exclamation of disgust, holding the pen by its cap as though it were a dead cockroach. The other debate team members crowded around to look. Fisher looked at the pen he had handed back to her, and then down at his own hands, in horror. Both had bits of Einstein's and Heisenberg's droppings all over them. His face turned fire-engine red.

"Remind me not to lend you my toothbrush!" said Jen Keller, giggling.

"It's m-mouse poop!" stuttered Fisher. "I had to feed Granger's mice today!" The other kids were starting to break down into fits of laughter.

"Ugh, and all these little white hairs on here, too," Amanda said. "Fisher, I'm allerg—" Her words were cut off by a sudden sneeze. She raised her hand, barely able to ask to be excused in between sneezes, and then tore out of the room, sneezing every few steps. Fisher's teammates were still laughing and pointing at him.

At that moment, Fisher wished that he were a rodent himself. He would find a deep, dark hole, burrow into it, and hibernate. Forever.

His day went downhill from there.

He was bumped into by no fewer than four people as he made the long journey to the bathroom to wash his hands, and then four more on the way back to his locker, including Wally Dubel, who sweetened the deal by shoving Fisher into the wall and grunting, "Move it, loser."

Usually, bricks were a building material but apparently Wally had decided that one would make a good substitute for a brain. Fisher trudged to his locker, trying to distract himself from his dark mood with theorems and mental calculations.

Assuming a rate of naturally selected brain expansion consistent with early Homo sapiens *development, Wally Dubel's descendants should be able to fit into modern-day society in approximately 134,000 years, assuming the presence of suitable breeding partners, which is unlikely.*

On the way to his locker, he glanced up and immediately felt his throat seize and his chest tighten. Veronica Greenwich. The last time he'd seen her had been moments before diving into a shrub. This time, he promised himself, he would actually smile at her. Maybe he would even talk to her.

But the feeling of warmth in Fisher's chest turned to cold revulsion when he saw Veronica was already talking to someone. Chance Barrows.

Chance Barrows, who had a golden aura radiating out from his blond hair. Tall, athletic, with a smile that could make plants grow. Always accompanied by a pack of girls who wanted to be closer to him, and boys who thought that if they stood in his presence they might absorb some of his holy Chance Barrows-ness.

Fisher's stomach twisted as Veronica let out a chiming laugh in response to something Chance had said. Fisher spun around and stormed off in the opposite direction, forgetting all about his locker.

To add insult to injury, with Mr. Granger out sick, Fisher had no choice during lunch but to brave the off-white, leaky-ceilinged, straw-wrapper-strewn wasteland that was the cafeteria. When the time came, he took his place in line between two elbows that reached almost to his head.

He shuffled forward in line, trying to pick out one or two things that looked marginally digestible. He ended up with a turkey sandwich that was about 93 percent bread with a membranous layer of what may at some point in the past have been turkey, some stale chips, and a small carton of chocolate milk.

Fisher looked over the crowded tables, each occupied by one of Fisher's carefully observed and named groups. The Aristocracy sat around the sole round table in the corner with the best windows. They wore clothing that most students' parents couldn't even afford for themselves, the kind with a single European name on the tag. They didn't pick on Fisher for the same reason that they didn't pick on potted plants. This was where people like Chance Barrows sat.

In the middle of the cafeteria was the two-table domain of the Legion. These were the largest athletes, the ones whose mental capacity was even smaller than their necks. Fisher would have to constantly dodge elbows if he sat there.

At the smaller table nearest the door sat the Urchins. They wore torn hoodies and band T-shirts with words like *skeleton* and *witch* in their names. They enjoyed being thought of as delinquents, even though the worst crime any of them had actually committed was putting Krazy Glue on a chalkboard eraser so that it stuck when the teacher tried to use it.

Finally, there was the uneven-legged table by the trash cans. Its sole occupant was Gassy Greg. Of course. The kid was cursed with the world's most troubled digestive tract. But if Fisher was lucky he would be able to sit down, eat, and leave in between Greg's "eruptions."

He moved toward the table and almost jumped in the air when he caught sight of Leroy the Viking bearing down on him. Fisher braced himself for impact, but Leroy just swiped his chocolate milk. "Trade ya," he said, putting a carton of the cafeteria's regular, unappetizing, and probably past-expiration milk down in its place.

Fisher let out a small sigh of relief. All things considered, he'd gotten off easy. He took his seat, exchanging mumbled greetings with Greg, and tried to get his teeth to cut into the spongy bread of his sandwich.

Greg, in spite of his volcanic intestines, still sat a little above Fisher on the Wompalog social ladder. His father worked at TechX, and all the kids liked to wonder what he did there all day. Greg was the only Wompalog student who had ever been inside the TechX compound, and he kept what he'd seen to himself, which only made

Density of Gassy Greg's Farts

$$D = C\,(Q-R)\sqrt{\dfrac{W}{(x-xy)}}$$

$$w\left(\dfrac{f}{x}\right)^2$$

let:
D = density of farts
C = circumference of Greg's stomach bloating
Q = quantity of beans consumed (in liters)
R = quantity of roughage consumed
    (soluble fiber in grams)
W = weight in kgs
X = measurable day, where Monday = 1,
    Tuesday = 2, Wednesday = 3, etc.
y = day of most recent turd
T = # of turds
f = frequency of farts, in farts/min (fpm)

NOTE: Add additional variable mx^2
for days when cafeteria serves tacos
(every other Wednesday)

the other kids pay him more attention.

Greg grinned at Fisher, squinting his narrow blue eyes and showing his Dorito-colored teeth. Uh-oh. Doritos were a known trigger for Gassy Greg's condition. Fisher decided he better eat his sandwich as quickly as he could.

"Hey, Fisher." That voice. That bell-like, clear voice. Fisher's internal organs tap-danced around each other as he looked up and saw Veronica Greenwich, smiling at him. And *talking* to him. In *public*.

He tried to greet her in four or five different ways at the same time, then settled on nodding and smiling back, trying to keep his knees from knocking under the table.

"I was wondering if you could give me a hand with one of the science questions from last night's homework before class starts," Veronica said, lightly moving a strand of her long, blond hair out of her eyes. She sat down across from him, hardly noticing her proximity to Gassy Greg. Fisher could barely breathe, and his mouth felt like it was coated with sandpaper. He took a huge swig of milk and straightened up as Veronica got out her worksheet.

Suddenly, Fisher couldn't recall a single word in the English language. In a panic, he looked down at his watch. In addition to the compliment generator that had almost gotten him caught in Granger's closet, there was one button designed to measure the freshness of his breath, and a third that, when pressed, would suggest conversational topics and witty greeting lines. And he needed a greeting line.

Quickly tapping his watch, he looked up into her eyes, put on his best smile, and said, "Your breath is below acceptable social levels."

"What?" she said, looking puzzled. He stuttered a bit, looking down and realizing that he'd pressed the FRESH BREATH button instead of the GREETING LINES button. Great.

"Uh . . . I said, I'd accept the chance to help you with your grade level. Happy to help." Fisher tried to keep his voice from squeaking, and quickly popped a Tic Tac in his mouth. "So in question one . . ."

Grrrrrrl, his stomach growled loudly. Fisher cringed; he was sure Veronica must have heard. The butterflies in his stomach continued their frantic flapping, as they did whenever Veronica was in the same county. He took a deep breath. "In question one, it asks for a brief explanation of Newton's first law."

"I'm not sure I understand the principle well enough to properly word it," Veronica said, and as always Fisher marveled at the elegance of her speech.

"Well, to understand inertia you need to consider objects in both possible states, moving and still, and—"

Fisher broke off as once again his stomach gave an

SOCIAL SURVIVAL WATCH

(ver 1.2)

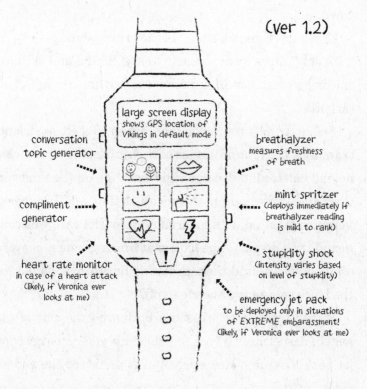

large screen display
shows GPS location of
Vikings in default mode

conversation
topic generator

compliment
generator

heart rate monitor
in case of a heart attack
(likely, if Veronica ever
looks at me)

breathalyzer
measures freshness
of breath

mint spritzer
(deploys immediately if
breathalyzer reading
is mild to rank)

stupidity shock
(intensity varies based
on level of stupidity)

emergency jet pack
to be deployed only in situations
of EXTREME embarassment!
(likely, if Veronica ever looks at me)

enormous, churning growl. Sweat began to bead on his forehead. Veronica was smiling at him encouragingly, and he felt the butterflies beating their wings faster. With some effort he wrenched his eyes away from hers and back down to the paper.

It was only then that he realized something was wrong. His stomach wasn't filled with butterflies—more like a swarm of angry hornets. He leaned forward, wrapping an arm around his stomach, willing the hornets to calm down.

"Fisher?" Veronica said. "Is something wrong?"

A few tables away, he saw Leroy, Brody, and Willard smiling wickedly at him. Leroy was rattling a small plastic bottle.

Fisher tried to say, *I'm fine*, when he felt a violent, cramping heave, and the sandwich and everything else he had eaten all day came right back up, on the table, on the homework, and on Veronica's clothes and backpack. Veronica leapt up with a horrified yelp. Her face was contorted with disgust. She looked at him as though *he* were a pile of vomit, and then, grabbing her things, bolted for the bathroom to try and clean off.

Fisher frantically pressed a button on the side of his watch, desperately trying to deploy his emergency escape jet pack. Nothing. He clearly hadn't perfected the gadget yet.

It was no use. Everyone had seen, anyway.

Laughter. Laughter roaring all around him.

"Ew!"

"Did you see that?"

"Foul, Fisher! Totally foul!"

Fisher sprang from his seat and fled the cafeteria. Even after he had made it into the hallway, Leroy's, Willard's, and Brody's leering faces still seemed to hover in front of him tauntingly. Whatever was in that plastic bottle had ended up in Fisher's milk carton, and then, all over his crush, in the form of acrid, vile vomit.

So much for getting off easy. This was the slimy garbage pile at the bottom of the hill Fisher had been tumbling down all day. No—all his life.

And he was *not* going to stand for it anymore.

≋ CHAPTER 5 ≋

Dear Stanford Admission Community—
My name is Fisher Bas, and although I have not yet taken
my SATs—or even entered high school—I would like to once
again petition seriously and earnestly to be admitted to
your undergraduate program . . .

              —College application, third attempt

Fisher kept running. He barreled down the corridor as other kids dodged and leapt out of his way. His stomach still felt like he was skydiving with a grand piano for a parachute.

Rows of lockers stood on either side like sinister metal walls. They glared down at him with their off-beige faces. The air vents looked like snootily upturned nostrils.

He barged through the double doors at the school's entrance. He continued his dash down the walkway and turned onto the sidewalk without slowing down.

He couldn't imagine going back to school again—ever. He would keep running and running, racing as fast as his short legs could take him on a straight line away from the school until he'd reached the exact opposite spot on the planet.

And once he got there he would build a towering space-craft with a module on top just big enough for him, and its massive rockets would fling him farther away from his middle school than any human being had ever been from anything.

After a few more blocks, Fisher slowed to a walk. He had calmed down a little, but his mind was unchanged. He had a three-day weekend ahead of him. But if this was the way things were going to be at school from now on, nothing could get him to return—not on Tuesday, not on Wednesday. *Never.* He would rather go to jail. He would rather get a *job*.

As Fisher passed TechX labs, he watched as a squad of robots marched in perfect lockstep out of one giant door, across the concrete surface surrounding the building.

One day, Fisher thought, he would create his own robotic army to follow in his wake and do his will. He could see it clearly: Robots pursuing the Vikings and tossing them headfirst into garbage cans. Robots tying the Vikings up in the gym and playing "It's a Small World After All" over the loudspeakers for twelve straight hours. Robots and Vikings in a baseball game: robots as players, Vikings as baseballs.

It wasn't until Fisher was home that he remembered his backpack, which was still sitting in the cafeteria. By now the Vikings had probably found it and were filling it with the vilest things they could find. Although they would be hard pressed to find China on a map of China, they were quite talented at locating all things disgusting.

Fisher stumbled into the kitchen, determined to eat anything he could find that was bad for his dental health. Certain times in life called for a mix of chocolate and Day-Glo-colored cheese crackers, and this was one of them.

Unfortunately, the closest thing to junk food he could find as he dug through shelves and pantries was his father's newest culinary innovation, Cookie-in-a-Thermos. The clear liquid inside the thermos tasted enough like a cookie, but Fisher wanted something he could chew. He kept searching until the clattering woke up one of the kitchen's permanent occupants.

"Young Fisher! Have I overslept, or are you home early?" Fisher looked up at the toaster, which looked essentially like any other toaster with the exception of two white, glowing eyes that had appeared on one of its sides, and a small speaker grille that functioned as a mouth.

The toaster was one of his mother's early experiments in sentient appliances. It—or he—brightened their mornings with clever wit, delivered in a clipped, upper-class British dialect. He was *far* friendlier than the refrigerator.

"Hey, Lord Burnside," Fisher said with a sigh. "I'm home from school early. I guess you could say I gave myself an unscheduled vacation."

"Oh!" said the toaster. "Lovely." Fisher continued to scowl at the floor, giving up his search. "Fisher, are you quite well? You don't seem to be pleased by your impromptu time off." The glowing spots narrowed slightly. It was the closest approximation to a look of concern that Lord Burnside was capable of. Fisher sighed again.

"I ran away. I couldn't stand to be in school anymore so I came back here to escape."

"I say! Was something bothering you, dear boy?"

"Vikings."

The glowing spots widened in surprise. "Goodness me! I have only the most basic of historical knowledge, but I was under the impression that those Norsemen had not been around for hundreds of years. If they have come back, I should worry for all our sakes, and I dare say you are fortunate to have escaped with your life."

Fisher cracked a narrow smile for the first time in what felt like days.

"Not *real* Vikings, Burnside. A group of dumb, ugly boys whose only source of satisfaction in their dumb, ugly lives is to torment people less ugly and dumb than themselves. They just call themselves that to feel cool and tough."

Lord Burnside clicked his toast basket up and down, a curious method he had developed to express sadness.

"I am indeed sorry to hear that, young sir." He paused for a moment. "I'm afraid I don't quite know how to advise you in this matter. I am rather untutored in human inter-action, and my only real expertise lies in the realm of darkening bread."

"That's okay," Fisher said. He did actually feel a little better. "This is something I have to get myself out of. I don't think anybody can really help me."

Burnside waggled his eyespots vertically in a sort of nod.

"Do you have any bread you need to be darker? I would be only too happy to oblige, if that might help lift your spirits."

"Not at the moment." Fisher patted the toaster lightly. "Maybe tomorrow morning."

"But of course, young sir. I would advise you to consult with your parents on this matter, but I'm afraid they're both out. Your mother is at her genetics lab in town, and your father is in all likelihood tramping through mud look-ing for new amphibian species, the dear fellow."

"Thanks for listening, Lord B."

"Anytime, my dear boy." Lord Burnside's eyespots winked out as he returned to sleep mode.

Having at last located a half-finished bag of Cheetos and some hot chocolate, Fisher walked out of the kitchen. His fury had cooled to a low, smoldering anger.

Fisher's parents were out, which meant that Fisher had free rein of the whole house. A small side door beyond the living room led to a narrow spiral staircase that wound down to Fisher's father's basement laboratory.

Most kids seek out beds, couches, and other soft surfaces in times of distress, but Fisher was most at home among the buzz of miniature generators and the burble of simmering chemical solutions. When Fisher was an infant, his father had carried him in one arm while working experiments with the other, and the sounds and smells of the lab were deeply comforting to him.

He settled down between two stacks of data-storing servers. Running against one whole wall was a large glass enclosure full of animals. There were a few cats, a handful of birds, and five sheep. Not five different sheep, but five copies of the *same* sheep.

The animals were all clones. His father was working on perfecting a cloning mechanism that allowed clones to be created from the smallest bits of genetic material. The five sheep had all been grown from a single strand of shaggy wool.

As Fisher watched them trotting around the enclosure, he heard the familiar snuffling and light hoof steps of his small, blunt-snouted pet.

"Hey, FP," Fisher said. His pet curled up on Fisher's lap, pressing his flat nose into Fisher's leg and snuffling contentedly. "Man, it's good to see you. You know what I think? I think humans are overrated."

FP let out a snort that Fisher took for agreement. "Maybe I should just clone myself a bunch of pets. They'd keep me company and wouldn't throw me into trash cans or make me barf up my lunch."

He smiled, then looked down at the little animal in his lap. "What do you think? Would you like to play with another flying pig?"

FP squeaked and blinked rapidly at Fisher, which made Fisher laugh.

"Don't worry, FP. I don't think I could handle another pet just like you—how would I scratch you both at the same time? And how would I keep track of which FP was the real FP? It's be too weird." He shook his head. "*You'd* feel weird, too, if you walked into the room and there were suddenly two of *me*."

As soon as the words were out of his mouth, Fisher froze. "Two of me . . ." Fisher looked again at the duplicate animals in the tank. And in the reflective glass, he saw his own reflection—the crazy hair, the bony shoulders, the three prominent freckles on his nose. "Two of me . . . two of me . . . That's it, FP! *Two of me!*"

Fisher leapt to his feet, sending FP sprawling with an outraged squeak.

"My flat-nosed friend, I am going to make *another* me. *He* can go to school and be beat up and tormented, while you and I hunker down here, and ride out middle school

Supplies Needed for
Operation H.I.M.R.W.C.G.T.S.
(hide in my room while clone
goes to school)

Cheetos
Doritos
Cheez-its
gummy worms
gummy bears
M&M's
Starburst

in safety. I'll reconsider going back when I get to ninth grade or so. In the meanwhile, I'll have a substitute student. A scholastic stunt double!"

The pig cocked his head slightly in response to all of this, twitching his nose with a look of utter incomprehension.

All of a sudden, Fisher was flooded with energy. With hope.

"Come on, FP," he said. "We've got work to do."

FP trotted along behind Fisher as he strode out of the lab.

CHAPTER 6

Like attracts like. Ergo: the best companion a boy can have is his own clone.

> —Fisher Bas, *Scientific Principles and Observations of the Natural World* (unpublished)

Fisher stepped into his mother's chemical storage locker. It was the size of a large walk-in closet and completely lined with shelves. Fluorescent lights clicked on, one by one, filling the space with a bluish glow and illuminating rows of sealed bottles, flasks, test tubes, copper wire, and centrifuges, as well as three dozen cans of McGinty's Old-Fashioned Cherry Fizz Soda. His mom was addicted to the stuff and always needed it when she was working.

Fisher walked the rows until he found a clear canister with a titanium latch on its seal labeled, AGH-X3, and below that, UNTESTED.

Below that were the words: EXTREMELY VOLATILE. VERY DANGEROUS. DO NOT TOUCH.

And then, in tiny letters: THAT MEANS YOU, FISHER.

Fisher gulped. His mother had been working on the project for over a year. If he destroyed her work, and was caught stealing from her—stealing dangerous and highly experimental chemicals, no less—something terrible would happen. Maybe he'd be the test subject for his mother's next project—developing an effective angry-squirrel repellant. Fisher thought about being dropped into a vat of squirrels. He twitched reflexively. He definitely couldn't take much of the hormone without her knowing—certainly not as much as he needed—but if he could siphon off just a tiny bit and take it to his own lab to study, he might be able to re-create it himself.

The canister was on a high shelf and Fisher didn't have a ladder. He considered trying to balance on FP but decided the pig would never stand still for long enough.

Fisher raised himself up onto his very tiptoes and eased his hands around the container as quickly as he dared. He wiggled the canister off the shelf . . . a little farther . . . and a little farther, and then . . .

The slick canister slipped right through his fingers.

Icy panic shot up Fisher's back. For a moment, time seemed to stop. The canister pinwheeled, plummeting to the ground. His eyes followed the path of the falling canister, helplessly, until it struck the hard steel floor.

And bounced.

Fisher exhaled. Of course! It was plastic. His mom was far too smart to keep an important chemical in a container made of glass.

Fisher slipped a sealable test tube out of his sock—he

always had one there, just in case—connected it to the small built-in port on the canister's seal, and eased out a bit of the advanced AGH. He quickly replaced the canister, made sure that he had not disturbed anything else in the room, and slipped out again.

The first part of Mission: Fisher Bas Number Two had been a success. Fisher allowed himself a small smile. Not even space hero (and scoundrel) Vic Daring could have done it better.

An hour later, FP lay on the floor, slowly chomping his way through a green apple, as Fisher began the process of re-creating the Accelerated Growth Hormone in his room. He had put on his white lab coat, custom-tailored to his small frame, and his gloves and goggles. A variety of laboratory supplies and materials mingled with boxes of cookies and bags of barbecue-flavored potato chips on his lab table. He had three days to make this experiment a success.

Fisher cracked his knuckles and began his work.

Clone Log. Friday, 7:00 P.M. The first stage of the process will be to establish a proper balance of the AGH, cellular tissue, and other substances to begin rapid cell division. Also, to keep a small, hungry pig with the power of flight away from my snacks. Constant vigilance will be required!

Clone Log. Friday, 7:40 P.M. Am leaving chemicals to stew while joining parents at dinner table. Have a cover story prepared in the event of fire, explosion, or fiery explosion.

Clone Log. Friday, 8:25 P.M. Have been experimenting with different chemical combinations. Have not as yet found the correct quantities. Now taking necessary pause for recalibration. And Babylon 5 *reruns.*

Clone Log. Friday, 11:46 P.M. Balance may be properly achieved with a rapid jet of oxygen to help set the process in motion. However, volatility of oxygen is causing some possible flammability issues. Small flames causing setbacks. Hope Mom won't notice the smoke damage. Also: running low on ginger ale.

Clone Log. Saturday, 12:13 A.M. After many oxygen-jet trials, am increasing to higher levels in a more rapid jet, which according to calculations should set things into motion quickly without undue risk. I think this is going to work.

Clone Log. Saturday, 12:14 A.M. Note to self: in future, make sure that the last words you use before combining volatile substances are not "I think this is going to work." Side note: AGH is very effective at stimulating the regrowth of eyebrows.

Clone Log. Saturday, 8:15 A.M. Slept for roughly 3.2 hours. Am now—

"Good morning, Fisher! You're up early today." Fisher leapt up from his keyboard, his eyes sliding rapidly over the collection of petri dishes and test tubes on his worktable before landing on his mother. She was holding a test tube, which sent a thin blue mist into the air, and she wore a sophisticated eyepiece over her right eye.

Fisher pushed away from his worktable, casually brushing a key that made his log blink off the screen.

"Hi, Mom!" he said, plastering a broad, innocent grin across his face. "How did you sleep?"

She frowned slightly, and set down her test tube on Fisher's lab station. He tensed as she walked toward him. He forced himself to keep smiling.

"Fisher, I can see through that idiotic grin on your face, so you might as well drop the act. Don't think I don't understand what's going on."

Fisher's heart began thumping in his throat. It felt like he had swallowed a bullfrog. Had she checked the levels of AGH in storage to the centiliter and noticed the missing quantity?

Fisher's heart stopped, and he began to stutter frantically. "I . . . I . . . er . . ."

She put a hand on his shoulder.

"When your dad and I were in school, we were just like you," she went on, her expression softening. "And there were bullies and social orders then, just like there are now. But that doesn't mean it's okay to be skipping classes and coming home from school early. Don't give me that look— Lord Burnside told us everything. I promise you, I truly

70

promise you, that these things will get better as you and the other kids get older. And I want you to know that you can always talk to us about it. Okay?"

The reassuring look she gave him was somewhat less effective with one of her eyes completely concealed behind an elaborate system of lenses and lights, which made her look like the world's most technologically sophisticated housefly.

"Thanks, Mom," he said. Of course she didn't know about the AGH. How could she? "I think I'll be all right. If it's okay with you, I'd like to get back to work. Helps me keep my mind off things."

"Of course, Fisher," she replied, straightening up. "I've got plenty of my own work to get to. Dad said he'd fix lunch at one, okay? Let's hope he and the oven don't get into it again. I think it's been charring the meat on purpose—it's still upset about what your father said about the broiler." Fisher nodded sympathetically as his mom backed out of the room and closed the door. He breathed an enormous sigh of relief.

Then he was back to work.

Clone Log. Saturday, 10:00 A.M. Trying a new combination of the AGH and other chemicals. Confident this new combination will not result in fire.

Clone Log. Saturday, 10:10 A.M. Confirmed, new combination skipped the fire stage and went directly to smoke. Previously untested laboratory venting system working very well.

Clone Log. Saturday, 2:00 P.M. After time taken off from experiment to brainstorm and perform new calculations, have decided that formula needs more external stimulation for process to begin. Stand by.

Clone Log. Saturday, 2:15 P.M. Preparing to apply stimulating electrical feed, after rerouting certain laboratory wires. Stand by for upda—

The screen went black in the middle of his log entry. The lights followed. With all of his blinds closed, the room was plunged into darkness. Fisher heard FP's hooves clicking as the pig jumped in surprise, then let out a squeak of fear.

Fisher felt around for his battery-powered emergency light. Finding it, he flipped the switch. The light beamed on—directly into his eyes. Blinded, he stumbled backward just as FP crossed his path. He pitched over backward and lay in a heap for a few minutes.

"I guess I'm lucky I'm short. I don't have very far to fall." He sighed. FP walked over to him and started prodding him with his nose. "And I'd have to rely on your snout-based first-aid skills."

Fisher pulled himself to his feet, walked to his door, and slid open a wall panel. Ever since his mom had caused a short circuit that set the living room couch on fire, each room in the Bas house had been connected to its own circuit breaker. Fisher switched the circuit breaker off, then on again, bringing his lights, equipment, and computer humming back to life.

The power's return made FP jump again, and this time he took off, landing squarely on Fisher's head.

"Mmmn grrrnf," Fisher said, reaching up to peel the terrified FP from his forehead. "Relax, boy. This isn't that bad. Remember when Mom made that robo-teapot, and it was running around the house dousing everything with scalding-hot Earl Grey? *That* was scary." FP shuddered a little bit, and Fisher put him down. "Now let's get back to work."

Clone Log. Saturday, 2:36 P.M. After a brief electrical setback, attempting to stimulate again at reduced voltage.

Clone Log. Saturday, 3:40 P.M. Apparently, I made a calculating error. I have produced not a human body but a large, cushion-shaped mat of hair. The pig is finding that it does, in fact, make an effective cushion.

Clone Log. Saturday, 5:00 P.M. Further unsuccessful attempts to begin cell division have produced results including a single large tooth, a circular object made entirely of biceps, and finally a one-fifth-scale skeleton. Unfortunately, an action figure is not the desired product of this experiment. Must sleep now. Still have two days to go. I'm not giving up yet . . .

Fisher collapsed onto his bed and was asleep almost instantly.

He dreamed of an army of Fishers, completely identical, faces blank, marching in lockstep along a road. The sound of hundreds of Fisher feet striking the pavement seemed to make the world jump and dance like a chimpanzee on a trampoline.

Then the dreams switched, and he was watching as his clone grew in the lab, just like it was supposed to—except the clone didn't stop. The new Fisher kept getting bigger and bigger, knocking shelves over, splintering and crashing through the ceiling, and the whole house began to collapse. . . .

Fisher jolted upright, breathing heavily. He was covered in a cold sweat. He looked at the clock. It was almost 4 A.M. He rubbed his eyes, shaking the remains of the dream out of his head as his heart gradually slowed back to normal.

As frightening as it had been, the last dream had given him an idea. . . .

He pulled his chair up to his desk, slapped down a few dozen sheets of white paper, and began frantically scribbling down new formulas and notes.

Clone Log. Sunday, 4:00 A.M. Have recalculated entire experiment—proportions of AGH need to be LARGER. Must sleep again so that I can make an appearance at breakfast, otherwise certain parties may become suspicious of my activities.

Clone Log. Sunday, 11:00 A.M. I believe I have finally

achieved the proper balance of elements and can begin the growth process. Stand by for updates.

Clone Log. Sunday, 3:00 P.M. Growth process underway. Partial skeleton has formed in the isolation tube. FP is confused. I should probably eat something before the process of watching myself be grown in a vat causes appetite loss.

Clone Log. Sunday, 8:00 P.M. Nervous system and blood vessels mostly in place. Organs are now forming. I am considering the philosophical implications and scientific importance of viewing a replica of myself slowly developing in a plastic vat. It is . . . weird.

Clone Log. Sunday, 8:01 P.M. Note to self: research vocabulary more appropriate for expressing philosophical implications.

Clone Log. Monday, 1:00 A.M. Organs continuing to grow at rapid rate, muscles starting to grow. Trying not to look at clone too much. The presence of excess fried-potato consumables in stomach may cause difficulties with over-observation.

Clone Log. Monday, 2:00 A.M. Skin beginning to grow over now fully formed muscles and organs. This experience may or may not be extremely philosophical.

Clone Log. Monday, 10:00 A.M. Subject is fully formed. Will now attempt to awaken. If clone turns into rampaging creature and takes my life, I bequeath all of my laboratory equipment to my parents, and my mint condition Issue #1 of

Vic Daring, Space Scoundrel to Harold Granger, Wompalog Middle School. My snacks I leave to FP, although he probably won't wait for the will to be read.

Fisher looked the boy in the oversize tube up and down, studying him. Proportions were all correct, bone structure seemed perfect, his muscles (or lack of them) appeared to be properly formed. His limbs pressed up against the glass. The tube had once been used by his father to incubate giant squid eggs. Fisher hoped he had cleaned the tube sufficiently before beginning the experiment; he would hate to think that his clone was part-squid.

Fisher had to build up his courage for a minute before he could bring himself to more closely examine the clone's face. *His* face.

Or almost exactly his face; Fisher had three freckles on his own nose, while the clone had only two. But surely nobody would notice a difference so slight.

It was time to bring the clone out of stasis. Its organs were being held in suspension at low temperature while direct nutrient and oxygen flow kept them alive. In the final step, Fisher would give the clone the jolt it would need to truly live, like the Frankenstein monster coming to life with a bolt of lightning.

Fisher *really* hoped that his clone would not turn out to be like the Frankenstein monster.

"This is a glorious way to begin your existence, eh, Fisher-2? In a dark, little room full of equipment and empty potato-chip bags? Too bad the only witnesses to your birth are a sleep-deprived seventh grader and a winged pork chop." He adjusted various knobs and dials in preparation for the final step of the process. "But I've got quite a future in store for you. In theory, if middle school is the first environment you're exposed to, you won't realize how horrible it is. To you, it'll just be how the world works. Hey, you might even like it."

With that, he initiated the sequence.

The IV carrying nutrients and oxygen to Fisher-2 abruptly withdrew, and the tank began to warm up. Two metal probes whirred into place, one at the clone's chest, the other below his stomach. While the tank was instantly flooded with oxygen, the probes shocked his heart, which gave its first beat.

The clone's lungs contracted, then expanded. The clone took its first breath.

Fisher, meanwhile, couldn't breathe at all.

If Fisher had calculated correctly, once the clone's pulse and breath had been set into motion, his brain should be able to take over and keep them going. A few tense seconds passed as Fisher pressed another button, and the glass tank unfolded like a flower opening its petals, exposing the clone to the atmosphere for the first time.

The only sound in the room was the low hum of the equipment, and the background babble of his lab TV.

Seconds passed. Fisher's hand hovered over the emergency button that would shut the tube again and plunge the clone into a deep freeze to keep him alive if his breathing and heartbeat didn't continue on their own.

Three seconds. Four. Five, six, seven . . .

Then the clone's chest expanded as he took another breath, and a second tiny bleep came from the heart monitor.

Fisher threw his goggles off and almost shrieked out loud. He had done it! It was alive! Fisher did a little dance of joy, making FP snort and run off into a corner to avoid being trampled.

The clone's eyes moved back and forth under their lids, and his hands twitched. Then the clone opened his eyes.

Fisher looked at his new brother and smiled cautiously. He tilted his head to one side. After a moment, Fisher-2 imitated him. Fisher slowly raised his right arm, and the clone mirrored the movement exactly. Fisher raised both arms above his head, and Fisher-2 did the same. His eyes and basic hand-eye coordination appeared to be in perfect order. Now it was time for phase two: the Knowledge Implant.

Fisher lowered a machine with a curious assortment of lights on the end of a long arm down to the clone's eye level. He had designed it to help him study for big English tests, since he never did understand why a subject with no correct answers should be studied at all.

The machine began blinking rapidly, sending complicated light signals to the brain, like a subconscious Morse code, to activate certain learning centers. Simultaneously, a probe descended and clamped around the clone's ears. Fisher knew that the clone would be hearing rapid-fire speech patterns and vocabulary words, that would help him gain command of English—as well as basic lessons in biology, math, and history—in less than thirty minutes.

He began the process, and the clone's eyes darted up at the machine as it began pulsing rapidly. Within the first twenty or thirty seconds, a basic vocabulary should be in place.

Fisher decided to test its language center.

"Fisher-2? Fisher-2? Can you hear me?" The clone did not respond. Only the sound of the TV, playing an ad for the household cleaner Spot-Rite, answered him. "Can you hear me, Two? Blink if you can hear me."

Once again, the only sound in the room was the Spot-Rite ad, with its irritating jingle. "Mommy likes to keep her whites brighter than the light of day . . ."

Fisher furrowed his brow. He couldn't understand why his clone, whose senses appeared to be functioning, wasn't reacting. Had he messed something up in the early development stages? Was the brain-activation-upload machine not working?

Then Fisher-2 said his first word.

"Mommy!"

Fisher froze in place. He realized that Fisher-2's eyes were focused just over his right shoulder on the television behind him. Fisher whopped around and saw the "mother" character in the commercial, an apron-wearing blond with a blindingly white smile, kneeling on a spotless carpet with a golden retriever.

"Spot-Rite!" she beamed, holding the bottle up toward the camera. "Get your spots right out!"

"Mommy!" Fisher-2 repeated with an anguished cry as the Spot-Rite mom faded out and another one began.

"No, don't go!" The clone took another step toward the television. "Mother! Where are you going?" The clone lunged forward.

"Wait!" Fisher said. "The machine hasn't finished . . ."

But Fisher-2 ignored him completely and kept right on going . . . pushing the delicate uploader onto the floor, where it cracked, sparking. Fisher lunged for the fire extinguisher and doused it.

The clone kept charging toward the TV.

Sitting right in front of Fisher's lab TV was a delicate assembly of beakers and tube work from an earlier experiment. One of the vinelike plastic tubes wrapped around the clone's leg as he stumbled toward the TV, and just as Fisher caught up to him, he tumbled to the floor and brought the whole mess of equipment down around him.

Fisher reached down to untangle his clone, but before he could, the clone began thrashing and punching as if he'd fallen into a nest of rattlesnakes.

"Let go of me!" he shouted at the inanimate mass tangled around him. "You'll never keep me away from her!"

"Stop it!" Fisher shouted. "Listen to me, this isn't a—" He was interrupted by the test tube that flew up and smacked into his nose.

There was a knock at the door.

"Fisher?" came his dad's voice. "Everything okay in there?"

The clone spun around to face the door and took a single running step toward it. Fisher dove and tackled him to the floor. Fisher, with strength he didn't know he possessed, held Fisher-2 down and clamped a hand over his mouth.

"Everything's fine, Dad!" he said. "Just pushed over an experiment setup by accident! I'll have it cleaned up in no time, no need to help."

"All right then," answered his dad as the clone struggled in Fisher's grip. "Just let me know if you need anything."

Footsteps retreated from his door.

"Hey!" Fisher said. *"Hey!"* He jostled the clone, and finally his new twin looked back at him.

Fisher-2 squinted for a moment.

"Father? . . . No, no. Fathers are *old*. You are not old enough." The connections in Fisher-2's brain were obviously working correctly, even if he was not exactly mentally up to par with the original. Then his eyes widened again. "Brother!"

"Uh . . . Yes, Fish—I mean, Two!" Might as well make him think that was his name. "It's me, your dear twin brother. How do you feel?"

"Where did Mom go? Why did she leave us?" Two's face fell into a frown.

Fisher sighed. He picked himself up off the floor and helped his clone do the same.

"Look, that's just a commercial. She wasn't really your mo—"

"I want to see her!" Tears started to form in the clone's eyes.

Fisher fought his frustration. At least the clone was rapidly proving that all of his basic functions were in working order.

"You don't understand, it's just a TV, that woman's an actor, and she—"

"Please go get her and let me see her!"

"Oh, for Pete's sake, kid, will you please listen—"

Without warning, the clone dropped to his knees and began to wail.

"I need to see her! There's a spot on my heart, and only she can get it right out!" Two buried his face in his hands and let out a shuddering sob.

Fisher couldn't believe it. Was it possible—was it remotely, humanly possible—that Fisher's clone was even *lamer* than, well, Fisher?

For a moment, Fisher wished he had never brought his clone out of stasis. If the clone kept wailing, there was no way his parents wouldn't come and investigate.

Then he caught sight of an old book of his, *The Iron Corsair*, lying on his desk (Fisher had been using it as a coaster for his cans of Dr Pepper). The book was about a swift-sailing soldier whose mother is kidnapped by an evil cult.

Suddenly, Fisher had an idea.

"Two. Hey, Two!" he said. Two stopped crying. "I know what's happened to Mom!"

Fisher-2 looked hopefully at Fisher and climbed to his feet. "Tell me."

"Mom's been taken away somewhere—captured, that is—and we have to rescue her. We're being kept in this house against our will, though, so we have to be clever about it. The bad people holding us here don't know that there are two of us. They think we're the same person! If we want to find Mom, they can never know the truth! Understood?"

Two nodded.

"Here's what we need to do," Fisher went on. "I'll stay here and work in this lab, and you have to go to a secret institution the enemy is using to train their evil agents. You go there every day, and you will learn things. Some of these things may not seem important, but with enough information you can gather the clues we need to find her!"

Fisher-2 stood up straighter, looking suddenly determined, like a man on a noble and heroic mission. "Anything for her, brother! I will keep my mission a secret and blend in with the evil henchmen around me. What is this institution?"

"It is called middle school, and it's the most fiendish, torturous, and horrible place ever conceived in the darkest corner of man's mind." At least he didn't have to lie about *that* part.

"Very well. I shall covertly attend this middle school while you research rescue methods here in this prison. I will spend as much time as it takes to gather the knowledge we need."

"Good man," Fisher said, patting his clone on the shoulder. "Now get some sleep. You need your rest. The mission begins tomorrow."

CHAPTER 7

School teaches you many things. For example, it teaches you to really not like school.

—Fisher Bas, *Personal Notes*

Fisher lay under his covers, tense, with FP curled up next to him. It was Tuesday morning. This was it. Two was dressed for school and on his way downstairs. Fisher counted sixty seconds, then crept after him.

Two's steps were light and purposeful as he descended to the first floor. So far, so good. Fisher heard the distinctive ringing sound of a spoon scraping the sides and bottom of a cereal bowl.

Fisher had carefully typed up an "intelligence document" about the "mission" for Two. Because Two had destroyed the info-upload machine, he'd been forced to turn to the Internet. He'd directed Two to Wikipedia, and Two had stayed up reading all night.

Additionally, Fisher had typed up a simple overview of all the information Two would have to know in order to imitate the original Fisher. Two had so far shown himself a remarkably quick learner, and his mind was nearly as sharp as the original's. The document read like this:

YOUR COVER NAME: FISHER BAS.

YOUR ASSIGNMENT: INFILTRATE WOMPALOG MIDDLE SCHOOL. GATHER INFORMATION AS IT BECOMES KNOWN TO YOU. (PLEASE TAKE NOTES NEATLY ON COLLEGE-RULED LOOSE-LEAF PAPER, WITH BLACK OR BLUE PEN.)

—YOU WILL NOTE THAT MANY OF THE TEACHERS AT WOMPALOG ARE CAPABLE OF HYPNOTIC POWERS OF SLEEP-INDUCING SPEECH. TRY TO REMAIN ALERT THROUGHOUT CLASSES TO AVOID ATTRACTING TOO MUCH ATTENTION.

—ALSO, TO AVOID ATTRACTING TOO MUCH ATTENTION: DON'T TALK TOO MUCH IN CLASS, NEVER WEAR BRIGHT COLORS, AND AVOID EYE CONTACT WITH FELLOW STUDENTS IN THE HALL.

—THERE IS A SQUAD OF THUGS THE ENEMY MAINTAINS AMONG THE SCHOOL POPULATION. THEY ARE CALLED THE VIKINGS. THEY ARE TRAINED IN CLOSE COMBAT, SPYING, AND ADVANCED RESTROOM-BASED INTERROGATION TECHNIQUES. AVOID AT ALL COSTS.

Fisher had also listed his classes, teachers, and classroom numbers, and advice on which food in the cafeteria was edible, since most of it was not.

"Good morning . . . Mom and Dad," Two said. Fisher, listening on the landing upstairs, flinched a little at the slight pause. But if his parents noticed it, they didn't say anything.

"Morning, Fisher!" came his dad's voice. "Sleep well?"

"Indeed," Two said cheerfully.

Wompalog Middle School
Class Schedule

Name: Fisher Bas
Grade: 7
Homeroom: Mrs. Thurston

Period 1 - Math - Mr. Mael, Room 213

You know this. Don't worry about it.

Period 2 - Computers - Mrs. Visulian, Room 220

Vikings share this class. Steer clear! Don't correct them
no matter how wrong they are!

Period 3 - Debate - Mr. Hart, Room 317

Don't upset Amanda! She can hurt you. Also, Mr. Hart is never there.

Period 4 - Activity Period

Monday - Gym

Try to stay out of sight.

Tuesday - Music

No solos!

Wednesday - Art

Art teacher is nuts. Recently divorced. Don't ask how she is.

Thursday - Gym

Friday - Study Hall

No comment.

Period 5 - English - Mrs. Weedle, Room 302

Mrs. Weedle is super boring. Just try to stay awake.

Period 6 - Biology - Mr. Granger, Room 104

Sanctuary! Best class + teacher ever!

Period 7 - Lunch Don't eat: well, anything.

Go back to Mr. Granger + he'll share something better.

Period 8 - History - Mrs. Shorza, Room 324

U.S. history is pointless. Just get through it.

Fisher's stomach flipped. *Indeed?* But again, his parents said nothing, and there were more cereal bowl clinks.

"Ready for a new week?" said his mom.

"Yes," Two replied in the same flat voice. "Could I have some grapes to take to school?"

Fisher stifled a gasp and clenched his fists.

"Grapes?" said his dad. "Don't you hate grapes? You always say it feels like you're eating human eyes."

Please think fast, please think fast, Fisher pleaded silently.

"I, ah . . . yes, exactly," said Two. "They're not to eat. I'm doing a physics experiment to test the effects of impact stress on the human eyeball."

"Oh, how lovely!" said his mother. "Let me get you some. Would you prefer green or red eyeballs?"

As Fisher heard his father get up from the table, he quickly retreated to his room. He hopped back into bed and rolled himself up in his sheet to wait. After a few more minutes, he heard the front door open and close. That must be Two headed for the bus. Another few minutes, and he heard his father leave for work and, finally, his mother.

With his parents safely out of the house, Fisher swept the covers off, leapt from his bed, and threw a fist in the air in triumph. In the process he wrapped his sheet entirely around his left ankle and came crashing to the floor in a heap, but he was too happy to care. The first part of his plan was a complete success. If he could keep everything running smoothly, he might *never have to set foot in middle school again.*

"Waaahhooooooo!!!!!!" Fisher screamed, throwing his head back as he did. FP oinked and bounced around him.

Fisher had the whole day ahead to himself, and it was the best feeling in the world. No classes, no obnoxious kids, no toxic-sludge lunch, and, most important of all, no Vikings. He'd have to spend the day in his room; if he ventured into the rest of the house, some of the intelligent appliances might tattle on him. Being the kid of two genius inventors had its perks, but also its drawbacks: it's tough to keep your presence at home a secret when the toaster can mention to your mother how interesting it was that you came into the kitchen for a snack at 11:13 A.M.

But Fisher had already stocked up on necessary supplies and had plenty of food to get him through the day.

Fisher pulled his leg out of the sheet and leaned against his bed. FP trotted toward him, and Fisher reached down and lightly stroked one wing-flap. "I think I've done it, boy. I'll be around a lot more from now on."

At 10:00 A.M., third period, he'd ordinarily be sprinting full tilt down the hall, trying to stay far away from any object of head-stuffing-in size. Today he was sitting at his lab table, petting FP, and testing out a new growth-accelerating formula. He usually spent fifth period listening to a teacher whose voice made a foghorn sound chipper and excited. Today he was playing video games, saving a tiny peasant village from the wrath of elder snake gods. Lunch period on a normal day would involve feeding crumbs of unrecognizable "food" to ants to see if it killed them. Today he was on his bed, popping Cheetos into his mouth and reading the latest issue of Vic Daring, Space Scoundrel—flipping pages with the non-cheesy hand, of course.

The rest of the school year—which Fisher usually imagined as an endless prison hallway, each day a separate cell—now stretched before him like an endless sunny day. As he hummed happily around his room, checking on various experiments and munching on his favorite post-meal dessert of M&M-coated Starbursts (one of Fisher's favorite inventions), he could barely stop himself from bursting into song. Even FP seemed happier than usual—happier than he *ever* did, except when he was eating.

There was no doubt about it. The lying, the stealing—even the singe marks on his ceiling from one of the more fiery, failed cloning experiences—had all been worth it. In this case, the ends really did justify the means.

In the afternoon, Fisher put the finishing touches on a little chamber that he'd been building. Underneath an older lab table near the back of his personal lab space, he had placed a small mattress, a lamp, water, and food. This was to be Two's hidden living area. Fisher's room was so big and cluttered, that the little nest would go completely unnoticed.

But as the end of the school day approached, a faint twinge of guilt started to build in Fisher's stomach. Two might be Fisher's creation, but he was still a living, breathing, thinking being. And Fisher had just thrown him into a pit of lions. Who knows what could have happened to him on his first day at Wompalog? What if he'd wandered into the wrong room and gotten laughed at by a whole class? What if the Vikings had tossed him into the cafeteria Dumpster with his underwear pulled up to his ears?

Fisher was imagining his duplicate stumbling through the door battered, bruised, covered in grass stains or chocolate pudding or sea kelp. Maybe his first day was so bad, he'd refuse to go back. Maybe he'd be transferred to a mental asylum.

All of the terrible possibilities tumbled through Fisher's head as he sat at his worktable, trying for the several hundredth time to re-splice the DNA of his attack mosquitoes. Making a duplicate of himself hadn't involved any genetic rewriting. Strangely, the mosquito work needed a lot more fine-tuning. And it was hard to focus, worrying about all of the terrible things that could have happened to Two.

He heard the front door open and close. He heard Fisher-sized footsteps coming up the stairs, and then a frantic banging at his door. He sprang up from his chair and ran for the door, ready with a medical kit, some anti-bacterial soap, and a case of anti-radiation medicine (in case he'd eaten the Cobb salad), just in case.

"It's okay, Two. I'm coming. I'm—oh, no."

There he was. He had some kind of orange sauce dotting the top of his shirt and striping his hair. Little scraps of paper and plastic wrappers clung to his clothes.

But in spite of all of that . . . he looked perfectly calm and collected. He walked . . . no, not just walked, *strode* into the room, picked up Fisher's bag of BBQ potato chips, and set himself down in Fisher's reading chair, nodding to Fisher.

"Hey. Get some work done?" he asked, reaching in and pulling out a chip.

"I, uh . . . yes. Yes, I did. How was school?" Fisher could barely choke out the words past his disbelief.

Two shrugged.

"Fine. I didn't get any leads, but I guess this operation is going to take time. Anything valuable is probably buried pretty deep."

Fisher's eyes went wide. "Er . . . what about the, uh . . ." Fisher gestured at the food and junk on Two's clothes.

"Three guys gave me a hard time," Two said casually. "Probably the agents your document mentioned. I have to say, I'm not impressed. Their brains process information about as fast as sponge cake, and I told them so. Besides which, they have a totally bad vibe." He popped another handful of chips into his mouth.

Fisher swallowed. "You *said* that to them?" He could barely choke the words out. "You can't—you're not allowed to—you shouldn't have—"

"Why not?" Two asked, shrugging again. Fisher realized he didn't know how to explain, or where to begin. *That's not how things work*, he wanted to say. *You just don't understand.* But his mind was spinning so fast, no words would come out.

Two threw his feet onto the desk. "I also told them I'd seen better-looking larvae than their little trio. They didn't seem to know what larvae were, but they understood when I said 'worm.'" Two chuckled. "That's when they upended a garbage can over me. But they're gonna need a lot more than a bad-smelling ambush to stop me. Did you know that most aggressive behavior comes from having inherited unevolved ape genes?"

"That's not true," Fisher said.

"Is so. Read it on Wikipedia," Two said.

"You shouldn't believe . . ." Fisher started to say, but Two cut him off by springing out of the chair, chips in hand, and whipping out a small plastic case from his backpack. It was a video game disk case.

"*Super Bayonet Frenzy 6*?" said Fisher, his eyes lighting up. "Where did you get a copy of that?"

"Borrowed it from a friend," said Two.

Fisher opened his mouth to reply, but no words were in his head, and so a simple *hhhhsssmmpphh* sound escaped him as Two dropped his things on the other side of the room.

A friend? He borrowed it from a friend?

"I'm gonna go change, then watch some TV," Two said. "I'll do it downstairs so I don't disturb your work." As he headed out the door, he paused, leaning his head back in. "By the way," he said, pointing to the petri dish where the mosquito engineering was taking place, "there should be another TCCAG sequence at the end of your third artificial RNA strand." He followed this remark with a wink—*a wink*—and closed the door behind him.

Fisher sat in his room, dumbstruck. Who *was* this kid? And where did this swagger come from?

What was going on?

An hour later, Fisher sat staring at the dining room wall, slowly lifting forkfuls of chicken and vegetable stir-fry from his plate and down to FP. The pig was sitting on his lap and happily snapping up each bite. His mind was still whirling, and his parents' conversation, which he picked up in bits and pieces, sounded echoey and distant. Two was hiding upstairs. Fisher had promised to smuggle up his dinner when he was done.

"I just can't believe what they're up to this time," said his dad in a fretful tone.

"You mean the plans to expand the King of Hollywood into an arcade complex?" asked his mom.

"Exactly. It's going to take up thousands of square feet more, and that could . . ."

Fisher's mind drifted. Two had borrowed a video game *from a friend*. The closest thing to a friend Fisher had ever had was Mr. Granger, and he risked a heart attack every time he played Go Fish.

". . . and the lesser pink-mottled ganglebird has never been closer to extinction than it is now!" came his father's voice again.

"That's unfortunate. . . . How exactly do these birds 'gangle'?" asked his mother, sounding puzzled.

"Well, you see . . ."

That meant that Two had made *a new* friend. Even *normal* people didn't make friends close enough to borrow from after a single *day*!

There was only one explanation: Fisher must have done something wrong. Maybe he'd been too hasty in his cloning process. Maybe he'd missed an essential part of the formula. Or maybe the problem was in the hormone itself! It was still in early stages of development. That must be it.

"Mom?" Fisher asked.

She turned to face him, blinking, as she tried to sink

Revaluation of 3rd level calculations on "Two."

$$O = \frac{1/2\ G^1 a f^2}{9.4M(.5)(7/9)}$$

$\downarrow$

$$(2.7\text{fer})(2.76\text{mL}) = C$$

$\downarrow$

$$q = \frac{2d}{f^2} = 7.2\ (.29\text{mL})$$

$\downarrow$

WHAT WENT WRONG?!?!

Vic Daring never had these kinds of problems.

her teeth into a zucchini the size of a baseball bat, gnawing it like an ear of corn. "Mmmph?"

Fisher tickled FP behind the ears, to avoid making eye contact. "Oh, I was just curious about your work on the AGH. Have you noticed any strange . . . um, effects?"

"Don't be silly, Fisher. We're still in a developmental phase. There hasn't been any kind of testing yet, so we have no way of knowing its effects. And, Fisher," she went on, "while your father and I encourage your scientific curiosity, I need to make very clear to you just how delicate and sensitive my work is. You can't go around talking about AGH, not to anyone, you understand?"

Fisher nodded, trying to stop his mouth from twitching.

"A lot of people would be interested in getting a hold of it," his mom went on, her brow wrinkling with worry, "and there's no telling what lengths they'll go to. Criminals, foreign governments, biotech corporations . . . if they found out just what I'm working on, they might try to hurt me to get it. Or your father. Or even you."

Little sweat beads rolled down the back of Fisher's neck, leaving icy trails.

"Speaking of which," she said, turning to Fisher's father, "a brick in the perimeter wall was out of place today. I think someone might've been trying to bypass security."

"You check the wall, brick by brick?" Fisher's dad asked.

"I am *not* letting anyone get their hands on this formula," she said, bringing her fist down on the table for emphasis. "No one. Anyone who tries is going to have to answer to me."

The table's arm popped out and removed her plate, mistaking the impact of her hand for an order. She quickly tapped it again to get her dinner back.

Fisher spent the rest of the dinner in anxious silence.

Later that evening, Two crawled into his little makeshift sleeping space as Fisher climbed into bed. The plate that Fisher had snuck up with dinner for Two sat on the floor, and FP contentedly lapped up the little bits left over.

"Ready for tomorrow?" Fisher asked.

"If it's as easy tomorrow as it was today, I'll have no problems," Two answered as he rolled onto his back. Almost immediately, he was asleep.

As Fisher closed his eyes and tried to block out the sounds of Two's snoring, it occurred to him, for the first time, that maybe this hadn't been such a great idea after all. The fact that he had proved that the AGH worked would make it even more valuable—and his family even more of a target—if the truth ever came out.

One thing was clear: no one could *ever* find out about Two.

CHAPTER 8

Every experiment has unforeseen complications. Keeping a good ten feet between yourself and the experiment is a good idea, too. It doesn't matter what you're working with; things have a tendency to explode.
—Harold Granger, A Lab Enthusiast's Handbook

Fisher was woken up by the sound of his two-day-old twin going through the closet. He blinked the blurriness away and had to stifle a laugh when he saw what Two was wearing. He had on an old T-shirt, full of holes and fraying at all edges, which his mother used as a hand cloth for cleaning the furniture. It had been his dad's years ago, with a now completely worn-down and unreadable rock band logo.

Fisher was about to ask him about his choice of outfit when a sharp citrus aroma hit his nose. It was the scent of Spot-Rite. Two must have been wearing the shirt so that he had a reminder of his "mother" in his nostrils at all times.

He was also wearing an old, short-brimmed gray fedora that Fisher had inherited from his grandfather. It was still in pretty good condition, though the peak was starting to lose its shape. Two looked in the mirror and cocked the hat slightly to the side, so it almost hid his right eye. Then he noticed that he was being watched and turned to Fisher.

"How do I look?" he asked, spreading his arm wide.

"Like you tripped, fell through a thrift store, and landed in a bucket of floor polish," said Fisher, trying to make the remark sound as pleasant as possible.

"Cool," Two said. Fisher winced.

Two shouldered his backpack, a much more stylish replacement for the one that Fisher had left in the cafeteria. When Fisher had asked where he'd gotten it, Two had replied simply, "Traded it for a favor." He had given Fisher no other details.

"See you in the afternoon," Two said with a wink. And out the door he went, a wake of lemony-fresh scent trailing through the air behind him.

Fisher pulled himself out of bed, stretching his arms. In the morning, with the sunshine streaming in, his concerns about Two seemed silly. No one would find out. How could they?

Another day of glorious freedom spread before him. He sat down at his worktable. He was still tinkering with the genetic structure of the attack-squitoes, helped in part by Two's suggestion. He carefully stuck his arm through the seal into the tank. When he pulled it back out, it was only lightly bitten.

Hmmm. Could Two be even smarter than the original?

Fisher pushed aside a twinge of envy. He would *not* be jealous of his own clone.

At lunchtime, Fisher realized the only food he had left in his room was a half-squashed chocolate bar and some stale Doritos. His stomach grumbled.

He would have to risk a trip to the kitchen.

Fisher crept into the hall. Getting downstairs was relatively easy—the night-light was always sleeping during the day. He tiptoed down the hall toward the kitchen. This would be dangerous.

Fisher took a quick look inside to check and see that the appliances weren't on alert. The oven was intelligent, but when it was cold it had sluggish senses and a terrible memory. The dinner table was technically intelligent—but, thankfully, it couldn't see. And Fisher knew that the fridge spent much of its time pouring off wine into its own box, and was generally out of it.

As long as he didn't bump anything, he would be fine.

Carefully, slowly, he extended a single foot onto the pale linoleum, hoping it wouldn't squeak.

He froze when a faint blubbering noise came from just a few feet away.

His eyes darted to one side of the counter. Lord Burnside!

For a second, Fisher considered darting away. Then he realized the toaster was asleep. A faint, cheerful snoring sound emanated from its wire baskets, which rose and fell in a rhythmic fashion.

Fisher sucked in a deep breath and took slow, careful steps into the kitchen. To his relief, the snoring continued. Unfortunately, he wouldn't be able to open the fridge without waking it up. He tiptoed toward the pantry, hoping to scrounge up something decent.

"Oh my!" came a high-pitched exclamation from the toaster.

Fisher jumped a foot in the air, landing unsteadily. He was about to sputter excuses when Lord Burnside went on. "Lady Wheaton-Rye, however did you get up the narrow staircase to my chambers in those petticoats? And is this visit entirely proper?"

Fisher stifled a laugh. Lord Burnside was dreaming! His dad loved to tinker with the AI programming his mom had originally installed. Apparently, the latest update actually allowed the toaster to dream.

Fisher reached into the pantry, grabbed the first edible thing he found, and bolted back to his room.

But just as he sat down to enjoy a pack of granola bars, the house alarm began to wail.

"Intruder alert!" the house blared. "Intruder alert!"

Fisher was so surprised he toppled backward out of his chair. Someone was trying to break into the house! Forgetting all about staying quiet, he made a dash for the nearest security console, which was in his parents' bedroom.

"Intruder al—!"

Before he could reach the security console, the alarm abruptly went silent. Fisher tapped at the console frantically, trying to figure out why it was no longer working. The alarm should still be blaring, automatically notifying his parents at their jobs, but it wasn't.

Fortunately, the cameras were still working. Fisher tapped and swiped at the screen, and brought up the front yard on the monitor. His heart was hammering.

Two dark-clothed, masked figures were making their way across the front yard. They'd gotten past the outer wall, and Fisher realized they must have managed to disable the alarm system. The house's automatic defenses should have been running in response, but nothing was activating.

Fisher looked at the array of controls in front of him. His heart was jackhammering inside of his chest. He couldn't call his parents, and reactivating the security system would take more time than he had. The intruders would reach the door in less than a minute even at their creeping pace.

Fisher took off at a run back to his room, where he began tearing through his closet, looking for anything to help him fight off the intruders. FP circled Fisher's ankles, squealing nervously.

He plucked a small pouch out of a cardboard box full of in-progress inventions. "This won't stop them," he said to himself, "but it might slow them down and buy me some time."

He raced down the stairs just as scratching sounds emanated from beyond the front door. They were picking the lock! Fisher opened up the pouch and removed what looked like an ordinary clump of dirt. He tossed it into the foyer, then raced to the hall bathroom. After soaking a towel in water, he returned to the front hall.

"I was hoping to test you under more controlled conditions," Fisher muttered as he squeezed and wrung the towel out onto the dirt clump, "but this'll have to do."

Fisher jumped back as the clump started to move and pulse, making scratching, snapping noises. Wooden spines shot up into the air, splitting off into branches, and these sprouted full, richly green leaves. Roots crawled out along the floor and gripped the walls for support. Within moments a fully grown shrub decorated the Bas entranceway. His shrub-hiding incident by the bus had reminded him of this old project of his dad's. Insta-Growth was intended for use to quickly repopulate flora in deforested spots. Fisher had been hoping to modify it for hiding purposes. This prototype was decent, although the presence of enormous, thick thorns on its branches made it impractical to stand in.

Fisher gave the creation an approving nod before

racing back up to his room. He heard the dead bolt click back and the door swing open behind him, followed by the surprised shouts of the thieves as they came face-to-face with the most bizarre interior-decorating choice they had ever seen.

"What's *this* doin' here?" said a gruff male voice.

"Doesn't matter. Get out the special shears the doc gave us. We'll get through it in no time," answered a smoother voice.

Fisher backed out of the front hall and into the kitchen, frantically trying to hatch a defensive plan. Every snap of a twig made him jolt like a live wire. He tried to keep his hands steady as he ducked beneath the half wall separating the dining area from the kitchen, to keep the fridge from seeing him.

All that he could find was a stack of small plates sitting on the table. The men he was up against weren't about to get slowed down by a bunch of flying dishware.

Was this it? Was he fated to meet his end cowering under a dinner table?

The dinner table.

Suddenly, Fisher knew what to do. Gathering an armful of plates, he hunkered down behind the table and waited.

A final crack, and what was left of the shrub toppled over, revealing the two thieves, clad in black and wearing full face masks.

"All right, let's go!" said the smooth-voiced one. "We're looking for the laboratory."

"I thought I heard something over this way," said the other.

"Okay, okay. We'll check it out. But let's make it fast."

They strode purposefully in Fisher's direction.

Fisher took aim and hurled a plate. It sailed past the leader's face by over a foot . . . which was exactly Fisher's intention.

As the thief turned to see where the plate had come from, there was a loud *clank!* One of the table's automatic arms shot out to catch the airborne dinnerware . . . and smacked the intruder right on his forehead, knocking him onto the ground.

"What the . . . ?" he started to say, clutching his head, and staggering to his feet.

As the second thief started forward, another plate whizzed past his head, and a second wooden arm shot out from the table and floored him.

"The table!" he shrieked. "The table's attacking us!"

Fisher took a deep breath and ramped up the barrage. As the thieves got to their feet again, dizzy and dazed, Fisher sent a flurry of plates in their direction. The table arms grabbed each one, battering the two men relentlessly. At last, they lay in a heap on the floor, one clutching his arm, the other grabbing his sides. Fisher stayed low behind the table, keeping out of sight.

"I think I mighta broke a rib," said the gruff one, holding his side.

"I ain't gettin' paid enough for this," the other one replied, cradling his elbow. "That doc guy didn't say nothin' about a fightin' table. Let's split."

The thieves picked themselves up and limped out of the house, one angrily slamming the door behind them. Fisher collapsed backward on the tile floor, as the table arms retracted neatly. The hall was filled with shattered plates, and he had no idea how he would explain that to his parents, but the important thing was this: the intruders were gone.

"Nicely done, Woody," Fisher murmured to the table, reaching up to pat it on the side. The table flapped its leaves once.

When his breathing had slowed, Fisher climbed to his feet, rebooted the security systems, and swept the hall clean of shattered porcelain. He decided it was best *not* to let his parents know about this little incident. There's no way he'd be able to explain why he was home when the attempted break-in happened. Really, his parents should be thankful! If it hadn't been for Fisher's incredible foresight in cloning himself (and sending that clone to school in his place), the Bas home might be under siege. Working quickly, Fisher deleted the security logs from the past hour and replaced them with normal status reports.

Someday he'd tell them about the break-in. Maybe.

Later that afternoon, Fisher was working hard on his latest project: a device that would give him remote access to the house's security system. By altering one of his old calculator watches into a mobile command station, he would theoretically be able to control the security system from anywhere in the house. This would allow him to move through the house undetected and help him be ready in case of another intrusion.

He was so absorbed that he hadn't even noticed that Two was back from school until he heard water running in the bathroom and the jazzy sounds of cheerful humming: Two was singing the Spot-Rite commercial jingle over and over under his breath. Fisher couldn't help but feel a twinge of irritation. Two couldn't even *pee* without having fun.

A few minutes later, Two had still not emerged from the bathroom, and Fisher's fourth orange soda of the day had just taken its toll. He walked to the bathroom door and rattled the handle.

"Hey," he said. "You almost done in there?"

"Hang on a minute," came Two's voice, and then Fisher heard him continue talking. "Are you sure that's a good idea? . . . I don't know. Is it really going to work? Eighty percent of protests end in arrest . . . Yeah. Wikipedia . . . You're

Schematics for
MOBILE COMMAND CENTER WATCH

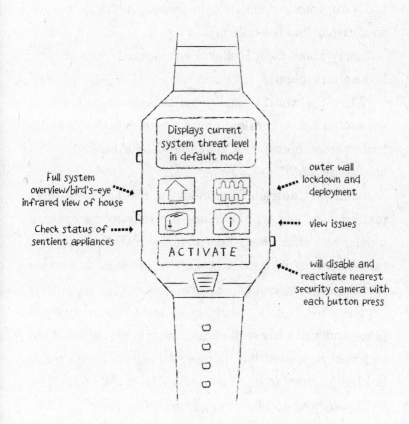

Displays current system threat level in default mode

Full system overview/bird's-eye infrared view of house

Check status of sentient appliances

outer wall lockdown and deployment

view issues

will disable and reactivate nearest security camera with each button press

ACTIVATE

probably right, now that I think about it. . . ."

Fisher's mind began racing. *Uh-oh. Two is talking to himself! Is my creation slipping into madness? Did the AGH turn his brain to bread pudding? Will he turn violent? What can I do to save my—* Then the door opened, and Two, with a perfectly calm look on his face, breezed past Fisher into the hallway.

"Sorry about that, Fisher. I just wanted some privacy. I was on the phone."

"The—the what?" Fisher spluttered, even as his eyes fell on the black, cordless phone clutched in Two's hand. Fisher sometimes forgot that they *had* a phone. "But—how? With who?"

"Amanda Cantrell. I'd promised to call her later. She's planning to protest the King of Hollywood's opening tomorrow. I think I'm going to go down there and try to talk her out of it. But for now we've got more important stuff to focus on, right?"

Even FP, trotting along at Fisher's side, stopped in place and stuck his ears up at that remark. Fisher himself was surprised that he was still able to blink, which is what he stood in place doing for a minute or so as Two went snapping and humming into the bedroom.

It was official: something was wrong. *Very* wrong.

Not only had wearing a torn shirt and a hat six decades out of style earned Two a friend, it had earned him *two*

110

friends—and one of them *was a girl*! Two had done in two days what Fisher had yet to accomplish in his whole life.

Whatever was going on at school, Fisher had to find out about it. Tomorrow, he was going to get to the bottom of this mystery.

≋ CHAPTER 9 ≋

A lot of people say they trust themselves, but most of their "selves" don't have the power to wreak havoc while they aren't looking.

—Fisher Bas, Personal Notes

It was Thursday, after school, and the day before the new King of Hollywood's grand opening. Fisher had spent the day in anxious agitation. Even a new issue of Vic Daring: Space Scoundrel hadn't been able to calm him down.

He knew that Amanda Cantrell had planned a big protest, and he knew that Two would be making an appearance of his own.

Fisher was also planning on making a cameo. Two was obviously up to something. He'd been standing up to the Vikings, and making friends—friends!—which meant that he was already calling attention to himself. Fisher needed to see whether the clone was in danger of breaking their secret wide open.

"Disguise, disguise," Fisher mused, looking around his room. "What should I use for a disguise?"

Half an hour later, a short boy walked toward the King

of Hollywood restaurant. A strangely puffy plume of long hair spilled out of his pulled-up hood, and he was wearing tropical-themed souvenir sunglasses with little palm trees on the frames.

It was not, Fisher admitted, the most brilliant disguise he could have imagined. All the same, it was a good use for the extra hair Fisher had accidentally engineered during the early stages of the cloning process, which had looked kind of creepy just sitting on the floor of Fisher's room.

The remains of the marshland made a strangely prehistoric-looking setting for the restaurant, as if a herd of *Iguanodon* might emerge at any moment to graze on spicy fries and milk shakes. Fisher could see a crowd gathering in the parking lot already, many hoisting signs in the air. He really hadn't expected that many to turn up against the popular chain. Maybe the ducks had really earned a place in people's hearts.

When Fisher got closer, he took a look at some of their signs: LONG LIVE THE KING; TWO BILLS IS ONE TOO MANY; I BET YOU DON'T EVEN KNOW WHAT BILIOUS MEANS.

The big crowd had formed to protest *against* the protest.

Fisher elbowed through the crowd, trying not to draw too much attention to himself, and finally broke free of the tightly knit pack.

In front of the King of Hollywood restaurant were

Amanda Cantrell, a handful of Wompalog kids he recognized but didn't know, and . . . a giant duck.

Or rather, somebody in a human-sized double-billed yellow-bellied bilious duck costume.

Amanda had handcuffed herself to the front-door handles of the new restaurant. The other kids looked nervous, probably because the only people watching their protest had joined the *counter*protest. The only member of the protest who seemed really enthusiastic was the giant duck, who was walking back and forth shouting various pro-duck statements.

"Ducks don't knock down your houses for bread crumbs!" it shouted in a voice that was muffled, but very familiar. "This marshland is their only habitat! You are bringing them to their doom! Do you really want a doomed duck on your conscience?" Very, very familiar. "We can coexist with this peaceful species! Live in harmony! Their double-billed quacking really is quite harmonious!"

The giant duck paused for a moment, breathing heavily. "Man, this thing is hot," it said, before reaching up and pulling off the duck head. Fisher gaped.

"Dad?" he gasped.

There was no doubt about it. There was Mr. Bas, wearing a giant duck costume in front of the entire town. Fisher buried his forehead in his hand and wished he could rocket himself into a new solar system. This would make things even worse for him than they already were. The other kids at Wompalog would mock and push him around even *more.* . . .

No. They would push *Two* around even more. He knew that he had created his clone just for this purpose, but rather than feel triumphant, he felt a little sickened by the idea. But maybe, at least, Two would start to realize how things worked at Wompalog: it was best to lay low.

Fisher retreated a little farther into the jostling crowd as his dad took off the rest of the duck suit. The counter-protesters began chanting "Holl-ly-wood! Holl-ly-wood!" until someone shushed them to silence and stepped forward.

Two.

The clone walked back and forth in front between the two groups, raising his hands to the much-larger counter-protest to get their attention.

"This fine establishment is not the great invader that they're making it out to be!" he said, affecting a heroic tone. "Don't be fooled! The ducks aren't the big victims here, but our taste buds will be if they get their way!" The counter-protesters shouted and waved their signs in response.

"Fisher?" Mr. Bas said, tossing the second huge duck foot aside. "How could you be doing this?"

"I'm sorry . . . *Dad,*" Two said, "but I've been analyzing your data on these ducks very carefully, and I'm afraid you're wrong about them."

"What are you *doing*, Fisher?" Amanda hissed, rattling her cuffs. "King of Hollywood is destroying their only habitat!"

Two reached into his pocket and pulled out a map, which he unfolded and held above his head.

"The double-billed yellow-bellied bilious duck is not native to marshlands!" he proclaimed, pointing at several spots on the map. "This species moved here after their old woodland habitats were drying up from drought! Evidence I've collected indicates that the species only lives on this marshland because it was the only place wet enough at the time." He produced another piece of paper with a graph on it. "That drought ended five years ago. The original habitat of the DBYBBD is more than capable of supporting them again."

There was a moment of stunned silence. Fisher's dad and Amanda looked at each other with puzzled surprise on their faces.

Fisher gritted his teeth. Two was drawing more and more attention to himself with every moment. Was making friends not enough for him? Did he need to be a celebrity, too?

"Well . . . ," Amanda said, searching for a comeback, "what about their food source? The frogs in the waters of this marsh are keeping the ducks well fed, and the ducks are keeping the frogs from overpopulating!"

"In the short term, yes," said Two. Then he reached into a pocket and pulled out yet another piece of paper with a chart on it. "But what's really happening is that the ducks are eating up the small marsh frogs that the badgers used to thrive on. Now those badgers are losing their food source, and in the long term, the ducks will throw off the whole ecosystem."

There was a longer silence. Fisher's dad scratched his head, and Amanda looked down at her handcuffs, kicking the toe of her shoe against the pavement. Fisher adjusted his wig but remained hidden in the crowd.

"Well . . .," Mr. Bas said, looking bashful. He had finally wrestled out of the duck costume, and was wearing (to Fisher's dismay) a full suit of long underwear. "Well. They aren't going to move back to the woodland all by themselves. Will you help us organize an effort to help move them?"

Two was about to reply when a high-pitched screech pierced the air. A pair of hawks circled rapidly above one of the small patches of marsh untouched by the construction.

"The nest!" Trevor cried out. The hawks were circling lower and lower, closing in on a nest of baby DBYBBDs.

"Do something!" someone cried out, but nobody moved. Everyone was frozen in horror.

Then, suddenly, the giant duck was flapping and

squawking and tearing toward the nest. Fisher saw that his dad was still standing next to Amanda. Someone else had slipped on the suit and was honking and quacking and beating its enormous wings furiously.

The hawks let out a final screech and shot back up into the sky to escape the wrath of the giant waterfowl. Fisher watched as, with feathered wings, the duck impersonator reached up and removed the costume's head.

And, of course, it was Two.

Fisher ground his teeth as the whole crowd cheered and shouted his name. Two just beamed and shrugged as he took off the rest of the duck costume.

Two walked over to Amanda, who was tugging at her handcuffs. Fisher slipped his way through the crowd so he could get closer and hear their conversation.

"I tried to get the key out of my pocket," Amanda said shyly, "but it fell."

"Let me help," Two said, reaching down and fetching the key. He unlocked the handcuffs and set Amanda free. Fisher watched as they stood for a moment, smiling at each other. Then Fisher's dad came up behind Two and clapped him on the shoulder.

"That was pretty amazing, Fisher," he said, beaming. "I got so caught up in closely studying the ducks that I lost sight of the bigger picture! And the trick with the duck suit was pretty inspired."

"Anything to save a baby duck," Two said, not taking his eyes off Amanda, in a voice so syrupy sweet it made Fisher choke.

"Wow, Fisher." Amanda beamed at him. "I always knew you were smart. But I never knew you had such a big heart, too."

Fisher decided he'd seen enough. He had to sneak away soon, anyway, to make sure he got home before his dad and Two did. Luckily, his mom was going to be working until later in the evening.

Feeling outmatched, unloved, and inches away from disaster, he slunk out of the crowd. He didn't know why he'd been worried that somebody would notice him. Nobody ever did.

"What were you thinking?" Fisher shouted, hours later. That night it had been *Two* sitting down at the dinner table, and Fisher waiting upstairs for whatever leftovers his clone brought up. Fisher himself had been too upset to do much besides sit on his bed and fume. Even FP seemed nervous about Fisher's mood.

"What do you mean?" Two said. "Your dad and Amanda were wrong. Their conclusions were faulty, and they could've hurt the animals they were trying to protect. I was helping both sides."

"And what about the heroics with the duck suit?" Fisher

119

said, crossing his arms. Two tried to pet FP, who snipped at his hand.

"I wasn't just going to let the hawks eat those defenseless ducklings," Two protested. "They're endangered as it is."

"Listen," Fisher said, holding up his hands. "You can't just run around doing anything you like," he said. He fought down a twinge of guilt; he knew that he had created Two because that was exactly what he wanted for himself. "If you keep pulling these big flashy stunts, we're going to get found out. Do you want that to happen?"

Two shook his head.

"Then we need to keep things more quiet and focus on the mission. All right?"

"Right," Two said, sighing. "The mission."

"Good."

Fisher hoped that his speech—and his continued lies— had served their purpose. Still, as he got ready for bed, he couldn't ignore the whirling anxiety in the pit of his stomach. Tomorrow, he decided, he would keep tabs on Two, and make sure the clone followed his instructions.

It was time for the spy-cam.

⇛ CHAPTER 10 ⇚

I like precise, clearly defined rules. How else would I be sure I was breaking them?

—Vic Daring *(Issue #1)*

It was Tuesday morning, and Fisher held the old fedora his clone had been wearing in his hand. Two watched with a hint of a frown on his face.

"I think I know a way to keep you under con—I mean, to help guide you through the school day so that this operation goes as well as it can." In Fisher's other hand was a self-camouflaging camera produced by none other than TechX Enterprises. He affixed it to the front of the hat and then pressed a locking switch. Instantly, it vanished, its active camouflage blending it perfectly into its surroundings.

A window on Fisher's computer popped up with the live feed from the camera, and Two's look of mild annoyance appeared from two angles. "With this, I can see everything you see during the day. And *this*," he went on, slipping a tiny microphone pad under the front of the brim, "will allow me to hear as well. If you need any advice I can provide it with this earbud." He attached a tiny, ear-fitting

121

speaker to the inside of the hat. "Any objections?"

Two took a slow, deep breath, exhaled, and shook his head slowly. Fisher could tell that he had at least two or three objections. But Two remained silent.

"Good," Fisher said, satisfied that the experiment was getting back on track. Clearly Two respected Fisher enough to listen to his direction. Fisher was pleased to see his clone defer to his wishes.

After all, Fisher *had* given Two life—that had to count for something, right?

As Two left for school, Fisher got comfy in front of his computer, stretched his neck back and forth, and put his feet on the desk, next to the keyboard.

The video window was open. At the moment, it only displayed the wrinkle-textured, brown vinyl back of a school bus seat, but at least the picture was clear. Fisher could also hear the sounds of the trip: cars outside, a dozen conversations, and sometimes, faintly, Two's own breathing all came through the speakers just fine. Fisher flicked a control on his keyboard and spoke softly into the little headset slipped over his ear.

"Mic check. Tap the seat in front of you if you can hear me."

An arm and hand came into the picture, and Fisher shivered slightly. Watching someone identical to himself doing things he had done before was like hovering slightly behind his own eyes.

The hand that looked just like his own tapped idly on the seat in front. "Good, good. Okay, carry on. I won't talk unless it's really necessary." The hand gave a thumbs-up that Fisher couldn't help but feel was more than a little sarcastic.

He turned away from the image as the bus made its way to school. FP was trotting lightly around the room looking for discarded bits to eat, and Fisher's lab machines were conducting their own work. A few were running computer simulations of a new growth formula he was testing for himself, one was incubating the next generation of attack-squitoes, and one was collecting data from an automated telescope that scanned the sky for radio signals.

Fisher decided to kick back in his chair and catch a few minutes more of sleep. He felt what little muscle he had relax, the tension in his neck and eyebrows releasing. He breathed slowly and deeply. Having two Fishers might be a lot of trouble, but at moments like this, it *still* felt worth it.

He was jolted awake when he heard his name being called. A single, jerking, two-arm flail tipped his chair over and spilled him into a jumbled pile on the floor. FP trotted over to check on him, and Fisher lightly pushed him out of the way so that he could sit up. He scrambled back into his chair, staring in disbelief at the video screen.

"Hi, Fisher!" said Trevor Weiss, adjusting his enormous glasses.

"Hey, Fisher," said Wally Dubel, blinking with the concentration he normally needed in order to speak.

"Fisher! How ya doin'?" said a tall girl Fisher didn't know.

"Hey, Fisher. What's up?" Corey Devonshire called from down the hall, with a quick wave.

The barrage of greetings almost pushed Fisher out of his seat all over again. Smiling faces streamed at him through the video screen as Two sauntered through the halls. His loping stride made the image bob slightly.

As Two walked down the familiar dull beige hallway, almost everyone he saw was talking to him. Being friendly to him. And Two was responding! He knew all of their names, asked them about things Fisher had never even *heard* of, like football tryouts and glee club. One boy came up, extending his arm, and Fisher saw that familiar-looking hand dart out and give the kid a fist bump.

A *fist* bump.

Fisher turned the sound knob down as dozens of conversations, laughter, and shouts drummed in his ears. His substitute kept right on going, hellos left and right and calling out names as if he had them all written on the inside of his eyelids.

Then a massive *whud* sound, like an oak tree falling

onto a whale, made Fisher's teeth rattle, and he flung the headset off his ear. The world in the computer monitor whirled around, spinning crazily until it stopped short at a mouse's-eye view. The hat had been knocked off. Fisher heard one voice pierce through the others.

"Sorry about that, Fisher! Didn't see you in the crowd." The hat was lifted from the ground, and Fisher regained his clone's-eye view.

Staring him in the face was Chance Barrows—football player, basketball player, sunglass-wearing, slick-blond-haired, Veronica-talking Chance Barrows, who had a swarm of admirers buzzing all around him like an electron cloud.

Fisher gaped at his computer monitor. Not only did he know who Fisher was, he was apologizing!

The way the camera angle shifted slightly suggested that Two was shrugging in response.

"No big deal, Chance," Two said. "Say hi to the guys on the team for me, will ya?" Chance nodded and smiled, walking off.

The bell for first period rang, and as Two turned a corner, Fisher reflexively recoiled.

Vikings.

They were on the prowl, and they had Two in their sights. This wasn't their normal hunting routine, either. Normally, they looked like they were having fun, laughing, shoving each other, their grins like sickle blades. Today, they looked completely serious. They stepped together like soldiers, fanned out in formation to minimize the possibility of escape.

And they made straight for Two.

Fisher fought the urge to hide, an urge that almost overpowered his knowledge that he was merely watching a transmitted image.

"Vikings dead ahead!" he whispered frantically into the microphone. "They're after you. Get out of there while you can!"

"I see them," came the half-whispered answer. "I'm not running from anyone."

"You *what*?" Fisher said. The Vikings kept lumbering forward. Brody was in the center, his jutting forehead leading the way. Leroy on his left, legs rolling forward like he'd learned to walk by watching truck pistons. And Willard on the right, his sneakers slapping the ground rhythmically like a sword banging the side of a shield.

Two looked around, and Fisher saw through his camera that the hall was empty. No witnesses. The three stopped a foot from Two, and glowered down at him. *Run,* Fisher thought. *Run run run run run run run run run.*

"Looks like our friend Fisher has been making a new name for himself!" sneered Brody, clapping a hand on

Two's shoulder so hard it made the camera jump.

"Y-Yeah, he's, he's getting around, isn't he?" answered Willard.

"He's really flipped over a new flower," finished Leroy, a satisfied, smug grin on his face.

Brody closed his eyes in frustration and turned to him. "*Turned over* a new *leaf*, Leroy. He's . . . whatever. Just grab him!"

The camera was suddenly a whirl of images, like the shaken-up pictures of a kaleidoscope: first the floor, then the ceiling, then Brody's face, then a series of rapid sideways jerks.

In the middle of it all, though, Fisher saw something that made his jaw drop. He saw a familiar-looking elbow shoot out and catch Brody in the stomach. He saw one of his own sneakers kick Leroy right in the nose, as Leroy let out a yelp of pain.

Two was fighting back. And he was fighting hard.

"Ack! Hold him steady, guys!"

"My nose, Brody! He broke my nose!! What do I do?"

"You don't have to smell him, idiot, just hold on! We're almost there!" The three were using all their strength to hustle him into the bathroom. As Two struggled, he looked down, and Fisher saw a freshly bleached toilet bowl, flecks of blue cleaner still clinging to its sides.

More shouts of pain from the Vikings as they finally

managed to wrestle his head into the toilet, and the camera was submerged. Fisher closed his eyes and turned away from his desk, feeling like he might throw up.

The torrential roar of the flush nearly overwhelmed the microphone. On the one hand, it was fortunate that the equipment on the hat was waterproof. On the other hand . . . Fisher wouldn't exactly have been upset to be spared the view it was giving him.

"I can't feel my nose, Brody," came Leroy's voice in the background over the slow exiting footsteps of the Vikings.

"I-I think he broke my toe," said Willard, who was grunting in pain with each step.

"Come on, you two," Brody's fading voice responded. "Don't be wimps. Let's just get out of . . . aagh, I think a tooth is loose. . . ."

The bathroom door opened, and closed.

"Are . . . Are you okay?" Fisher asked into the microphone. He felt a newfound respect for his clone. Two might be reckless, but he was also brave. Where had he gotten the courage? That desire to fight? Fisher, the original, had never once stood up to the Vikings.

Water dripped off the camera lens as Two picked himself up, and the view wobbled a bit as he walked a little unsteadily to the mirror. Fisher watched drips of water fall from the fedora's brim. Then Two turned to face the mirror, and Fisher was overcome with the weirdness of it.

He was looking at a mirror image of himself looking at a mirror image of himself.

Two reached up and adjusted the tilt of his fedora. He reached up and brushed a spot of the blue cleaning fluid from his cheek and another from the tip of his nose. His expression was blank. "Fine," he said shortly. "I'm fine."

"I told you, you should have run," Fisher said quietly. "You should listen to me next time."

Two just scowled into the mirror, then turned around and stalked out of the bathroom.

Mid-morning, the bobbing camera turned down the familiar—and dreaded—dull red-painted cement hallway of the gym, and Fisher was glad he hadn't built any kind of smell-transmitter to go with the camera and microphone.

Two walked to Fisher's locker, spun the lock to Fisher's combination, which was the first five digits of pi—3, 14, 15—and tossed the hat in, turning it around so Fisher was staring into his own face. Two wasn't looking as smug as usual, but considering his recent encounter with the toilet bowl, he didn't look too bad, either.

"I'll see you after gym," said the mirror image, and then the locker door slammed shut.

Fisher breathed a sigh of relief. Things were looking up for the long-term success of his experiment. The incident with the Vikings was unfortunate, but hopefully it had shown Two exactly where he belonged in the scheme of things at Wompalog. He turned from the computer and walked over to what had been his father's platypus-egg cold-storage unit, which Fisher had inherited after an especially adventurous brood had hatched early and sought warmth in his parents' bed.

Fisher opened it up and withdrew turkey, some sourdough bread, and honey mustard. He'd converted the storage unit into a makeshift refrigerator to avoid going into the kitchen when he was supposed to be at school. As he made the sandwich he felt himself jostled at ankle level, and looked down to see FP bumping his forehead against his shins.

"Didn't I already feed you today?" *Bump, bump bump.*

"You know this is my food, not yours, right, boy?" *Bump, bump bump.*

"You're not going to stop until I feed you more, are you?" FP looked up into Fisher's eyes, his expression seeming cheerful. "All right, all right." Fisher reached into the fridge again and took out a little bowl of corn, which he set at his feet. "Happy?" He took the crunching, snuffling noises for a yes.

Fisher returned to his work as he ate, fetching from a rack over his worktable a device that looked like a weapon. It had a long, cylindrical barrel, a handle with a trigger, and a rifle-like stock at the back. In fact, the device looked almost like an actual rifle, except that the chamber the

Blueprints for
POPCORN GUN

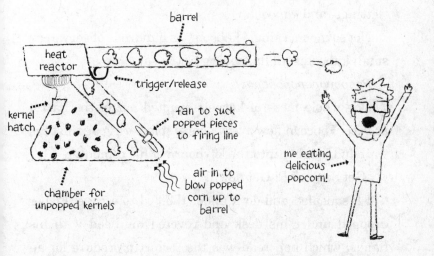

barrel

heat reactor

trigger/release

kernel hatch

fan to suck popped pieces to firing line

me eating delicious popcorn!

chamber for unpopped kernels

air in to blow popped corn up to barrel

barrel was attached to was bulky and oddly shaped.

Fisher pulled a small bag out of a drawer and, as FP watched eagerly, he poured a large number of tiny, brown pellets into it. Popcorn kernels.

If his calculations were right, the main chamber should heat up at specific intervals. That would allow him to fire individual kernels of popcorn up to one hundred fifty meters. As he powered it on, he thought of all of its uses: long-range popcorn mouth-catching. Popcorn marksmanship events. Two teams, both armed with popcorn guns: the winning team would get to eat all the ammunition at the end.

Fisher's popcorn fantasies distracted him from realizing just how hot the main chamber was getting. When his fingers started to burn, he reached down to adjust its settings, and *kaboom*.

Not so much a single kaboom, as hundreds of very, very small kabooms all happening at the same time.

Poppopopopopopopop!

The whole mess of kernels erupted out of the barrel at once. Popcorn flew everywhere, splattering against his wall and lodging into the keyboard of his computer.

"Get down, FP! Get down!"

FP squealed and dove under the bed to escape. Fisher dropped under his desk and covered his head with his hands, which he'd read was the correct procedure for an earthquake, a bombing, or an invasion of flying popcorn.

Pop! Pop! Pop!

When the barrage of popping had at last slowed, Fisher uncovered his head. His floor was coated an inch deep in popcorn kernels. They were on his bed, his desk, his equipment. Fisher got up and started crunching through the mess, trying to find his way to the automated cleanup-bot in the corner.

FP was happily running around the room and vacuuming up the popcorn with his mouth. By the time the cleanup-bot warmed up and got going, FP had taken care of an impressively large amount of the mess. The cleanup-bot whirred and buzzed and beeped, sweeping up the kernels into its built-in trash receptacle. Fisher put the defective popcorn gun back in its place, pulling a kernel out of his left ear and vowing to reexamine the blueprints.

After the robot had finished cleaning, Fisher looked at his computer screen. Still the dark inside of a locker. He looked at the time. Funny, gym should have ended ten minutes ago. He wondered what was . . .

Oh, no.

Fisher's train of thought came to a crashing halt like . . . well, like a train crash. It was Friday. Gym was on Mondays and Thursdays.

Two had tricked him.

CHAPTER 11

People will always do what they want to do, no matter what you ask of them. That is why, while most people have children, I have robots.
—Dr. X, Notes on Human Weakness

Fisher's desk chair was left spinning on its swivel, pieces of paper blown into the air, and a jar of pencils and pens making a clanking waterfall over the desk's side. There was almost a dust trail leading out of his room, down the stairs, across the front hallway, and out the door.

After Fisher disabled the alarm, he eased open the front door very slowly and tiptoed across the yard. The movable paving stones matched his tempo, gliding sneakily along the grass to arrive silently under his feet. He was almost to the front gate when he heard a faint clopping sound behind him. He froze, almost afraid to turn around, wondering if his parents had invented a new yard inhabitant he didn't know about.

Then he turned and saw FP doing his best to move stealthily across the yard. FP delicately placed one hoof in front of another, looking left and right with narrow eyes. He kept sneaking forward until he bumped into Fisher's leg.

Fisher crossed his arms. "Where do you think *you're* going?" Fisher promptly scooped up his pig, marched back to the front door, and tossed him inside. He closed the door behind him as FP squeaked and glided to a haphazard landing on the kitchen floor, narrowly missing the recycling bin.

Two minutes later, Fisher was halfway down the sidewalk when he heard a familiar squeal. He turned around just in time for FP, having leapt from an open window and over the wall, to crash headlong into his face.

"W—!" was all Fisher had time to get out, before the force of FP's landing carried him backward and off his feet, and pet and master were rolling, entangled, on the sidewalk. Fisher ended up on his back, with FP bouncing excitedly on his chest.

"FP, I don't have time to . . ."

Fisher trailed off as FP nuzzled his face. He sighed. "You really have a taste for stupid adventures, don't you?" He stood up, dusting off his jeans. "Come on, then. Just try to keep up."

Fisher kept his head down as he walked to school, trying to keep cars or buildings in between himself and anyone he saw on the street. He wanted to avoid being seen walking around in the afternoon on a school day if at all possible. People would ask questions, and he didn't want to make up any more new answers. This lie was getting big and complicated enough as it was. To give himself courage, he reminded himself of great heroes of legend creeping into the lair of the enemy. Odysseus smuggling himself into Troy. Robin Hood climbing silently up the walls of Nottingham Castle. Vic Daring flying a stolen Venusian patrol craft to land on the Forbidden Satellite.

Two was extremely smart, and if he had deliberately given Fisher the slip, it had to be because he was up to no good. He could be getting into all kinds of trouble. He could be flooding the basement with chicken broth. He could be sticking unremovable clown noses to every teacher's face. Fisher might get to the school and find it burned to the ground, or covered in twenty acres of aluminum foil, or relocated to the dark side of the moon.

As Fisher got closer to school, he picked up his pace, until he was practically running. His lungs were burning, and his legs felt like a thousand rats wearing golf shoes were scampering across them. FP was moving as fast as his stubby legs would allow, his hooves clanging against the pavement, in between brief spurts of gliding. A gust of wind from a passing bus threw him off course once, and he veered left and right in front of Fisher, squeaking as he tried to regain his course. Fisher reached up and pushed, and FP nose-dived into a soft hedge. Fisher plucked him out as he ran past, and the pig resumed his half-running, half-flying routine.

The school was still standing when it came into view, and Fisher breathed a small sigh of relief. So far, it didn't look like any massive explosions had occurred. There weren't any strange glows coming from the windows or multicolored smoke plumes rising out of the roof. Fisher mentally crossed off a few worst-case scenarios.

He knew he couldn't just charge in the front doors. There already *was* a Fisher in school, even if he didn't act at all like the original. Luckily, Fisher had plenty of practice getting around school without being noticed. He'd been making it his business to be as unnoticeable as possible for the past few years.

He made straight for a little-used maintenance door whose lock had broken years ago. FP ran along behind him, whipping his head from left to right. Pig and boy slipped inside, and found themselves in a storage room that probably hadn't been used since color TV was invented. Fisher started to pick his way through decades of discarded stuff to reach the door into the basement.

"Squeeeee!"

FP squealed in terror and dove behind a box when he came face-to-face with what seemed to be a huge, fanged beast. Fisher whipped around, heart hammering, and then laughed.

"It's okay, boy," he said, holding out his hand and beckoning FP back over. "It's just an old-school mascot. Let's

Go, Furious Badgers!" he said sarcastically, twirling a finger in the air.

Wompalog's basement was a place Fisher had unfortunately gotten to know before—but not of his own choosing. In sixth grade, the Vikings had once tossed him into the boiler room and locked the door behind him. When a teacher had walked by and asked why they were standing against the door and what the banging sounds were, they'd said that the radiator was on the fritz again and they were keeping people out, for their safety.

Fisher remembered that he had found an escape route that day: an old dumbwaiter that used to carry supplies up to the cafeteria. The door was still loose. Fisher took off the cap and sunglasses, lowered his hood, and crawled into the little compartment, reaching down to pull FP up after him. He reached behind him for the rope and hoisted the contraption up, hand over hand, until he reached the main floor.

Fisher and FP slipped out of the dumbwaiter and found themselves in the very back of the cafeteria kitchen. Weak lights flickered off grease-stained oven doors and floor tiles. Strange creaks and odd hisses echoed around the room. Fisher tensed, looking left and right, but didn't see anyone. Even the cafeteria workers avoided coming this far back into the kitchen when they could help it.

Fisher could hear the commotion from the busier part

of the kitchen as the cooks prepped the school lunch. He looked back at FP, who squinted his beady eyes and waggled his tail a little in a show of excitement.

"All right, boy," Fisher said, petting his pig on the forehead. "Let's get out of here."

Fisher and FP crawled their way to the main kitchen, where the lunch servers were bustling around, ladling what looked like slop into large metal dishes.

A row of counters ran the width of the room, and on the other side was a door, hidden in a small alcove. Fisher didn't know where it led, but he knew he needed to escape the kitchen before somebody saw him. He turned to FP.

"Stay behind me, boy," he said, and lurched forward as fast as his hands and knees could carry him. A third of the way, halfway, two-thirds . . .

Then he saw one of the cooks—massive, lumbering—heading straight for him. As soon as the man rounded the corner, Fisher would be caught dead in his tracks. He glanced wildly right and left, looked for a cabinet or something to conceal him, but found nothing. He froze. Any moment now . . .

Then a shower of pots and pans from a high shelf made both Fisher and the cook jump. Fisher saw a pot of soup cascading to the floor. And he caught just a glimpse of a curled, pink tail darting along the shelf.

FP!

The cook pivoted and hurried over to clean up, giving Fisher just enough time to slip over to the door. Trusting FP to find his way, Fisher turned and tried the knob. It was locked! He snatched up a pair of forks from a sink and went to work trying to pick the lock.

"Hey! What is this pig doing here?"

Fisher's limbs locked in place. Fear froze his blood, and he could barely force himself to turn around.

The cook was standing over the counter, looking down at FP, who was lying on a plate, with an apple in his mouth. One of his ears was twitching, but the cook didn't seem to notice.

"Huh," he said, scratching his head. "Didn't see this on the menu. I guess I'd better ask admin." He walked away without another word. FP's eyes tracked the cook until he was inside his small, windowed office picking up his phone. Then FP hopped down and trotted over to rejoin Fisher, just as Fisher managed to work one of the fork tines into the lock and slide it open.

"You are the best four-legged spy I've ever seen," Fisher said as he and FP slipped out of the kitchen. "Come on."

The door, as it turned out, led to a back stairwell. They made their way up the stairs until they reached another door that Fisher believed, according to his memory of the school's layout, led to the main hallway on the second floor. He gently pushed the door open.

And saw Brody, standing no more than two feet away—thankfully, facing the opposite direction.

The bullying hulk wasn't moving. He was just standing in the hall, arms crossed. No doubt patrolling for prey. Fisher gulped. He *had* to find Two. That meant he had to find a way past Brody. He considered his options. He searched his pockets. He still had the sunglasses on him that he'd worn to the King of Hollywood protest, but that wouldn't be enough to camouflage him. He also found several popcorn kernels buried in the back of his jeans pockets, but he didn't think *that* would help, either.

Then his fingers closed on a small vial. Yes! He must've have left an extra dose of his chicken pox–simulating formula in a pocket by accident. It was crazy, but crazy was his only play.

"Let's go," he said, and scooped FP up with both hands.

A minute later, Brody saw a short kid in a tightly cinched hood and sunglasses walk past him, coughing dramatically. He had a wriggling potbelly, and his sleeves were rolled to the elbow.

"Hey, you," Brody barked. "Take off the hood, freak."

"I don't feel well," Fisher responded in a low, gruff voice. "I need to get to the nurse."

"Not so fast," Brody said. "What's with the getup?" He reached out and grabbed Fisher's arm, then immediately pulled back. Fisher's arm was covered in dozens of bumpy red blisters. "What the—!" Brody shouted. "What *is* that?"

"I think I might be contagious," Fisher said gruffly again, then leaned over and put his hands on his stomach. A whining squeal rang out through the hallway. Now *Brody* looked like he was going to be sick.

"Get away from me!" Brody bolted in the opposite direction.

And just in time, too. Fourth period was just about to get out.

The bell rang. Fisher slipped FP out of his shirt, took two quick steps, and dove into an unused locker. Students started filling the hall. Through the narrow slats, Fisher spotted a torn-up old T-shirt and a gray fedora bobbing out of a classroom. He'd found Two! He pressed his face to the locker slats for a closer look. Too tall, hair wasn't the right color . . . He remembered, also, that Two's fedora was still moldering in a crusty gym locker.

Somebody else was dressed exactly like Two. Fisher was confused for a moment, then saw someone else in the same getup, and a third person a minute later. He fell back, bumping his head against the back of the locker.

His clone had started a fashion trend.

After the second bell rang and the halls emptied, Fisher and FP slipped out of the locker, scanning the hallway to check that it was clear. Fisher slid low along one wall to keep out of the line of sight of the small windows in each classroom door.

He had almost reached the stairwell when a door opened out hard and fast in front of him, turning Fisher into instant wall-pancake.

"Urrroommfff," he couldn't keep from saying as he twitched, the door flattening him against the wall.

"What did you say?" said a teacher's voice.

"Me? Nothing," said another as they walked out of the teachers' lounge. "Must've been the air vents again."

They walked away down the hall as the door swung back, leaving Fisher tottering dizzily for a moment before he could continue. FP had ducked behind a potted plant, and he slipped out to rejoin Fisher.

The English classroom was wide and had two doors, and as the class filed in through one, Fisher and FP took advantage of the before-class bustle to sneak in through the other. They concealed themselves behind a partly extended retractable wall that was sometimes used to split the room in half. Mrs. Weedle began the class, as kids filed into their seats. As she began droning on about *Romeo and Juliet*, most of the students' eyes glazed over. Some desperately searched for something interesting outside the window, others focused on the clock and tried to push its hands forward with their eyes.

Mrs. Weedle was lecturing about Romeo's friend

Mercutio in her Jell-O-in-a-garbage-crusher speaking style when a hand shot up in the middle of the classroom. Oh, no. Two.

Why did Two insist on drawing attention to himself? When would he learn?

"Yes, Fisher?"

"I don't get him, Mrs. Weedle. Mercutio invites Romeo to a party, gets him this girl, and then Romeo thanks him by letting him get stabbed? He should know better if he's so smart."

Several students snickered. The kids at the back were exchanging hushed whispers. The teacher stiffened.

"I'd give Mercutio more respect if I were you, Fisher," she said, raising her nose and tilting her eyes upward as she always did when she was about to make a point. "The way Mercutio observes the action of the play makes him a stand-in for you, the reader."

"He's standing in for me?" repeated Two, looking around to see the reaction he was gathering. "Wow, I do respect him now! I guess I'll be going then, and let him do the reading. He can do my homework, too!" He stood up as if to leave, and the class was split between laughter and applause.

Mrs. Weedle managed to restore order and get Two back to his seat, but her hold on the class had slipped.

Fisher sat out the rest of the class, crouched in his

hiding spot, his panic increasing. When the period was over and the kids started to leave, he and FP snuck quietly back to the door they had entered through. Fisher looked out into the hallway. Unfortunately, since classes were changing, it was full of people.

Fisher knew he had to move quickly if he was going to get to the biology classroom in time to observe Two. He spotted an old backpack with a broken strap and a stray textbook lying on one side of the hallway. He swept them up. FP went into the bag, flailing his short legs and squeaking in protest.

Fisher held the open book in front of his face and slipped into the crush of people, moving quickly. He navigated as best he could by sneaking quick glances over the top of the textbook. He was jostled from all sides, as usual, but nobody seemed to notice him . . . also as usual. Small hooves pushed into his back, and he tried to hold the backpack tightly enough so that the movement inside of it wasn't obvious.

After a minute, the crowds began to thin. Fisher ducked into a smaller side hall, just next to Mr. Granger's classroom. He collapsed back against the wall to take a quick breather and felt something give way behind him. He turned around, but not in time to avoid plunging backward . . .

. . . into a large air duct.

He sat up, sneezing out dust. The air duct extended for dozens of feet into the darkness, and Fisher realized that it must connect with all the classrooms. It would be a perfect place from which to spy on Two. He freed FP, who was wriggling and squeaking, from his backpack prison.

Fisher and FP crawled several feet through the narrow duct until they reached another vent. Fisher's bet had paid off. Through its metal grille, they had a full view of Granger's classroom.

Mr. Granger was overseeing an experiment. The students stood behind rows of Bunsen burners, solutions carefully simmering in their beakers. Chemical smells wafted through the air, and FP wrinkled his snout and squeaked.

"Shhh! Quiet, FP," Fisher commanded, reaching out to put a hand over FP's snout.

Two had been partnered with Amanda Cantrell. Fisher watched as they began to set up their equipment. Amanda would start to arrange it on the table, and when she looked away, Two kept switching things or rearranging them. She would turn back to find the equipment out of place, then he would chuckle and she'd laugh with him, shaking her head. This happened several times.

It took Fisher a few minutes to realize that Two was flirting. Fisher shook his head in disbelief. Had someone spliced different DNA into his petri dish when he wasn't looking?

MAP OF WOMPALOG
MIDDLE SCHOOL AIR DUCTS
LARGE ENOUGH FOR TRAVEL

1ST FLOOR

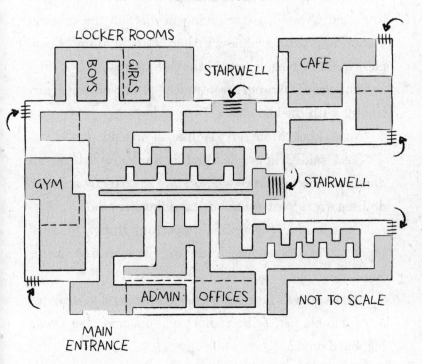

LOCKER ROOMS

BOYS

GIRLS

STAIRWELL

CAFE

GYM

STAIRWELL

ADMIN | OFFICES

NOT TO SCALE

MAIN
ENTRANCE

FP snuffled restlessly, and Fisher scratched his neck to keep him calm.

Once they had their equipment set up and the lab got going, Mr. Granger walked over to Fisher's lab table.

"Hello, Fisher," said Mr. Granger. Fisher thought his

smile seemed kind of tight—although it was somewhat difficult to tell from this angle.

"Hi, Mr. Granger," responded Two flatly.

"How's your lab going?" asked Mr. Granger.

"According to plan, I think," said Two. Fisher started to sweat. Two wasn't behaving at *all* like the original Fisher, and Granger knew Fisher better than most people. Would he be able to spot the differences?

"Oh, good," Granger continued. "Did you have any trouble with the homework?"

"Nope. I got through it just fine," Two said.

"Say," said Granger, leaning forward and setting his hands on the table. "How'd you like to come by at lunch and see my newest white-shrimp-migratory data?"

"I'm afraid I've got more important things to do at lunch," said Two casually, turning his eyes back to his Bunsen burner.

Mr. Granger's face fell. Fisher wished he had invented a retractable fist, so he could reach out and give Two a big, hard punch.

"Oh. Well, all right then." He started to turn away, then stopped and reached into his pocket. "I almost forgot—you left your pen in class last week. I found it at your desk." With that, he took out a large, black pen that Fisher had, without question, never seen in his life.

That's not mine! He wanted to scream at Two, but of course he couldn't.

Two reached for the pen and pocketed it. "Thanks, Mr. G."

Mr. G? Fisher could feel sweat crawling down his neck. He heaved a sigh of relief as Mr. Granger—after shooting one last puzzled look in Two's direction—continued circulating through the class.

It was only when Mr. Granger's back was turned that Fisher saw Two smile.

And it wasn't a sweet little-boy smile. One corner of Two's mouth curled up, and he looked like he was stifling a chuckle under his breath. Fisher gulped. Two was planning something. He could feel it.

Fisher scanned the classroom, searching for something amiss.

Then he saw them. At the back-most lab table, where no one was working, were little air nozzles sometimes used in experiments. The four on the back table were all turned on, and each one had a balloon around its end.

The balloons must have been inflating slowly for the whole period. Fisher wanted to shout and warn Mr. Granger, but he couldn't. He could only wait in silence, despairing, as they got bigger and bigger, nobody noticing.

Two had planned the prank perfectly. At exactly ten minutes before the end of class, just as the students were all about to clean up the lab, the balloons slipped off the nozzles. One, followed two seconds later by another, and by another after two more seconds, until all four were flying around the room in crazy loops as their air rushed out.

Beakers got knocked off their stands. Kids went diving for cover. Mr. Granger spun around in a panic as he tried to tell his class *not* to panic. A balloon smacked straight into his nose, and his thick, round glasses flew off. He crawled on the floor, scrabbling with his bony arms until he scooped them back up.

As he was about to stand up again, a pair of tiny white blurs ran straight up one of his sleeves. Einy and Berg! The balloons had toppled over their cage, and in the panic of screaming kids and zooming balloons, they sought the safest, most familiar thing they could find. Mr. Granger stood up, waving his arms in a crazy dance as the rodents scampered around under his shirt. It took him almost a minute of spinning and twitching to finally reach inside and fetch them out.

When he finally regained his composure, he stood up and saw that Two was the only one in the room not dodging or gasping, but smiling. A look of disbelief came to his face.

"Is this your work, Fisher?"

"Some of my best, Mr. Granger," answered the clone. "I

hope I taught the class a valuable lesson in ducking."

Mr. Granger struggled for a reply. "This is, this is absolutely . . . G-Go, go to the, the . . ."

But before Mr. Granger could even pronounce the word *principal*, Two had already sauntered out the door.

"My God, FP," Fisher whispered. "I've created a monster."

CHAPTER 12

Hypothesis: Two identical organisms occupying the same environment make each other less important. To escape this, they will naturally tend to act in wildly different ways.

—Fisher Bas, Scientific Principles and Observations of the Natural World (unpublished)

Fisher was clenching his fists in anger. Standing up to Weedle was one thing, but Mr. Granger was his friend. His close friend. His *only* friend. And now this clone was turning him into a laughingstock.

Besides, Granger was a biologist, and a very intelligent man. What if he began to suspect something? If Two kept acting like this, Mr. Granger could blow Fisher's plot wide open. Three days and this new Fisher was on the brink of bringing *both* of their lives to a crashing, crumbling halt.

Lunch period was next, and Two had said he had "important things to do." Fisher backed away from the vent overlooking the bio lab as quickly as he could and headed in the direction of the cafeteria through the narrow air ducts. FP trotted along behind Fisher. They crawled in a straight line for about a hundred feet. The tunnel took a turn to the right and began slanting steeply upward, and Fisher followed.

Then, suddenly, it turned sharply downward. He reached out a hand to steady himself, but the metal surface was too slippery. He felt himself sliding, sliding . . . then tumbling, head over feet, a hollow *thump-thud-thump-thud* accompanying his long fall. FP was sliding on his stomach, squealing in terror.

At last he struck the bottom with a gong-like crash. He heard a thin, wheezing squeak, and FP landed right on top of him, flapping his forelegs wildly to try and slow himself.

Fisher's arms were tangled behind his head. He felt a weird twinge in his spine and hoped he hadn't turned his torso around backward when he landed. He was reassured to look down and see his stomach rather than his back.

"Oof!" he said as FP put a hoof directly in his collarbone.

FP snorted excitedly. He was obviously still thrilled about the expedition. Smells of week-old potato soup, concrete-hard wheat bread, and charred hot dogs drifted through the duct, and those were just the recognizable aromas. Fisher took as few breaths as possible as he began to unknot himself.

Once he had recovered from the fall, Fisher crawled farther along the duct, FP still behind him. They were getting close. It wasn't long before the smells were joined by sounds. Excited voices were filling the space, and Fisher quickly heard his own name popping up in conversations. Arm over arm, he pulled himself up until he reached the wide duct whose vents opened into the cafeteria's ceiling and found one he could see from. FP pressed up next to him.

The cafeteria was buzzing with chatter, and Fisher was able to catch snippets of it from his high vantage point. There were too many conversations going on at once for him to hear one completely, but he was able to piece together the story.

"Hey, did you hear what . . ."

". . . Fisher pulled this crazy stunt . . ."

" . . . Vikings were in gym class, playing softball . . ."

"Fisher replaced the softball with some kinda rocket!"

Fisher seized up for a moment when he heard the rocket mentioned. Had Two actually blown the Vikings to smithereens?

". . . kablooie! All over the Vikings! And you'll never guess . . ."

". . . full of King of Hollywood spicy sauce! They were covered in it! Brody's still trying to get it out of his ears!"

Fisher exhaled. Not a real rocket. He could be thankful for *that* at least.

". . . just don't know how he comes up with this stuff!"

"Brilliant, totally brilliant!"

As the chatter about his clone continued, Fisher tried to sort out his own buzzing thoughts. In a matter of a few days, his clone had gone from making new friends, to starting fads and gaining popularity, to becoming nothing less than a full-blown hero. And although the Vikings deserved all they'd gotten and more, now Two was the center of attention of the *entire* school.

Fisher remembered what his mom had said: no *one* can know about the AGH. *It will put us all in danger.*

This did not bode well.

And yet . . . for all of Two's troublemaking and carrying on, Fisher couldn't help but admire him. Two was everything that Fisher wasn't. He had courage, self-confidence, pride. Charm, even. Thanks to him, everyone at school was starting to think differently about Fisher. People liked him. They laughed at his jokes. Girls exchanged those *looks* with each other. About *him*.

Fisher had never envied someone so much in his life, and part of him wanted nothing more than to see the clone humiliated the way that he had always been. But another part of him knew that Two had *earned* his new-found social status.

Something he had never imagined, never could have predicted, was taking place.

Fisher—at least, Fisher-2—was becoming popular.

The scattered gossiping and chatter turned into a single, huge cheer as the main door into the kitchen swung open and Two walked in. Or, actually, rode in: he was driving a long, motorized food cart, and though its cargo was covered, a new, delicious, and distantly familiar scent began to waft up, cutting through the unknowable smells of the cafeteria. Fisher's mouth began to water.

Two plucked a small microphone from the side of the cart, check-tapped it, and motioned the crowd to silence.

"Boys and girls, thanks so much for your appreciation! The Vikings have been pushing and shoving their way through this school for too long, am I right?" Another cheer went up. "I'm sick of it, and I'm sure you all are, too. That's why I decided to let 'em know that in the only language they understand: humiliation." More cheers and laughs. "Now you may be wondering, where did Fisher get all that amazing sauce? I'm glad you asked. You see, the new King of Hollywood franchise needs to promote its opening. And we all just happen to be their target market. So we made a deal: I get lots of their stuff for free, and in exchange I get you all pumped for its opening. The only catch is this. . . ." He snapped his fingers and two smartly uniformed KOH employees jumped seemingly out of nowhere and took hold of the two lids covering the long cart. "We have to eat all of the merchandise!"

The lids came up to reveal rows and rows of the

restaurant chain's signature star fries, alongside cleverly softball-shaped containers of the very sauce that was still seeping into the pores of the Vikings. The final ounce of restraint the kids had been showing collapsed, and the cafeteria exploded in shouting as more King of Hollywood assistants started distributing fries to everyone.

The chanting continued. Fisher watched as Two approached Amanda Cantrell. He reached behind his back and smoothly pulled a model of a duck nest from behind his back. It contained more of the fries and sauce.

"To coexistence," he said. Amanda smiled and took the gift. Then Two got back on the microphone. "I would also like to announce our new school mascot! I don't think a badger, however furious it may be, can really represent us anymore. That's why I'd like to introduce you all to . . . Billy!"

A student wearing Fisher's dad's giant double-billed yellow-bellied bilious duck burst into the cafeteria, waving excitedly to the crowd.

"Fish-er! Fish-er! Fish-er!" The chant grew in intensity until Fisher had to cover his ears. The only thing that cut through it was the shriek of the loudspeaker turning on and the announcement that followed: "Fisher Bas, please report to the principal's office. *Immediately.*"

CHAPTER 13

The principal is just a person. It's the office that gets you. It sits there, smirking with its wood paneling and worn-down furniture, dozens of books on its shelves, and seems to say, "I have always been here, and I will always be here, waiting. Waiting for someone like you."

—Fisher Bas, Personal Notes

Fisher turned himself around in the duct as quickly as he could and wracked his memory, trying to recall the layout of the air system. With chants and cheers still echoing in the tiny metal tube, he crawled up the steep incline he had tumbled down.

FP, still engrossed by the spectacle in the cafeteria, was trying to squeeze and push his way through the vent to get some of the food. He kept on trying until Fisher's hand reached back and pulled him by the tail.

At the top of the incline, the tunnel once again dipped downward. Fisher scooted along hastily, and FP slid down on his belly. Fisher took a moment to look at the three branches of the duct in front of them, closed his eyes to picture the plan, and turned left.

Fisher checked each classroom as he crawled along

above them, looking for the principal's office. In each one of them, there were kids with KOH fries, slurping special sauce with their fingers and bartering with each other for extra spoils.

"If you give me half of your fries, I'll do your homework for three days . . ."

"I'll do it for a week!"

"Kids!" Mr. Gertzweinner, the eighth-grade German teacher, held up a hand to silence his class. Fisher froze in the duct. Gertzweinner wasn't even his teacher, and Fisher was terrified of him.

"I won't assign homework for a month," Mr. Gertzweinner resumed, dropping his voice to a whisper, "if you all agree to turn over your fries to me. . . ."

Fisher shook his head in disbelief and continued crawling.

Finally, he found it: he recognized the leather armchair and the enormous desk. Fisher had been to the principal's office before (on more than one occasion he had gone there on purpose to avoid the Vikings) though he had never been *sent* there. Through the narrow slats of the vent, he saw his clone, sitting patiently in a chair.

Fisher wasted no time. He removed from a pocket the Screw Liquefier he had been working on in his home lab and drained the four screws holding the vent in place into a small bottle.

BLUEPRINTS FOR
SCREW LIQUIFIER

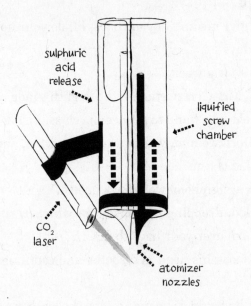

sulphuric
acid
release

liquified
screw
chamber

CO_2
laser

atomizer
nozzles

"Stay where you are, boy," he commanded FP.

He carefully removed the vent and slipped out, dangling from the ceiling by one hand as he fumblingly pushed the vent back into place. With his free hand, he replaced the screws in seconds by applying the liquefier's spray nozzle to the proper spots.

"Argh!" Fisher's arm strength gave way, and he dropped from the ceiling and landed, clumsily, in the middle of the office. Two sprang to his feet, grinning broadly.

"Brother!" he exclaimed. "Did you come to join in the invest—"

But before he could complete his question, Fisher exploded. "Don't 'brother' me! What were you thinking? You were supposed to avoid drawing attention to yourself, and now the whole school's in an uproar!"

"I wasn't going to let the Vikings keep pushing me around like that," Two said, obviously pleased with himself. "It's like Napoleon said: don't stomp a slug unless you want goo on your shoes."

"Napoleon did not say that!" Fisher clenched his fists.

"But Wikipedia—"

Fisher cut him off. "And what about the spectacle in the cafeteria? We're in an extremely delicate situation, and every time you pull something like that, you get more eyes on you. Who knows what could happen next?"

Two's grin faded. He grew serious.

"This is a bad place, Fisher, but lots of these kids are still good! It would be selfish to work only for our own goals when we could undermine the evil powers-that-be and free others like us."

Fisher was on the verge of simply blurting out that he had made everything up about the evil plans, and that Two's obsession with a cleaning-product commercial was reaching unstable levels, but before he could get out another word, he heard the doorknob rattle.

He had just enough time to take two running steps and dive into a closet, wrapped in coats and jackets, before the door opened and he heard Mr. Teed's soft but precise footsteps. Something that felt like an enormous, furry spider fell on his head, and Fisher stifled a yelp, swiping it away. Then he realized it was just one of Mr. Teed's ridiculous tufted toupees, which had fallen on him from above.

The footsteps continued their slow, methodical plod across the soft office carpet until Fisher heard the famous *crrrreeeaaakk* of Mr. Teed's office chair.

"Hello, Fisher."

Fisher tried to squeeze himself into a position where he could look out through a crack in the door. In the meanwhile, Mr. Teed went on by asking the traditional principal's question: "Do you know why you're here?"

"Yes, Mr. Teed," came a meek-sounding reply. Fisher bumped a leaning umbrella over with his shoulder and had to stretch out an arm to keep it from falling into the door. He breathed shallowly for a few seconds before reaching over and very gingerly setting it back into place.

"Over the past two days, it seems the Fisher we all knew and admired has gone away. You have always been among the best-behaved and most respectful students at this school, and your record is exemplary. Spotless, in fact. In terms of academic work, you are leaps and bounds ahead of your classmates. You've shown yourself to be dedicated to learning and the pursuit of knowledge. Few people your age have your respect for education.

"I don't know where this sudden change has come from. Frankly, the entire faculty is mystified. We all know that middle school presents many pressures and problems. And I am aware that some of the other students have taken it upon themselves to pick on you and mistreat you, but I believed you to be a young man intelligent and mature enough to handle them. Now, I am not so sure. I'm very disappointed in you, Fisher."

Still no reply from Two. Fisher finally got close enough to see through the narrow slit and saw his clone sitting with his head bowed.

Could it be that Two actually felt bad for what he had done? Unlikely. Two didn't seem capable of feeling sorry. He was surely just pretending to feel bad so he could get out of the office as fast as possible.

Teed continued, "You've caused a great deal of chaos in the past few days, Fisher. Now, don't you think your intellectual powers would be much better put to use if focused on your studies? I will be giving you a week's detention during which to contemplate this. In addition, I think you owe your teachers, and your fellow students, an apology. I've got paper and a pen for you, and you can take the next class period to write something appropriately well thought out."

Teed reached into his desk and slid a small stack of paper and a pen to Two, whose head stayed down. Then, with the hint of a sniff, Two reached into his pocket and pulled out a single tissue.

Maybe, Fisher thought, Mr. Teed's stern coldness had actually succeeded in upsetting Two's perfectly calm and cool exterior.

Two started to lift the tissue up toward his face, and Mr. Teed's expression lost some of its sharpness.

"Now, listen," he said. "Maybe I was a bit harsh . . ."

At that moment, Two flung it down onto the ground, and with a crackling *whisshh*, a blinding-white smoke cloud filled the room.

An acrid, rotten smell emanated through the office: it was the stench of a thousand rotten eggs being hard-boiled in a sulfur pit.

Mr. Teed coughed and sputtered.

"Fisher!" he roared as Two bolted for the door, obscured by the cloud.

Fisher, barely able to see or breathe, pushed his way out of the closet after him, groping wildly in the smoke-clotted air. One hand hooked an adjusting loop on Two's backpack strap. He felt Two thrash back and forth like a bull trying to buck its rider, and he clung on for dear life as the awful white cloud stung his eyes and filled his nose.

Then, something gave way, and Fisher went toppling

backward. The backpack flew toward him, hitting him squarely in the head as he collapsed onto the floor. Two had wriggled out of his shoulder straps. Fisher tried to get to his feet when he felt Mr. Teed's arms close around his ankles, and he fell flat on his face.

Two was long gone, and Mr. Teed's iron grip was locked in place.

"Not so fast, Mr. Bas," he growled.

CHAPTER 14

Have you ever been framed for a crime you did commit?

—Fisher Bas, Extended Clone Log

Fisher kept his head down as he walked across the school parking lot to his mother's waiting car. A creeping dread spread over him like an upended bucket of icy snails.

Pulling a prank in a bio class was one thing. Detonating explosive stink bombs in the principal's office fell into a whole new category.

The principal had decided, after consideration, that Fisher's punishment would be extended to *two* week's detention, and had counted on Fisher's parents to handle the rest.

Fisher would rather have been chained up in the school's boiler room for a day or two. At least then he would've gotten some peace and quiet.

His mom's car was equipped with a number of automatic functions added by his parents. Fisher knew all of them well. Nevertheless, it still always startled him when the back door opened by itself. His mother's silhouette in the front seat remained motionless.

Fisher slipped into the backseat, wondering if he could do it quietly enough that she wouldn't notice he was there. That idea was foiled when the popcorn kernels still in his back pocket crunched loudly as he sat down.

"Let's go home, Fisher," said his mother in a frosty voice, and the door slammed itself shut. Fisher slid as far down in the seat as he could.

There had been no sign of Two since his escape. Fisher's hands bunched up into nervous fists, imagining what he could be doing. Setting zoo animals loose and riding an elephant at the head of his own critter army? Pumping powdered sugar into the water supply? He was just waiting for the sirens to start wailing.

This was it. The experiment, and all of the hard work that Fisher had put into it, was an utter failure. More than that: it was a disaster. Most failed experiments you can just clean up and try again. But Two was in the world now, and Fisher couldn't un-make him.

"Kitchen," his mom commanded as soon as they were inside the house.

Fisher sat down at the kitchen table, feeling like a prisoner waiting for his sentence in front of a judge. His mom paced back and forth, her hands twitching like caffeinated octopi. The only other motion in the room came from the faint twin glow of Lord Burnside's eyes, which followed her back and forth in her pacing. Even the fridge seemed like it was humming less loudly than usual.

"Frankly, we were shocked when we heard about your antics today," said his dad, punctuating his remark with a swoop of his crayfish net. He had been working in the bogs earlier. "We're completely at a loss. Where did this aggression come from so suddenly?"

Fisher sat at the kitchen table, arms crossed in front of his chest, watching his parents do their best tough-parent pace back and forth in front of him. They'd never really had to give him a talk like this before and probably weren't entirely sure how it was done.

His mom spoke up next. The miniature microscope lens dangling in front of her eye bobbed up and down. "Fisher, we know that things are difficult for you at school. We had a tough time, too, remember. But there are ways to deal with that frustration and ways not to."

"What you did today showed great disrespect to your teacher and to your fellow students," his dad continued. "You disrupted class, *and* someone might have gotten hurt."

Fisher looked down at the floor. He was filled with a white-hot fury. Two was to blame for all of this mess. And every second that passed gave Two time to wreak more havoc. So far, there had been no major explosions in the vicinity, but Fisher didn't count on that to last.

"Excuse me!" said the toaster. Fisher's parents turned

to look at Lord Burnside with mildly annoyed looks on their faces. "I thought I might offer what little wisdom on the subject I can muster." The glowing eyes made half-squinted thinking expressions for a few seconds. Fisher drummed his fingers on the table. "It seems I cannot presently muster any wisdom. Carry on!"

"I haven't got time to be dealing with this, Fisher," Mrs. Bas said, continuing to pace. "The AGH project is attracting attention from a lot of bad people. I have neither the time nor the energy to deal with your antics."

Fisher opened his mouth to protest, then closed it quickly. He wanted to tell her that he had battled some of those bad people just yesterday and driven them out of the house! But, of course, he couldn't.

She brushed a stray lock of frizzy hair out of her eyes. "I don't know what it is you're trying to accomplish, Fisher, and you seem unable to tell us. I guess we just have to make it clear that we aren't going to tolerate this behavior. You're very smart, and you are capable of quite a lot. But using your brains to be disruptive and simply to please yourself, with no thought for the consequences to the people around you, is exactly what Dr. X does. Do you want to end up like him?"

Fisher could feel his cheeks heating up. He decided not to mention his evil mastermind fantasy. He kept his eyes on the oak table in front of him.

"We were there, too, Fisher. We were the students who outshone everyone else. And we got picked on and insulted and bullied. The kids around us were jealous, or they didn't understand, and they took it out on us. But that doesn't go on forever. Once they started to grow up, they realized they'd been wrong all along. Those same kids who had taunted and abused us began to admire and even follow us. *We* became the cool ones. Sooner or later, everyone realized what we had always known: humans don't have wings or claws or gills. We aren't that strong and we can't see very well in the dark. Our brains are what make us powerful, and what make us unique. Our minds are what make us special."

Fisher sat through her speech and didn't say what was really on his mind. Everything bad that had ever happened to him had happened because he was unique, because he was special. He didn't want to shine the brightest. He wanted to shine the same as everyone else so he could feel like he belonged with them. All being "special" did was make him feel alone.

"Dr. Xander," she went on, refusing to refer to him again by his nickname, "sent me a message today. It was a card congratulating me on my latest breakthrough. Vague, but clear. He knows about what I'm doing, and he plans to get his hands on the AGH. Do you understand that my work— that our *family*—is at risk? This project is extremely important. It could usher in an entirely new era of medical breakthroughs. But with any advancement this big, there are very big risks, and it's a delicate line for me to walk. I am close to having the balance disrupted, and I cannot let that happen."

She finally stopped pacing, stopping directly in front of the kitchen table and leaning toward Fisher, so he had no choice but to look at her.

"I have to be more creative in disciplining you than most parents," she said, crossing her arms. "I can't just send you to your room. You're never happier than when you're there. No, I have to go further." She took a deep breath, looking regretful for what she had to do. "Fisher, you are forbidden to do any scientific research or lab work, outside of school, for one month."

The room seemed to grow darker. Fisher heard the word *month, month, month, month* . . . echoing as if his mom had shouted it down a bottomless well. She might as well have said three months or six months or six *years*. He would never last that long.

Fisher sucked in a deep breath. Ever since Fisher had created the clone, things had been spiraling out of control. He didn't think he'd be able to keep Two a secret for much longer, especially not with the forces of Dr. X closing in.

Fisher looked up into his mother's eyes. He had to come clean. The situation would just get worse if he kept it a secret. She'd be furious, of course, but if he waited until she found out for herself it would be apocalyptic. He steeled himself and quickly imagined a list of small island countries he could flee to if she took the news badly.

"Mom," he said. "I have to tell you something. I—"

Just then, the doorbell rang. Fisher nearly jumped out of his chair. His mother sighed in frustration.

"Computer, identify!" she barked.

"Single visitor, youthful, female," said the computer. "Shall I apply discouraging electric shocks? Or release the poisonous darts? Should I immobilize and apply frizzing hair treatment?" it asked, eerily eager.

Fisher's dad gave his mom a surprised, questioning look.

"No, no," she said, looking slightly guilty. "I'll get it."

She walked out of the kitchen and to the door. Fisher gripped the sides of his chair. Now that he had decided to spill his secret, he could barely keep himself from blurting it out. He looked at his dad, who tried to keep a stern look on his face. He wasn't very good at being stern. Ordinarily his mom wasn't, either, but her recent stress seemed to have brought out a much scarier side to her.

"Fisher," she said, walking back into the kitchen, "there's a girl here to see you." She was trying, unsuccessfully, to conceal her surprise. No girl had ever come to see Fisher before.

Fisher felt his eyes widen and his cheeks flush.

"There is?" he said, also trying not to seem shocked.

"She's waiting at the door," she replied. "We'll continue our talk later." His dad followed her out of the kitchen with a final swoop of his crayfish net.

Fisher slid out of his chair, snuck to the hall, and peeked around the corner.

Standing on his front porch was Veronica Greenwich.

Fisher's pulse flipped from a piano sonata into a punk rock tune on fast-forward. He felt his legs wobble slightly, and he rubbed his eyes and blinked several times.

Veronica Greenwich was still standing on his front porch.

"Hi, Fisher!" she called, spotting him, just as he was about to duck back into the kitchen. He walked up to her slowly, feeling slightly off balance. "How are you?"

"I, uh, I'm . . . ," he started, trying to keep his vision focused, " . . . that is, I've been, er, busy. You know, with . . . business. Busy, busy business. And stuff."

Nice going, he thought to himself. *That's just how you want to talk to a brilliant scholar of English and French literature.*

He put his hand out to steady himself on a display case. Unfortunately, the case held Mr. Bas's very top-heavy and imbalanced buffalo camouflage suit. As he leaned, the case started to fall toward him, and he had to catch it on his knee. A horn slipped out and punctured him in the thigh, and he stifled a yelp as he stuffed it back into the case.

Veronica laughed her soft, tinkling laugh, which nearly made him lose his balance again.

"Listen, you want to get together to study sometime? I could use a hand with my chem work, and I could help you out with the trickier parts of Shakespeare."

Her warm, bright smile had a crippling effect on Fisher's brain functions.

"Study? Study . . ." What did that word mean again? "Sure. Yes. Great!" He tried to smile back and had no idea if he succeeded.

"Good!" she said, her own smile getting even bigger. Fisher could swear he saw gleaming ribbons of sunlight streaming from it. "Maybe even tomorrow? Like around two P.M.? I know it's a Saturday, but if you don't have anything else to do . . ."

"Yes," he said. "Shakespeare is. Totally. Saturday study. Yes. I could very certainly use your help with pants—er, pent—pentameter."

Veronica giggled. "Great. See you then!" She turned and walked away. Fisher stood watching her, half expecting her to reach the front gate and turn into a cloud of mist or a flock of doves.

He closed the door behind her and leaned back against it, sliding to the ground.

Sonnet for

nica Greenwich

our hair is so nice
eyes are pretty as well you know
da I bet you like to drink ice
Because you're classy so that's the way you go

When I see you across the hallway there
It makes my heart skip some beats
Even though that's scientifically square
You make science seem like it's a creep

You are so smart and beautiful to me
I like you more than I like genetics
You make me want to study more chemistry
'Cause talking to you makes me feel so sick

I mean that in a good way though I swear
Your smile shines as bright as your hair

His thoughts were spinning. Veronica had never paid him any kind of attention before, and now she had *come* to his *house*.

There was only one explanation: Two. That must be why she was suddenly interested in spending time with him. Two was confident and cool. He had charm.

If Fisher tried to study with Veronica, he'd just start gibbering again and make a fool of himself. Two would have to go in his place. As much as Fisher longed to spend an afternoon with Veronica Greenwich, he knew he could never pull off pretending to be his clone. Maybe in a few months he would be ready to make the switch . . . maybe by freshman year of high school . . .

Fisher's mouth tightened in resolve. If the truth came out now, if Veronica ever found out that this new Fisher was an impostor, she wouldn't like him anymore.

He had to find Two and keep him a secret, at *whatever* the cost.

≋ CHAPTER 15 ≋

Human error is the most reliable thing on earth. Except when they mess it up.
—Harold Granger, Margin Scribbles

Fisher pushed the door to his room open with enough force that a rack of test tubes rattled on its shelf. He almost flung his bag in the air in shock when he saw who was there: Two, twisting himself around and around in circles. FP had clamped onto the clone's ankle.

"Ow, ow . . . uh, little help, Fisher?"

"You!" Fisher said. "When did you get here?"

"Just a—ow! Let go of me, you stupid pig!—a little while ago," Two said, trying to shake the pig off the cuff of his pants. FP held on for dear life, grunting.

"And how did you get past the house systems?" Fisher demanded, remembering to keep his voice down just enough that his parents wouldn't think he was yelling at himself. Even though he was, sort of.

"I rigged up a special ladder to your window," Two said, his rhythmic stomping getting faster. "Just in case we needed a quick escape from the guards. It extends right over the wall."

Fisher crossed his arms and let FP continue gnawing

Experiments I can still perform with remaining lab equipment:

1. baking soda volcano
2. growing mold on bread
3. ~~drawing moustaches on my clone while he sleeps~~
4. this sucks!

for a few more seconds before snapping his fingers sharply and pointing down at his feet. "Come here, boy. That's enough."

FP let out a disappointed snort and trotted over to Fisher's side, shooting the closest expression to a glare that a pig could make in Two's direction.

"We need to talk," Fisher announced.

Two plopped down in Fisher's desk chair, swiveling in a full circle before, as usual, kicking up his feet on the desk. Two's smug, self-satisfied expression was really grating on Fisher. Seeing it on his own face made him cringe. He hoped he never looked like that.

"You know what I just sat through?" Fisher demanded. The clone shook his head. "A lecture about *the pressures of school life and the ways that are and are not appropriate to cope with them.* I was harshly interrogated by my par—I mean, er, the guards."

"Did you give up any information?" said Two, looking severe.

"No, but that's not the point. The point is it's *your* fault. We're only in trouble because of the pranks you pulled at school."

Two raised his hands. "I was just trying to interfere with the enemy's training schemes. Besides, it's so boring there I had to do *something* interesting. The other kids really seemed to appreciate it."

"The more trouble you cause, the more attention you call to yourself," Fisher said. He snapped his fingers again at FP, who had begun to creep back toward Two—even though Fisher was halfway tempted to let the pig use Two as a chewing post. "No one can find out about us and our plans. *No matter what.* Okay?"

Two nodded slowly, reluctantly.

"Besides," Fisher went on, "you were mean to Mr. Granger today. He's a friend of mine and a good teacher. You don't find many of those at Wompalog."

"Granger?" Two frowned. "He smells like Krazy Glue and his eyes don't focus. I don't like him."

Fisher shook his head, wondering whether some outside element—maybe something radioactive?—had gotten tossed into the vat while this second him was grown. He reviewed the cloning process again and again in his head, but couldn't think of anything that had seemed out of line with his predictions. If anything, the procedure had been even smoother than he had expected. So what was going on? He found it hard to believe that a simple lack of experience could explain everything his clone was doing and saying. This time, he did not try and stop FP when the pig made a run for Two.

"You're pushing this to the brink, Two," Fisher said angrily, slamming his hand on his bedside table for emphasis. His hand hit a ruler—half concealed by an open box of markers—that was sticking off the desk edge. The impact catapulted the box at his own face. He ducked quickly. "Do you have any idea how much danger you're putting us in?"

"I. Am. Tired. Of. Waiting," Two replied, accenting each word with a shake of his arm. FP had now determinedly grabbed hold of the clone's sleeve. "I'm tired of lying low. I'm not gathering any useful information, and every minute we delay puts our mother's life in more danger!"

Fisher's mind worked feverishly to come up with a way to reassure Two while still keeping him under control.

"Let—go—of—me—you—edible—menace!" Two kept flapping his arm up and down.

Fisher stepped in decisively and unclamped FP's jaws. After setting the pig down on the bed, at a safe distance from Two, Fisher straightened up and looked his clone in the eyes.

"I wasn't going to tell you this so early," he said, trying to sound like an allied general, "but I've made a contact that could be crucial to our success." He wished he had a wall-mounted map to pace in front of. He paced, anyway, for effect. "If we're going to get your—our—mom back, we need more than just your spying. The enemy will not give up information so easily."

Two looked at him attentively. If Fisher could sell this, then maybe, just maybe, he could buy himself enough time to fix the situation.

"This is dangerous to even talk about, so don't write it down. You never know who might be picking through your trash." Fisher was mentally running through every spy movie he'd ever seen, trying to pick out lines that sounded good. "We have a contact on the inside."

Two perked up.

"A double agent?" he said, his perpetual cool expression dropping away. "This could be just what we need to crack the enemy's defenses!"

Two's unusual excitement made FP stir for a moment. He looked at Two, probably considering whether or not to chew on him. After a moment, he decided it wasn't worth the effort and slumped down again and began snoring on Fisher's pillow.

"Yes," Fisher said, "it could be. But only if you stop making a wreck of the school. Thanks to the chaos you're causing, the enemy is tightening its security. Our double agent is one step closer to getting exposed."

Two slumped in his chair. He actually looked a little bit regretful. "All right," Two said. "I guess I got a little carried away. Tell me about this agent."

"She is another student and has earned the trust of the enemy's leaders," Fisher said.

"She?" said Two, perking up, an excited shine in his eyes. "Is it . . ." He paused and cleared his throat. "Is it Amanda Cantrell?" he asked in a lower, deliberately flat voice.

"No," Fisher said, sitting down in his desk chair and shuffling through a drawer, while Two did his best to hide a deflated expression. "Her name is Veronica Greenwich." Fisher produced a little black-and-white photo of Veronica that he had cut from last year's yearbook. "She has inside information that we can't get any other way, but getting it will be extremely delicate. You can't speak to her directly about any of this. She's in too deep to risk that. Instead, you're going to meet her tomorrow, under the guise of studying together. When she helps you, there will be very small clues hidden in the things she points out. Words, quotes, scenes. These messages will be very subtle. Record what she says faithfully—record *every-thing* she says—and we'll discuss the clues when you get home."

Fisher exhaled silently, praying that Two would buy this latest part of the story. This was the longest, most complicated lie Fisher had ever told. He was worried that he was going to get lost in it if he had to keep it up for too long.

"I'm sorry," Two said. "Tomorrow won't work."

"What?" Fisher said. "What do you mean it won't work?"

"I'm meeting with Amanda to coordinate the project to move the DBYBBD population back to the woodlands."

Fisher's jaw dropped.

"You're going to . . . to put our whole mission at risk in order to move some *ducks*?" Fisher could have throttled Two.

"If anything, I'm helping us out," Two said, crossing his arms over his chest and staring at Fisher defensively. "If you're so concerned about blowing our cover, then the best thing to do is to lie low and act normally for a while. If Veronica is in so much danger of being exposed, we should give it a few days before meeting."

Fisher stuttered for a few seconds. In the fantasy world he'd been crafting, Two's argument was actually . . . *right*.

"There is one other mistake I'll admit I've made, though," Two went on as he stood up. "And that's letting you boss me around and not questioning your instructions."

Fisher exploded. "I'm organizing the whole thing! I

HOW TO SEAMLESSLY CONVERT THE BADGER COSTUME TO A DBYBBD DUCK

by Two

BADGER **DBYBBD**

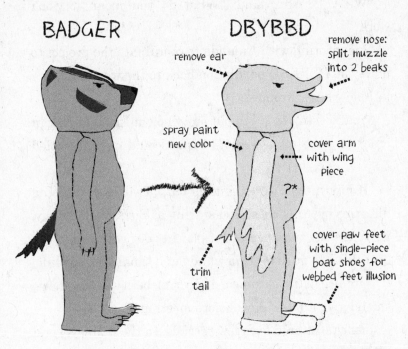

remove ear

remove nose: split muzzle into 2 beaks

spray paint new color

cover arm with wing piece

?*

trim tail

cover paw feet with single-piece boat shoes for webbed feet illusion

*Still unsure how to express bilious...

Get out of my notebook! —Fisher

know what's going on! Without me, there's no plan."

Two's stare turned hard and angry.

"And why is that, exactly? Why have you never asked me to help craft the ideas or make plans of my own? Even when I agree to go along with all of your plans, you *still* don't trust me. Spy cameras on everything I do. You keep telling me I'm putting us at risk, but what about when you snuck into school? If we'd been seen together at Wompalog it would've been disastrous. Your vibe is all wrong and I'm *sick* of it!"

"I just want everything to run smoothly," Fisher said. His face had heated up. Embarrassment and anger were coursing through him at once.

"Is that all it is?" said Two, narrowing his eyes. "Or is there something else going on?"

"What . . . What are you talking about?" said Fisher, taking an instinctive step back.

"You're making all the plans, telling me where to go, and watching what I do, but I don't know what *you're* up to. Are you trying to keep something from me?" Two took a step forward. "What are you scared that I'll find out?"

"N-Nothing!" Fisher stammered. "You know as much as I do! I'm just trying to keep everything from spinning out of control!"

"You're hiding something, and I know it," Two fired back. "You're terrified. And until you learn to mellow out a little, we won't get anywhere." With that, he turned and practically dove into his hidden bunk, leaving Fisher standing alone, hands balled into fists.

He had completely lost control of the situation . . . and Two was inches away from the truth.

CHAPTER 16

Humans always overexaggerate their own mental capacities. Thankfully, I have resolved that problem by being intellectually perfect.

—Dr. X, Notes on Human Weakness

Fisher woke up the next day with FP sleeping on his forehead, breathing pig-breath onto his face, which did nothing to improve his mood. After he'd pushed his pet off him, he lay in bed, staring at the ceiling. So far, the whole time Two had been alive had been nothing but a series of disasters.

He heard a rustling as Two climbed out of bed, keeping his eyes on the floor.

"Morning."

"Morning," Fisher said. A few seconds passed.

"Look," Two said, "I'm not trying to cause trouble. I just want us to be a little more open with each other, okay? I'll make you a deal. You take this one. Nobody can tell us apart, right? You go and meet with Veronica, and I promise I'll stay out of sight here and cause no trouble."

Fisher mulled on the idea for a bit. He didn't want to live his *whole* life through Two. And sooner or later, he would have to talk to Veronica himself. Otherwise there was no point. He sat up.

"All right," he said. "I'll do it." Two nodded.

"Good," Two said. There was a pause. "You want to play a game?"

Fisher looked up. Was that a touch of guilt he saw in Two's eyes?

Fisher hesitated for just a moment. "Sure," he finally said.

"*Uncanny Outlaws*?" Two asked.

Fisher grinned. It was his favorite video game. "Only if you're ready to get creamed."

Fisher and Two settled onto Fisher's bed and lay on their stomachs, controllers cradled lightly in their hands. Fisher got up to turn on the system, then settled down next to his clone, and in moments the two were assaulting the mountain fortress of a demon territory governor, Arizona gunslingers with six-shooters and warlock spells.

"I hate this part," Fisher said, dodging out of the way of a cannonball. "Right after the part with all the spikes, there's a ghost wall. You have to find the one little spot in it that you can jump through before the cannons blow you to pieces."

Two's brow furrowed as he leapt and dodged his way up, trying to keep up with Fisher.

"Do the demons keep coming, or can you wipe all of them out with pistol fire?" Two said.

"They keep coming," Fisher said, turning to pull off a

Stats for
Spaceblaster McGraw!

New Player for Two in Gunslinging Warlocks 6
(if he wants it)

RACE: Neptunian
> Slow, but strong. Two's strength with
> tactics would compensate for speed

SPEND INITIAL STAT POINTS ON (10 total):
- MP Max 3 → 5
- HP Max 5 → 10
- Speed 2 → 5
- Extra weapon slot 1 → 2

EQUIP (use code to give him some of my higher-
level equipment until he can level up)
- Helm: Helmet of knowledge (+2 intelligence)
- Gloves: Space sockems (+1 strength)
- Boots: Martian winged slippers (+1 speed)
- Armor: Asteroid plate (+1 defense)
- Weapon 1: Stardust canon (10-40 HP damage)
- Weapon 2: Blood staff (15-35 MP damage)

quick shot at an impish minion. For a few minutes, the only sounds in the room came from the explosions on-screen, and wails of the pixilated demons as they disintegrated into computer dust.

"Fisher . . . ," Two began finally. Fisher heard Two swallow and take a deep breath. "How can you tell when a girl likes you?" he blurted out.

Fisher was so stunned that his fingers stopped moving on the controls for a second, and a fiery skull plowed into and evaporated him. While he waited to pop back into the game, he turned to his clone.

"You're asking *me* for advice about *girls*?" His avatar reappeared and hastily dodged another projectile that threatened to wipe him out a second time.

"Sure," Two said, casting a mystical barrier around them to shield them from incoming fire. "You're the one who makes the plans. You seem to know what you're doing, y'know? I figured maybe you'd have more of a sense of this stuff than I do."

Fisher and Two were in the home stretch. They reached the mansion at the top of the mountain, and Fisher set dynamite in front of the door.

"But you always look so confident," Fisher said. "You never trip over yourself or blurt out dumb things you don't mean."

"Well, sure," Two said, making his avatar dive behind

a boulder as the door was blown to splinters. "Life at school can be intimidating: new people, new challenges. You have to meet it head-on. What else *can* you do?"

They stormed the mansion together, guns blazing, spells firing, dispatching the villain's guards quickly.

"As far as girls go, I can't say, honestly," Fisher admitted. "I'm pretty sure no girl ever has liked me, so I wouldn't know."

Two chuckled. "I guess we've got more important things going on."

"Yeah," Fisher said. *Like the lies I made up so I would never have to face school head-on.* An uncomfortable sense of guilt—and shame—began worming away in his stomach.

The final villain loomed on the screen, a huge man standing in a black cloud, a bowie knife in each hand.

"Ready?" Fisher said.

"It was good fightin' with ya, partner," said Two in an affected southern accent.

Fisher smiled. "Right back at ya," he said as both of them charged.

Fisher wished life were as simple as a video game: that if it got too hard he could just save, power off, and not think about it for a while before trying again. Or turn down the difficulty setting. Or even pop the disk out and put a different life in to see if he liked it any better.

He'd thought Two was completely sure of himself, that he really knew how to handle things. Apparently, Two had thought the same of him.

Were they both right . . . or were they both wrong?

Later in the day, Fisher came upstairs from lunch. As the meeting with Veronica approached, he was growing increasingly nervous. His stomach was doing the cancan, and his palms were sweating. Two was napping, and the sound of gentle snoring came from his hidden bunk. FP was also napping, although he had chosen a pile of socks as his place of rest.

"Okay, I'm heading out. Wish me luck," he said, taking a deep breath and trying to calm himself down. "Listen, make sure you keep FP in line, okay? He has a tendency to run out of the house to try and eat through my mom's vegetables." Two kept snoring. "Two? You hear me?" No response.

"Hey," Fisher said, walking over to the old desk, "Two, I asked . . ."

His voice turned into a tiny squeak as he lifted the covers draped over the mattress and found nothing but a pile of pillows and a tape recorder, playing the sound of Two's snores on a loop.

Fisher felt anger welling inside of him. He should've

known that Two's desire to make up had just been part of a larger trick.

He allowed himself a small, satisfied smile. Well, Fisher had tricks up his sleeve as well.

What Two *didn't* know was that while he and Fisher had played their video game earlier in the morning, Fisher had patted Two on the shoulder and stuck a tiny adhesive camera to it. It was a safe bet the camera was still in place.

Fisher bolted across the hall to his parents' bedroom. His parents were busy in their home labs. There was a chance they'd catch him here, but it was a chance he had to take. His mom had disabled the video-streaming capacity on his computer, but by meddling with a few wires, Fisher was able to establish a feed from the camera to the monitor in his parents' shower. Ordinarily, his mom or dad used this monitor to keep track of an experiment while showering. It was like a baby monitor, but the "baby" in this case often involved chemical reactions. More than once, Fisher had heard quick, watery footsteps sloshing down the hall just in time to stop something from exploding.

The screen fuzzed for a moment, then showed a Two's-eye view—or rather, Two's-shoulder view—of a street. Fisher squinted and tried to orient himself. The clone was walking up to a small park not too far from their house.

"Hey, Fisher!" The camera view turned quickly. Amanda Cantrell was standing by the curb.

Of course, Fisher thought. Two had tricked him, yet again, so he could make his meeting with Amanda.

"Hey, Amanda," Two replied, the cool, swaggering tone coming back into his voice.

"C'mere!" she was calling to Two, beckoning with her hand. "I've been brainstorming the best way to begin the operation."

"Excellent!" Two called back as he walked toward Amanda. Her smile was so big it looked like it was swallowing her whole face. Fisher tensed up. He didn't know what to do. Would this throw off the study plans with Veronica? Should he still meet her? What if it got back to the girls that Fisher had been in two places at once?

It was still only one o'clock. Maybe he should sit tight. Maybe Two intended to return soon. He *had* to know how important Fisher's meeting with Veronica would be.

"I've been putting together some ideas of my own," Two was saying. "Why don't we find a comfortable spot to compare notes?"

Fisher whipped out the notebook he had tucked into his pocket and started scribbling down Two's movements, tone, and speech. This was valuable data if he ever wanted to get out a full sentence in Veronica's presence.

"That sounds great!" said Amanda. Her smile still

hadn't budged, and Fisher began to feel uneasy. "How's your day so far?"

The camera shifted as Two shrugged. "Hasn't been great, but it's getting better."

Fisher was too bothered by the look in Amanda's eyes to marvel for too long at his clone's confidence. There was something weird about Amanda today . . . something scarier about her than usual. . . .

"How are you?" Two asked.

"I'm good, Fisher," Amanda was saying. Her face now took up most of the screen. "I'm . . . gooooooooooodddd. . . ."

Her voice thinned out into digital static.

Fisher's whole body seized up as Amanda's black eyes glinted at him through the camera.

Amanda Cantrell's eyes weren't black. They were green.

Too late, Fisher realized that Amanda's eyes weren't eyes at all. They were cameras. And this wasn't Amanda. It was an android.

An Amanda-bot.

"Two! Watch out!" Fisher shouted uselessly, just as Two must have also realized that Amanda was an imposter. Two tried to jump back out of reach, but the robot's arms shot out and gripped him around the torso.

The Amanda-bot was even stronger than the *real* Amanda! The camera shook and the view got blurry as Two was pushed down to the ground.

"Get up, Two!" Fisher shouted. "Get up! Get up and run!"

His mind was spinning in panic. Whose robot was this? What in the world was going on? Who even *had* this kind of technology?

Amanda-bot had Two in a hold, and Fisher heard tires screeching in the background. A black shape that looked like it might be the side of a van came into the picture. Fisher heard shouting.

"Secure the target!" a gruff male voice said. "Go!"

Black-clad figures jumped out of the van, and Two was pulled inside. Fisher saw the rectangle of light left by the van's open door narrowing as the door slid shut.

Then there was only sound. Two's screaming was muffled when something was shoved into his mouth.

"Target secure," said a woman's voice.

"Go!" said the man. The van's engine revved up and it sped away.

"Help!" shouted Two, breaking free of his muffle for a moment. "Heeelllllp!" Then his voice was muffled again.

"He's bugged," said the man. "Scramble it."

"On it," replied the woman.

One more muffled scream from his clone, and the picture turned to static and the sound to silence.

Fisher sat, staring at the black-and-white blizzard

on his screen, dumbstruck and terrified.

Two had just been kidnapped.

Clone-napped.

But who had done it—and why?

In a panic, Fisher punched wildly at the screen's controls, trying to erase all traces that he had used it. In the process, he accidentally hit the START SHOWER control. Instantly, he was blasted with cold water. He thrashed around under the spray, and smacked the KARAOKE button that his mom, who liked to sing in the shower, had put in. A background piano track for the Beatles' "I Want to Hold Your Hand" started to play as Fisher struggled, slipped, stood again, and finally managed to turn off the water.

Then he bolted to his room, where FP still lay on the floor. The little pig came up to him and nuzzled his shin. Fisher, soaked, was too shocked to notice.

It wasn't enough to say things had gone from bad to worse. Things had gone from disastrous to catastrophic.

He had to save Two.

CHAPTER 17

Telling a human being not to panic is like stealing a child's favorite teddy bear and then telling it not to cry. It's completely pointless, but it makes me laugh.
—Dr. X, Notes on Human Weakness

Fisher ran for his bedroom door, then stopped himself. He couldn't get outside without being seen by house security. He paced back and forth, his heart whomping in his chest like a giant's fist.

Then, out of the corner of his eye, he saw an object in his window. The ladder that Two had installed!

Fisher ran over and looked at it. It was a simple contraption of metal and plastic, camouflaged to look like a vine-encircled tree branch. Fisher scrambled down it as fast as he could, dashed to the front yard, burst through the liquid gate, and ran to the park.

But the park looked the same as it always did. Not a trace of the black van. The kidnappers hadn't dropped anything, and the robot must have gone with them. There weren't even any tire marks. Nothing.

Two could be anywhere. For all Fisher knew, the van could've taken him to a helicopter, or a plane. In an hour or two he might not even be on US soil anymore. He could be in a top-secret prison or a gloomy mob dungeon.

Fisher dashed back to the house. He scrambled across Two's emergency ladder, and accidentally clipped its manual release control. The ladder retracted out from under him and he only just managed to cling to his windowsill, pull himself over it, and collapse into his room, face-planting on his carpet.

He had to calm down, so he could think. He sat down at his desk, and FP curled up in his lap. He still shook as though his stomach had been replaced with a tumble dryer.

"Think, Fisher. Think," he muttered to himself.

Before he did anything, he had to reconsider the crucial question. Did the kidnappers know that Two was a clone? Or had they intended to grab Fisher?

Just then, he heard a chiming sound downstairs. It sounded like it was coming from the television. Fisher scrambled to his feet, tossing FP to the carpet, who landed with an outraged squeak. He cracked open his door silently, listening.

". . . middle of a lab procedure. What's that noise?" he heard his mom say.

"I was doing some very delicate telescope adjustments," answered his dad. "Fisher, is that you making this racket?"

Fisher crept into the hall. He heard his parents walk

into the living room. He tiptoed down the stairs, slipping behind one of his father's newest six-foot ferns, and saw his mother in full lab gear, one glove still on. His father, looking irritated, took off his own lab coat. The television screen was blank, but it was still buzzing and chiming.

"Looks like something's wrong with the TV," Fisher's mom said. "I'll have a look."

As she leaned in to look at it, the television turned on by itself. Fisher had to stuff his face into the fern's fronds to keep himself from gasping. His parents both jerked up in surprise.

The image took a few seconds to resolve itself: a man, from the shoulders up, entirely in silhouette.

Fisher's mother grew very pale.

"Dr. X," she whispered.

"You know me," said Dr. X. "That will save time." There was a detached, inhuman coldness to his voice. "You may have noticed that your son is not at home."

Fisher's parents looked at each other. Dr. X paused for a moment to let his first words sink in, and then continued.

"The reason he isn't at home is that he is, at this moment, in my keeping."

"You can't be serious," said Fisher's dad, the color draining from his face. His mom began to tremble, the goggles around her neck trembling with her.

"I do not joke," said Dr. X, tilting his head very slightly.

"I have, in fact, no sense of humor at all. But I will get to the real point of business between us. You, Mrs. Bas, have something that I want. I now have something that you want."

"You . . . ," she began, tears forming in her eyes. "You can't be talking about . . ."

"The Accelerated Growth Hormone. Precisely. I commend you on your work. I cannot replicate your success. I must, therefore, procure the hormone by different methods. Send a workable sample of the formula to me if you wish your son to see daylight again. You will come to my compound and hand over the formula to a guard in my service at dawn tomorrow. Do not attempt to contact the police. I am . . . *very* good at cleaning up *evidence*."

Then the screen went dark.

"Would he really— Could he even—" his dad stammered, his face flushing to an unusual shade of purplish red.

"I knew it. He's ruthless!" his mom replied. "He'll do whatever he can to get his hands on the formula!"

She snatched up the phone, then stared at it. Fisher's dad slammed it back onto the receiver.

"No cops," he insisted. "You heard what Dr. X said!"

Fisher sucked in a deep breath. He needed to come clean about Two at last. He couldn't bear seeing his parents so upset. And maybe they could convince Dr. X to release Two.

As he was about to step out from behind the fern, Mrs. Bas burst out:

"I don't know if the AGH even works. If it does, Xander could do terrible things with it. He could create armies from next to nothing. But how else can we get Fisher back?"

Fisher hesitated. His insides had turned to ice. If Dr. X found out that Two was a clone . . . if he knew the AGH worked . . .

Armies from next to nothing. The words echoed in his head.

"Come on," his dad replied, putting a hand around her arm. "Let's consult with the Crisis Computer at my lab. It can calculate hundreds of scenarios in seconds and predict the best course of action to take. Hurry!"

Fisher's parents tried to move in five different directions at once, and the result was a mad flailing. They looked like pinballs in a popcorn maker. Fisher's mom ran right into a sofa, tumbled over it, righted herself, and ran out the door. Fisher's dad *almost* got out the door, when one of the specimen nets sticking out of his coat caught on the banister. His feet flew straight out, and he crashed to the floor. His mom raced back inside, helped him up, and together they raced outside, leaving the front door gaping wide open.

Fisher waited until he heard his dad's ancient truck sputtering to life outside, closed and locked the front door, then ran back up the stairs and into his room. He hadn't realized just how much Dr. X wanted to get his hands on the AGH, and what he might do once he got it. If Dr. X knew that Two was an AGH-produced clone, he might try to see if there was enough of the compound left in his body tissues to provide the sample he needed . . . all he would need was a small sample of Two's DNA. Some hair. A skin sample . . .

Or blood.

There was only one option left. He had to mount a rescue.

FP trotted over, looking up at Fisher questioningly.

Fisher crouched down to pet his ears. "Hey, boy. You know how you're always wanting to run off on grand adventures?"

FP snuffled, nuzzling Fisher's hand.

"Well, now's your chance. I'll need someone to watch my back. Whaddya say?"

FP tapped his front hooves on the ground, one after the other.

"All right then," Fisher said. "We have some prep work to do."

If Fisher was going to get Two out of Dr. X's clutches, he would have to use all of the resources available to him. His mother had been careful to strip his lab of much of its equipment. Fisher was going to have to get some of it back.

As FP walked in excited circles around the room looking brave and spyish, glancing from side to side and attempting to tiptoe on his hooves, Fisher surveyed what remained in his room. Fortunately, he had a few items stashed in hidden places that his mom hadn't discovered.

Rolled up in the bottom of his shirt drawer was his Spy Suit. He'd never anticipated actually *needing* a Spy Suit, but no twelve-year-old boy with the capacity to make himself a Spy Suit will ever fail to do so.

He slipped it on. It was a flexible polymer suit allowing complete mobility and plenty of places to store gear. Fisher examined himself in the mirror. Its close fit emphasized his complete lack of shoulder width and muscle mass, but the mysterious air it lent him made up for his small size. He hoped.

Fisher picked up his handy Screw Liquefier and slipped it into the suit's tool belt. He also grabbed his special rope, which he kept in an airtight canister. Once it came in contact with air, the rope would slowly disintegrate into a colorless vapor. That way Fisher could tie it securely to something, leave it there, and in thirty minutes, there would be no evidence of its existence.

"Stay there a minute, boy," Fisher said to FP. He exited his room, doing his best stealthy spy walk. He would use his hallway as practice for the mission ahead. He crouched low, padding along quietly, taking cover behind any object

Schematics for
FISHER'S SPY SUIT

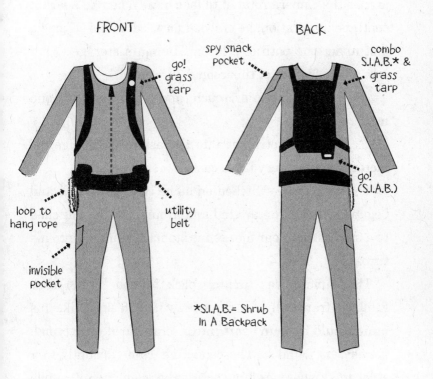

FRONT

BACK

spy snack pocket

go! grass tarp

combo S.I.A.B.* & grass tarp

loop to hang rope

utility belt

go! (S.I.A.B.)

invisible pocket

*S.I.A.B.= Shrub In A Backpack

big enough to hide him. Thankfully, most objects could. He steadied his breathing, thinking of Vic Daring sneaking down into the royal treasure house of Mars.

He slipped open the door to his mom's home lab, noting the security camera, which tracked slowly back and forth in a ceiling mount. Somewhere inside her lab was equipment she had confiscated from Fisher's room—equipment he now desperately needed.

He sucked in a deep breath and slid under a lab table just as the camera rotated to face him. When he heard it continue its rotation, he crawled forward on his stomach, just under the path of a laser. The main storage locker was at the far end of this room.

Fisher moved into a crouch, and leapt over a second laser . . .

. . . Crashing straight into a massive centrifuge his mother used for very large containers.

The centrifuge switched on as he collided with it and began whirling him around and around. Fisher clutched to a steel jar for dear life, as his stomach spun up into his throat.

The camera was turning back toward him. Fisher fumbled frantically for the OFF switch, feeling like his brain would be spun apart into a scramble at any second. Finally, he found it. The centrifuge came abruptly to a stop, and Fisher was flung across the room and into a pile of old, plastic machine parts. They avalanched on top of him just as the camera turned to face him.

Fisher dug himself out from underneath the pile as he heard the camera spin away from him. One final dash brought him to the locker door, and out of the camera's range.

The locker was fitted with an old-fashioned safe combination lock. He looked around the outside of the door for a few moments, then saw a small seam in the door near the lock. Reaching down, he pulled a tiny thread out of one glove, and fed it through the hole. The thread was a tiny wire with a micro-camera at its end. Reaching back behind his neck, Fisher pulled an eyepiece on a cord out of his suit, and fitted it over his right eye.

The tiny camera allowed him to see the inside of the lock. He was able to see when the gears lined up as he turned the dial.

108. October 8. The locker's code was Fisher's birthday. Fisher felt a pang, even as the locker opened with a satisfying clank.

Inside, jumbled up with his mother's gear, he found two things. One was a tiny Spy Suit for FP. The other looked like an ordinary backpack, but was, in Fisher's opinion, the most cunning camouflage device he had ever devised.

There was one last thing to do. Fisher snuck his way into his mother's chemical storage locker, just like that fateful day when he'd first gotten the AGH. He found the AGH canister in the exact spot he'd left it.

"Just in case they agree to give it to him," Fisher said, and took the canister down. "This is all my fault. No matter what, I can at least keep Dr. X from getting his hands

Schematics for
FP'S SPY SUIT

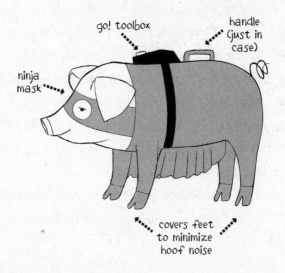

go! toolbox

handle
(just in
case)

ninja
mask

covers feet
to minimize
hoof noise

on it." He drained the AGH into his mother's perfume bottle, which he had swiped on the way downstairs. Then he
filled the AGH canister with water, and took the perfume
bottle back to his room.

He closed the locker carefully, retraced his path back
through the lab—minus the pit stop in the centrifuge—
and returned to his room, where FP was still trotting
around in excited circles.

"Okay, boy. Hold still."

FP did *not* hold still as Fisher tried to get his front legs
into the pig-sized Spy Suit. He finally managed one back

leg, but FP began trying to flap his forelegs to get away.

Sighing, Fisher reached into a food pouch in a drawer and pulled out a handful of raisins. He held the front end of the suit up and waved the raisins around until FP's eyes were stuck on them. One final swoop made FP lunge, and Fisher caught him with the suit, zipping it up around the pig's body before FP had the chance to wriggle out of it.

"Now try to get a little rest," he said. "We leave as soon as it gets dark."

CHAPTER 18

Some people go deep-sea fishing. Some people go rock climbing. I go on thrilling exploits of deadly peril.

—Vic Daring (Issue #41)

The sun was just setting when Fisher woke up, having slept in his Spy Suit for luck. He checked each piece of equipment one at a time. He was scared, but he had run out of options. His lying and sneaking around had only made things worse. He was the cause of this mess, and he had to fix it. He only had until dawn to save his clone. There was no time to waste.

"You ready, little pig?" he asked the sprawled form of FP, who continued to snore. "FP?" Fisher prodded FP with a toe. "You were really excited about this earlier."

More snores.

"I guess I'll just have to eat all of these spy snacks myself," Fisher said, sighing exaggeratedly. FP was alert and facing him so fast he almost left a blur trail. "All right then, boy. Let's do this."

As a thin rope descended from a second-floor window of the Bas house, the neighbors' houses remained dark, their inhabitants unaware of what was about to take place. A small, skinny boy silently climbed out of the window and lowered himself to the ground, and a pig glided after him gracefully, before crashing not so gracefully into an enormous cabbage.

Fisher snuck across his small side yard, avoiding security-bots by hiding between two of his mother's towering eggplants. After he heard the last security-bot pass, he padded lightly to the side of the wall.

He slipped a pair of gloves out of the suit's built-in pockets and onto his hands. He placed one hand on the wall, and the glove adhered to the brick like Velcro, its thousands of tiny strand-like hooks burrowing into the many cracks and chips in the brick surface. The soles of his boots were coated with the same material, allowing him to climb the wall like a spider. FP, with a running jump and some frantic flapping, managed to land right next to him at the top.

Fisher turned around and took a long look back at the house. He shivered, wondering if this would be the last time he ever saw it. His parents' room was dark. They had not yet returned from his father's lab. They were, he knew, already hard at work on their own plan to get him back. He just hoped he could recover Two before they found out what was really going on.

And if somehow Fisher managed to get himself—and his clone—out of this mess, he swore that he would never, ever, *ever* clone himself again.

They dropped down from the wall, FP using his wing-flaps to slow his fall, Fisher relying on his highly cushioned shock-absorbing boots. They cut across a neighbor's backyard, crushing a few flowers in the process. FP looked up at him when they reached the street.

"What is it, boy?" Fisher said, crouching low. "Do you sense something with your porcine instincts? Is there danger near?" FP poked Fisher lightly with one hoof. "Did we forget something essential? Are we in need of more gear?" FP gave a single, faint squeak. "Or are you already thinking about the spy snacks I promised you earlier?" FP hopped happily, and Fisher sighed. "Okay, okay."

Fisher reached into a small pouch on his back and got out a little pouch. He held out the mix of apple slices, raisins, and chicken he'd made for FP, and FP munched contentedly for a few minutes. Then, satisfied, he raised himself proudly on all fours, his snout pointing in the direction of their destination.

"Okay, boy," Fisher said, putting the food back. "On we go."

Cloaked by the darkness of night, the two companions crept along shadowy streets and sidewalks of suburban Palo Alto, ducking into bushes or behind buildings whenever the occasional car passed.

Halfway to their destination, the relative darkness of the streetlamp-lit night was interrupted by a blaze of light. Across the street, Fisher saw the King of Hollywood illuminated like a runway, spotlights crisscrossing back and forth to celebrate its opening. The place was packed, and a line of cars eight long trailed out of the lot.

Fisher ducked as one of the spotlights swooped down toward him. The scents of grilling onions, star fries, and spicy sauce drifted through the night air. Fisher forced himself to press forward. FP, on the other hand, was starting to veer off course, and Fisher had to reach over and grab his tail to keep him in line.

The bright lights of the restaurant receded behind them. The delicious food smells and the neon lights had been comforting. As Fisher left them behind, he felt like he was walking right out of the world and into a dark, cold place in the universe. He tried not to think that if the rescue mission went badly, he might never taste the spicy special sauce again.

After ten minutes, they saw the monolithic main complex of TechX labs looming ahead.

The main building was a massive, flat-topped pyramid, a dark gray concrete temple to technology. It was hundreds of feet tall, and illuminated by decorative floodlights. A logo spanning dozens of feet was emblazoned across the structure's front: a dark blue square with TechX in glaring white industrial font at its center.

Dr. X wanted his fortress visible at all times, as if to say,

Here I am. And you can't do anything about it. (So there.)

The first challenge would be the outer fence. This was a pretty simple obstacle, just a normal chain-link fence with some very discouraging-looking spikes jutting from its top. Fisher reached into his pocket and withdrew his Reversible Shears from the equipment belt of his spy suit. He'd used them once before, when backed into a corner of the athletic fields by the Vikings.

He clipped a small opening in the fence. FP slid through it first, and Fisher wriggled after him. Once on the other side, he pressed the REVERSE button on his shears. The blades flipped down and a small clamp flipped up. He applied this clamp to each cut in the fence, and it fused the metal back together perfectly.

Fisher crouched down in the brush, holding FP still with one arm. He was inside. There was no turning back now. His heart galloped in his chest, and he forced himself to breathe more slowly.

After the fence was a broad walkway, more grass, and then the main wall, twelve feet high and smooth as glass. Climbing wouldn't be an option. Fisher searched the walkway for guards. Seeing none, he picked up FP, and dashed across the walkway.

It was only when he felt a slight give under his foot that he realized he'd made his first mistake. There were pressure sensors underneath the walkway!

Blueprint for
REVERSE SHEARS

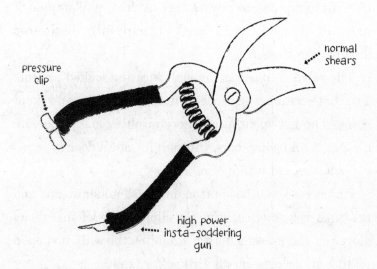

pressure
clip

normal
shears

high power
insta-soddering
gun

A quiet bleep sounded from the wall, and he heard automated systems chirping at one another. Fisher stifled a shout and looked around frantically for cover.

A small port opened in the wall several yards from the main gate, and a patrol-bot scooted out to investigate the tripped pressure sensor. Fisher dove toward the wall and dropped to the ground, pulling FP with him. Then he pushed a button on his shoulder straps, and a small tarp opened like a parachute and settled over himself and FP. This was one half of the camouflage capability his back-pack was equipped with.

The tarp's surface had spines colored and textured like grass, and automatically adjusted their color and height to match whatever grass it was next to—even the half-weed, half-dirt expanse that was the outfield of Wompalog's baseball diamond, as Fisher had thankfully discovered during gym class.

The robot stopped at the walkway and looked around. The bot's camera eye passed over Fisher, and kept going. The bot spent a few more minutes looking before giving up and going back through its small door.

Fisher let out a sigh of relief.

He pressed another button on his shoulder straps and the tarp retracted neatly. He slipped one of his sticky gloves on and pressed his hand against the wall. It slipped off like an ice cube on an air hockey table.

He frowned and looked for any sections of the wall that might be less slick. Nothing. There was no way to get a rope up the wall, either. Even if there was something on top of the wall to lasso a rope around—which there wasn't—the rope would almost definitely attract attention.

His eyes slid back to the little robot door. It was much too small for a grown spy, but Fisher could probably just squeeze through. He searched the ground and finally found a sizable stone. Then he and FP crept along the wall—being careful to stay at the very edge of the grass, where there would be no pressure sensors—until they were a few feet away from the little door.

Fisher tossed the stone onto the walkway, then quickly deployed the camo tarp. After a few seconds, the door opened and the security-bot rolled through it once again.

It buzzed its way to the path. While its back was turned, Fisher crawled through the door, with FP next to him, and the tarp concealing them both.

Fisher's heart was dancing the cha-cha in his throat. They were inside the main grounds now. Fisher pulled off the tarp and stared at the towering pyramid that rose in front of them. A pair of opaque windows was set near the top of the pyramid, and Fisher imagined that that was where Dr. X gazed upon the world he seemed to care so little about. Despite everything, and despite his anger at Dr. X, Fisher couldn't help but feel awed by the sight.

The pyramid was flanked by a pair of automatic guard towers. Fisher recognized the lenses on their sweeping cameras. Thermal. He and FP would have to get past without their heat being detected.

"Wasn't how I was planning to use this spy snack, boy," he whispered to FP, "but I've got no choice."

He withdrew a large bottle of orange soda from a pouch around his waist that had kept it barely above freezing, and shook it excessively. Then he laid the grass tarp in front of him and cracked the bottle, spraying it with the icy soft drink. Soon it was coated with soda and chilly to the touch.

"Come on. We have to hurry!"

The moving grass patch—now the moving icy-orange grass patch—made its way past the thermal cameras, stopping twice to let a security-bot roll by. Fisher and FP reached a hedgerow and crouched behind it. The single entrance to the building was now in sight.

Two human guards sat on a bench just outside of a large entrance. One was fat, the other scrawny. Neither seemed like a top choice for wanting to secure anything—and, in fact, the only reason they had not yet been fired by Dr. X is that he simply did not remember that they existed.

They never had anything to do. The occasional trespasser was almost always caught by the robots. And so they were drinking whiskey in the moonlight.

Each man had a flask in his hand, and they were in the middle of a heated discussion.

"King of Hollywood keeps their recipes locked up tight," said the fat one.

"So I've heard!" said the scrawny one. "In some kinda special vault."

Fisher looked around at the entrance they were "guarding," and saw a promising-looking air vent a little way off to one side, just around a corner. He could get in quickly with his Screw Liquefier, but he would need a diversion.

And then, an idea came to him. He could barely suppress a smile.

"Think anyone will ever be able to crack that spicy sauce recipe?" said the fat one.

"When pigs fly, my good friend, when pigs fly," said the scrawnier guard.

At that exact moment, a small pig flew through the air above their heads. They stared, their mouths gaping open.

"What in the . . . ?" said the fat man.

As they watched FP glide to a bumpy landing and then trot happily away, Fisher jumped the hedge and ran silently past them and around the corner, reaching the vent. FP snuck behind their chairs to rejoin Fisher without being noticed.

The guards, after witnessing this sight, looked at each other, then out into space, shaking their heads in confusion.

By then, Fisher and FP were already inside the complex.

⇒ CHAPTER 19 ⇐

*Spies have years of training and experience. I had half
an hour of panic and a pig.*

—Fisher Bas, Into the Dragon's Mouth,
(an unfinished screenplay)

Fisher lay on his stomach, pulling himself forward with
his elbows through the air duct. The popcorn gun was
slung over one shoulder, and every time Fisher moved,
it dug painfully into his bony side. He was, he reflected,
getting exceptionally good at the air-duct thing. It didn't
hurt that he now had gloves and boots that allowed him
to grip the duct instead of sliding around like a tilt-puzzle
ball. Spying on Two at school had been good practice, as
it turned out.

FP followed close behind, dutifully imitating his master and scooting along on his belly, even though he was
more than small enough to walk normally in the cramped
space.

They went a few inches at a time, Fisher's breathing
loud in his ears, trying to make as little noise as possible.
At any second, he expected an alarm to start wailing. He
knew that he was too far into the narrow duct to make a
quick exit. If he were discovered, that would be it, and he

could only imagine what kind of punishments Dr. X would cook up for him. Maybe he would be forced to toil forever in the depths of the complex, performing the same task over and over, like a human robot. Or maybe he would become a test subject for X's attempt to complete a human liquefication. Perhaps he'd just be tossed in a room with a defective robot that could do nothing but discuss the romantic plotlines in soap operas.

He shivered.

Fisher followed the duct deeper into the compound, twist after turn. He rapidly lost track of the way he had come, but it didn't matter: he had no idea where he was, anyway, and could only guess about the basic layout of the building. The last hints of the fresh air being drawn in from the outside gave way to the cool, sterile atmosphere of the facility.

After what felt like endless inch-by-inch creeping, Fisher and FP came to a small vent. Peering through the grate, Fisher saw that it looked as though they were directly above a maintenance corridor.

Fisher popped open the vent. He and FP slid into the corridor, following it until they reached a wide, vertical shaft. From below them, Fisher could hear the hum of extremely powerful generators. *The shaft must lead to the complex's power center,* Fisher realized.

"As much as I'd love to trot down there and just turn

the whole place off, boy," Fisher whispered, scratching FP's chin to cool both of their nerves, "Two needs us. We need to find him. He thinks I'm an ally, and he trusts me. Do you trust me, little pig? Do you believe in me?" FP's small, bright eyes winked back at him in the dark. "Maybe it's best you can't talk, so I can just assume that's a yes."

Fisher located a hatch low down on the wall, rotated its manual locking wheel, and eased it open a fraction of an inch. He pulled his goggles down over his eyes and extracted the camera wire from his left glove. He threaded it through the crack in the door. Slowly rotating his hand, Fisher received a full view of the corridor through the pinhead-sized camera on the end of the wire.

"Clear." He pushed the hatch open and stepped into the brightly lit hallway.

The interior hallways of TechX were made entirely of gray and white plastic. They were bathed in a uniform white light, but he couldn't see its source. Some doors were unmarked, others clearly labeled—EXPERIMENTAL RAT PARACHUTE, LASER RECALIBRATION CHAMBER, PROJECT: MAGIC 9 BALL . . . and on and on.

Twenty feet later, Fisher stopped, heart leaping up to jostle his Adam's apple. He fought the instinct to turn and run, forcibly steadying his legs.

The hallway came to a fork, one green-bordered passage left, a blue-bordered one right. A guard stood, motionless, a multibarreled beam stunner held over one shoulder. There was no way to go around or past him.

Fisher fought his rising panic. He could handle this. *Two* would handle this, if he was here.

Moving slowly and deliberately, trying to control the spasms in his chest, Fisher removed a small straw from his equipment belt, good for shooting off spitballs.

Or drugged darts.

Taking careful aim, he shot a tiny dart into the guard's neck from behind.

"Ow!" the guard exclaimed, slapping a hand to his neck. "What was that?" As he began looking around, the Memory Loop serum took effect. "Ow! What was that?" he said again, as his memory jumped back to three seconds earlier.

Fisher mentally thanked his mother for inventing the serum. Three seconds was the time it took for his father to recognize that *Arson Detectives: Spokane*, her favorite show and his least favorite, had come on.

Fisher grinned as he and FP walked past the guard, their images not registering with his senses, which would be tied up in the same brief moment for the next half hour. (*Arson Detectives: Spokane* was a half-hour show.) Fisher's confidence was slowly starting to build. He was working his way farther into one of the most secure laboratories on the planet.

That was when he heard the whine and hiss of pneumatic joints and the *clank, clink, clank* of metallic feet.

Something mechanical—and very large—was moving in their direction, and it was coming *fast*. As the footsteps boomed ever closer, Fisher ducked into an alcove and pressed a large button on his backpack. Plastic coils and arms shot out from it in all directions and set themselves into place all around Fisher, with mesh expanding into sections around the framework. A terra-cotta-colored cylinder surrounded his legs, a green camo net covered his body, and dozens of fake branches encircled him and sprouted thick, concealing leaves. This was Fisher's patented and perfected "Shrub-in-a-Backpack."

Simultaneously, the small device attached to FP's back expanded and surrounded the confused pig with the very convincing appearance of a toolbox.

In seconds, a large robot painted in the standard dark blue, with a white TechX logo on its chest, swept around the corner on its piston-driven legs. It approached the deployed Shrub-in-a-Backpack, examining it closely with dark-lensed camera eyes.

Fisher's pulse hammered in his head.

After what seemed like an eternity, the robot said dully, "New vegetation. Must log." And it turned away.

Fisher's sigh of relief got caught in his throat as the robot stopped, grabbed the disguised FP, and muttered,

SHRUB-IN-A-BACKPACK
(PATENT PENDING)

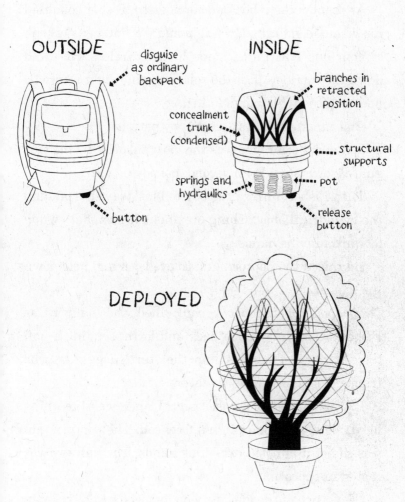

OUTSIDE

disguise as ordinary backpack

button

INSIDE

branches in retracted position

concealment trunk (condensed)

structural supports

springs and hydraulics

pot

release button

DEPLOYED

"Out of place. Take to maintenance." The robot then moved off at full clip, carrying Fisher's pig companion in its metal hands.

As soon as the robot was out of sight, Fisher collapsed his disguise, fighting a rising panic. FP had been taken!

Fear and frustration made Fisher careless. He raced down the corridor after the robot, veering right where he had seen the robot make a turn.

And ran straight into a security patrol.

It was not clear who was the most surprised—the four guards, or Fisher. For a second, nobody moved.

Then Fisher unfroze. He twisted his body sharply, and the cylindrical object slung over his left shoulder swung forward into his hands.

He raised the popcorn gun to eye level and held down the trigger.

Popopopopopopopopopopopopop! filled the hallway as Fisher swept his weapon back and forth, sending a hail of scorching-hot kernels into the startled guards, who tripped, leapt, and dove for cover.

It was over in a few seconds. Fisher was breathing hard, feeling his pulse in his forehead. The popcorn gun was so hot it almost burned his hands. The hallway was coated in popcorn.

"Hey!" one of the guards, who had taken shelter in an alcove, picked up a kernel of popcorn and tasted it with his tongue experimentally. "That's not a *real* gun. It's . . . it's . . . It's a snack gun!"

The other guards began picking themselves off the ground.

"You think you can scare us with one of your little toys?" another one said, scowling at Fisher.

"Er . . . um . . . extra butter, anyone?" Fisher stuttered. He tried firing off more corn, but he was totally out of ammunition. Too bad FP had eaten most of it for breakfast.

There was only one thing left to do. Fisher dropped the popcorn gun and bolted in panic.

"Hey! Get back here!" the leader roared.

Fisher raced down one corridor and turned onto another. Loud boot steps rang out behind him, getting closer and closer. He rounded another corner in desperation, and found himself at a dead end. No doors, no access panels, nothing.

He had one final trick up his sleeve. As his pursuers drew closer, he unsnapped an aerosol can from his tool belt and sprayed it liberally in front of him.

The four guards rounded the corner and found the corridor empty. "Must've taken a different turn along the way," said the leader. "You"—he pointed to one of the others—"stay here, just in case he tries to double back. Let's go." The other three hurried off.

Fisher stood pressed against the back wall of the

corridor. In front of him hung what appeared to be a hazy, translucent mist. The millions of nanomachines he had sprayed into the air had statically linked with one another and, using light-sensing and color-changing abilities, assumed the appearance of the walls.

The remaining guard shifted back and forth restlessly. There was a tiny crackle, and he raised a hand to one ear. "Mills here. Yeah, it's under control. I'm on sentry in A-17 and the search is expanding. We'll have him soon." He chuckled. "Yeah, just some twerpy, little kid like we used to throw around back in school. They just don't learn, do they? Guess we'll have to keep teaching 'em, right?" He laughed more loudly. "All right, we'd better cut the chatter. See you next shift. Out."

Fisher's mind shot back to the Vikings, to their taunts and their tortures. *Just some twerpy, little kid. Throw around back in school.* It sounded just like something Brody and his bonehead followers would say. *Guess we'll just have to keep teaching 'em, right?*

Fisher's fear began to tighten into anger and resolve. He smelled the damp pine of closet hiding places, he sensed the swirl of the toilet flushing around his head, he felt punches in the stomach, tasted dirt, and heard the never-ending laughter that seemed to follow him wherever he went.

And just then, Fisher realized something: he was tired of hiding.

His clone had been taken. His *pig* had been taken. He couldn't afford to sneak around on tiptoe and play shrub whenever a footstep spooked him. He was here to do a job, and he wasn't going to let any robots or guards or a scientist with a tic-tac-toe play for a name stop him.

Brazenly, he stepped beyond the haze of the fake wall and tapped the guard on the shoulder. The man jumped in surprise and whipped around.

"You! How did you . . . Don't move, kid. I'm going to call this in, and then we're taking you to the doctor for a little chat." He reached for his earpiece.

"I'm afraid," said Fisher, "that we're experiencing technical difficulties."

He tapped a control on his right wrist, and the guard's radio emitted a burst of static before going dead.

The guard fiddled with it for a few seconds before seizing Fisher's arm angrily. "All right, enough of your hocus-pocus. Move it."

Fisher squirmed away from the guard's grasp, punching another button on his wrist. There was a faint hissing sound.

"Are you sure you're up for dragging me around? You look awfully tired." A fine-mesh mask popped out of Fisher's shirt and snapped in place over his nose and mouth.

"What're you talking about, I'm not . . ." Suddenly, the guard's grip went limp and he collapsed to the floor.

Fisher, with some effort, pulled him back behind the cover of the camouflage wall. Then he cracked his knuckles.

"Your turn, Dr. X. Mess with one Fisher, you mess with all of us."

And drawing up to his full four feet eleven inches, Fisher strode mightily and confidently down the corridor.

≋ CHAPTER 20 ≋

Approximately 30 centiliters of New Drowse Vapor should render a 200-lb. man unconscious. This was proven conclusively by my dad, who thought that it was soup.
—Fisher Bas, *Experimental Notes*

At the very center of the complex was a narrow stairway that wound up to what must be the very top of the pyramid. As Fisher crept up the spiral staircase, he looked down at the heart-rate monitor on his wrist. He didn't like it when the number was *quite* that large.

At floor ten, Fisher stepped into a narrow, dark hallway, illuminated only by strange greenish light. A sign on the wall read, CENTRAL CONTROL AHEAD. DO NOT ENTER WITHOUT AUTHORIZATION, UNLESS YOU ENJOY BATHING WITH SHARKS. Fisher kept his back pressed flat against the wall as he advanced down the hall, trying to keep his knees from locking up. He tried hard not to think about FP in his little disguise as a toolbox, and what might be happening to him.

Though his first impulse had been to chase after FP, freeing Two first was the wiser option. FP was still in disguise, and Fisher could only hope that he would be sitting, ignored on a shelf. As long as someone did not try to open him to get at a screwdriver, he should be fine.

Two, however, was in immediate danger. And Two would be able to help get FP back—despite the less-than-perfect relationship between the clone and pig.

The narrow corridor ended at a small balcony. He eased himself up to peek over the guardrail, which sat on top of an opaque glass barrier.

Below the balcony was a massive chamber, the ceiling high above Fisher's head. It was a roughly rectangular space with rounded corners, the walls sheathed in dark gray plastic. There were banks of controls all along the far wall, and dozens of workers busily monitoring everything going on in the huge complex. All wore impeccably clean, identical dark blue jumpsuits with the TechX logo emblazoned on the back.

In the center of it all was a dark figure. He was dressed all in black: a gleaming black jumpsuit, black gloves, black boots.

As he turned to survey the room, Fisher saw that he was also wearing a mask. It looked almost like an old-fashioned gas mask, but was made of black metal, with completely opaque glass over the eyes.

The masked man wasn't large, but there was something to the way he held himself—feet planted like pillars, arms confidently behind his back, head up straight—that gave the impression of a much bigger figure.

It was Dr. X. In the flesh. Assuming, that is, he actually

had flesh. For all Fisher or anyone else knew, he might be a robot, too.

All of the frustration that Fisher had built up in years of being tormented by the Vikings was finally boiling over. Two's and FP's lives were in danger because of Dr. X's greed. Fisher had to put a stop to the power-crazed scientist. Fisher couldn't believe he'd once wanted to be just like him.

"I'm going to pluck that mask right off for what you did," whispered Fisher under his breath. At that moment, Dr. X raised his head. He seemed to be looking straight at Fisher. Those dark spaces where eyes should have been sent a column of frost down Fisher's spine. He practically threw himself behind the barrier, trembling. His new-found courage had its limits.

"Status on whale tank three?" Dr. X's low, soft voice drifted up to him.

"Whales appear to be reacting to the music," said a worker.

"I don't just need a reaction," came Dr. X's voice again, this time sounding more threatening. "I want them to *dance*. Are they *dancing*?"

"Um . . . our marine behavior specialist is working on determining that, sir."

"Good. Keep me informed." Dr. X then moved farther away, and his voice got too faint for Fisher to hear.

After waiting a few minutes, Fisher eased himself into

a crouch and took another peek. Dr. X's attention was still elsewhere, thankfully. Fisher scanned the wall of screens, searching for his clone.

But his attention was arrested by hundreds of images, showing the depth of Dr. X's operations, and the true purpose of his experiments.

The whale-dancing experiment wasn't about amusement or play. Fisher watched as a worker inside the whale tank controlled the whale's motions with sound piped into the water. The whale changed directions, flipped, and even breached on cue.

And on a different screen, Fisher saw a tankful of great white sharks, who were being trained the same way. . . .

Fisher shivered.

A different screen showed several of Dr. X's latest floor-mopping models, and Dr. X strode across the room to survey them.

"How is model M-13A functioning?"

"Perfectly, sir," one worker said. "They should be ready for mass production and marketing within a few months."

Dr. X had introduced many automated devices to the public; his robots took care of things like cooking and cleaning, and people loved them for it.

"Excellent," Dr. X replied. "Let's see it in omega mode."

"Yes, sir." The worker reached up to tap his headset and said a few words. A few seconds later, the mopper-bots stopped mopping the tile floor and began to buzz and shake. A few moments later they sprouted a variety of very unpleasant-looking weapons.

"Eliminate," they began saying in metallic monotone. "Eliminate."

Robotic assassins were being disguised as household-cleaning devices. Fisher's mouth turned to chalk. There would be one in every home in America. . . .

The largest screen showed two large, metal plates bolted into the floor. As Fisher watched, a group of lab-cloaked workers stepped onto the left-most plate. A few seconds passed, then there was a bright flash.

Suddenly, they were standing on the *other* plate.

Fisher boggled. He remembered when Dr. X had tele-ported that car from one side of the city to the other. Dr. X had said at the time that the technology to successfully teleport a human was decades away, if it was possible at all. But there it was. Fisher's blood turned to slush when he realized what would happen next.

AGH. Teleportation. The ability to create armies from next to nothing, and to transport them anywhere in the world—instantly.

Dr. X would be able to conquer the world.

All the more reason to find Two and get *out*, before Dr. X realized he already had a workable sample of the AGH.

At the far side of the control room, a screen was

switching feeds between different security cameras and stopped for a few seconds on a person in a small cell. Squinting, Fisher could just make out a mirror image of himself.

A guard was just removing Two's empty food tray—at least they weren't planning to starve him to death.

As Fisher turned his eyes from the screen, he saw the same guard walk into the main control room, carrying the tray. It had been only a few seconds. Two's cell must be right on the other side of the door at the far end of the control room.

Fisher fumbled through his equipment. He had just enough rope left to lower himself down from the balcony, even though it would mean descending into the pit of snakes. Or the pit of evil scientists, as the case would have it.

But he had no choice.

He fastened one end of the rope to the railing as securely as he could, grabbed hold of it with both hands, and slipped over the side.

Literally, that is—he slipped.

He was swinging his leg over the railing when he lost his balance. Tumbling toward the tiled floor below him, he frantically clutched at the rope. Flailing wildly, he managed to get the rope wrapped around his right arm and his left leg. He spun around and around, spiraling toward the control room floor. Just before he became a Fisher-puddle, the rope jerked and he came to a stop upside down, four feet from the floor. He clapped his left hand over his mouth to stifle his yelp of pain.

With his right arm and left leg still entangled in the rope, he spun, slowly, shaking his head to try and clear away the dizziness. As hard as he tried, he couldn't pull his limbs free. Each time he struggled, he spun himself one way or the other, moving in crazy, little circles and loops. If he were alone he would have considered waiting a half hour for the rope to dissolve, but the room was full of people. It was amazing that they hadn't noticed him already. He could only be thankful that their eyes were glued to the computer monitors.

He looked over and saw the room's attention held by one of the screens. Some kind of calculator-like device was being tested by a robot.

"How is the encouragement calculator progressing?" asked Dr. X. Now that Fisher was closer to him, there was something oddly familiar about his voice, although Fisher couldn't place it.

"Seems functional, sir," said a worker. "We're about to run another test. . . ."

Something flashed on the calculator screen.

"Five . . . ," the robot said in a tinny, emotionless voice, reading the question, "times two." It reached down and tapped two numbers. "Thirteen."

237

Possible ways to create faster dissolving rope:

- add acid? (test effects on skin)
- up dissolving solution
- add invisible ink (disappear before dissolve)

or

- learn how to smoothly climb ropes?

The calculator emitted a loud, harsh squawk, and a tiny boxing glove on a spring popped out and bonked the robot in the spot where a person's nose would be.

"Hmm . . . ," Dr. X said. "Better than last time. Keep on it."

This must be another one of the silly novelty inventions Dr. X was churning out by the dozens. And now Fisher understood why. They were a distraction. Little, amusing, bleeping gizmos to take everyone's attention away from what he was *really* doing.

Fisher was starting to panic. He was tied up like an antelope in the middle of a lion's den. If he could get to the pouch on the back of his belt, he might be able to reach his spy knife—which was a Swiss Army Knife, but painted black and with *Spy Knife* written on it.

He pulled at the ropes with his free hand, twisting his body and trying to use his entangled leg for leverage. His hand inched closer, grabbing hold of his backpack and tugging at one of the zippers. Close . . .

Then he felt something give way slightly beneath his hand, and heard a click.

"Oh n-*rrrghmp!*" was all he managed to get out as the trusty Shrub-in-a-Backpack deployed itself. The mechanical limbs shot out, the mesh camouflage wrapped itself around him, and the fake branches sprang into place, leaving Fisher completely wrapped up, more tangled than ever, and totally disoriented.

As he hung in his plant disguise, he heard quick footsteps approaching, and through the mesh was able to make out a guard.

"Uh . . . sir?" The man said, and then seemed to run out of words. He simply pointed.

"What is it?" said Dr. X in his distinctive low rasp. "I have very important work to . . . er . . ." His voice was cut off and another round of footsteps, extremely precise, echoed off the polished control room floor. "Why," Dr. X demanded, "is there a shrub dangling thirty feet off the balcony?"

"Well, I think it adds a nice charm," said another

console worker. "A little greenery to break up the industrial monotony really does . . . um . . ." Dr. X had turned his dark, masked glare on her. ". . . that is, I . . . erp . . ." Her voice trailed off in a nervous gurgle, and she turned back to her console.

"I . . . don't know what it is, sir," said the guard.

"Well, whatever it is, and wherever it came from, get rid of it," Dr. X snapped.

"Yes, sir." Fisher heard a click as the guard opened a large utility knife, and proceeded to sever the rope. "Oof!" he said, setting Fisher down. "This thing's heavy." His mouth was inches from Fisher's ear, and he flinched at the volume of the man's voice. Maybe, just maybe, if he kept perfectly still . . .

"Call down to maintenance. Maybe they know where it came from. In the meantime, put that thing in a corner." Fisher heard Dr. X's footsteps walking away, and then the guard hoisted him up, grunting. He was plunked down a few feet later, and the guard walked away, wheezing and gasping.

Unfortunately, the guard had placed him next to a wall, facing the corner. He had no idea what was going on behind him.

Fisher spent the next twenty minutes turning himself 180 degrees. Every minute or so he would turn a few inches, as slowly as he could.

Finally, he was facing the rest of the chamber again. The door to Two's cell was just thirty feet away. Maybe, he thought, he could manage to sneak his way to it.

Whenever no one was looking, the shrub edged a few inches along the wall. Fisher hadn't expected a sneaking technique invented by cartoon animals to be so effective, but after just a few minutes, he had cut the distance to the door in half. He couldn't believe his good luck. Just a few minutes more, and the door was right there!

Fisher sucked in a deep breath. He waited until everyone's attention was riveted by misbehaving monkeys in Chamber 17, and then dashed for the door.

That was when he realized he had never precisely calculated the branch spread of the shrubstitute. He tried to push through the doorway, but his branches were too big. He was caught in the middle of the door, wedged there like a baseball shoved up a drainpipe. Branches snapped and rustled, and every head in the room whipped around to stare at the shrub trying to force itself through a too-narrow doorway.

"Grab that thing!" Dr. X's thundering voice echoed through the room. Fisher tried to slip through the door one last time, but strong hands gripped him.

Fisher was dumped unceremoniously in front of Dr. X.

This was it, then. The end. His plan had failed. He'd been so close. So very close.

Dr. X leaned in and began examining the shrub. The cold, gloved hands got closer to Fisher's shoulders and he tried to shrink back, wishing he could just shrivel up into a little husk and blow away. After a few seconds, Dr. X brushed the hidden un-deploy switch. With a loud springing sound, the device collapsed. One of its twirling arms caught the underside of Dr. X's mask as he tried to back away, tearing it off to reveal his face.

A face that Fisher knew.

Fisher gasped.

It was Mr. Granger.

The instant in which the mask came off seemed to stretch into an hour. Fisher gaped, wide-eyed, this last horror freezing him solid.

But there it was: the most feared man alive, known only as Dr. X, was Fisher's seventh-grade science teacher.

CHAPTER 21

Even a calculated risk is always part clever, part crazy.
In this case, it was also part shrubbery.
                    —Fisher Bas, Into the Dragon's Mouth

Even though Fisher knew Mr. Granger's face like he knew the first three hundred digits of pi, Granger looked startlingly different. His unkempt, stringy hair was now slicked back. His glasses were gone, and his darting, nervous eyes were now calm and focused. His head no longer jutted forward, but was held perfectly straight. His long, hooked nose ordinarily made him look like a pigeon. Now he looked much more like a hawk.

"Mr. Granger?!" Fisher was finally able to blurt out.

"Fisher!" Granger shouted simultaneously in his oddly low Dr. X voice. Then, whirling around to his assistants, "How did he escape from his cell? I'll roast you all alive if you slacked off on security!"

"Negative, sir!" said one of the workers at the computer station. "Prisoner is still secure." He pointed up at a screen, which blinked to the cell camera, where Two was still sitting cross-legged in the corner. The expression of —Granger X? Dr. G?—became darker.

"Check the cell in person," he barked to the same guard

who had cut Fisher down from the rope. "He might have hacked the camera."

The guard walked quickly through the automatic sliding door.

Fisher was still in shock.

"I . . . thought you were my friend," he managed to choke out.

"Yes, Fisher, you were supposed to think that," Granger said, letting a quick laugh escape his lips. "I knew that I had to ingratiate myself with you in order to find out more about your mother's work and, eventually, to have the power to wrest it from her. You were a tool, Fisher. Just another piece of lab equipment, like all the rest."

Fisher was now clenching his jaw too tightly to respond.

"He's there, sir," said the guard as he returned to the room.

"Then what . . . ," began Granger, furrowing his brow in confusion. Then, as if a lever had been thrown in his brain, a fiendish smile spread across his face as he pieced everything together. "Oh my. Yes, now I see. How wonderful. All I wanted was a sample of the solution. I didn't know there was a *finished product* walking around. Even *I* didn't expect to have an AGH clone in my cell. That explains recent events quite a bit. I must admit, I had my suspicions . . . when you started to act strange. . . ."

"H-How do you know *I'm* not the clone?" sputtered Fisher, trying to regain any kind of advantage.

"He's been fighting and shouting ever since we brought him here," answered Granger as Fisher had now taken to thinking of him. "He has been brave, defiant, noble." Dr. X-G chuckled again. "I know you, Fisher. You are none of these things. *That's* why he's been causing such a stir at school."

Granger beckoned with one hand, and a guard came forward and bound Fisher's hands with a cord that felt like a live snake. It hung loosely on his wrists when they were still, but the instant he tried to wrestle out of his constraints, it coiled up tighter than a steel cable.

"W-Why?" Fisher managed to stutter. He was filled with a cold anger, which made thinking impossible. "Why are you doing this? Just who *are* you?"

"Oh, I think the answer to that question is very easy, Fisher," Granger said with a malicious smile. "Simply put, I am you."

"You're nothing like me," Fisher spat out.

Mr. Granger shrugged. "But I am. I am you, a little seed of anger, and a lot of time for that seed to grow." His eyes became unfocused, as though he were staring into the past.

"I had a brilliant scientific mind from a young age," Granger went on, clasping his hands behind his back. "I

245

What was that slinky rope made of? Possibilities:

- tiny chain mail
- Chinese finger trap weave (made of Kevlar?)
- rubber filaments
- snake skin
- elastic rope
- fabric/wire combo

was designing my first electrical circuits when most are still struggling to master the Tinkertoy. I thought that everyone would love and admire me for my talents. Then I found out, just as you did, what school is actually like.

"I was pushed and shoved and mocked and trampled through my early years. And at some point, I had had enough. If the world would not show me respect, why should I show it any? I have spent decades building up my empire. My mind has enabled me to produce a vast array of technology, as well as the patents that fund all of this. Did you know, for example, that it was I who invented the world-famous Automatic Cookie Cutter? No? What about the Self-frying Frozen Fries? Just add water and . . ."
He looked at Fisher expectantly.

Fisher was too angry to congratulate Dr. X on his many

food-product inventions, so he just scowled.

"Well, it is no matter," Dr. X went on. "Suffice it to say, I have contacts in governments the world over. And everything is about to culminate in the first part of my plan," he said, drawing in a deep breath for emphasis. "Ruining Ed Woodhouse." Mr. Granger chuckled nastily.

This was not what Fisher had expected. For a moment, confusion blotted out his fear. "Ed Woodhouse . . . ," he repeated, still secretly struggling against the coils that were binding him. Maybe if he could keep Granger talking . . . "You mean, the owner of King of Hollywood?"

"The very same," said Granger, taking a step closer to Fisher. "When he was your age, he was very much like those Viking boys you dread so much. He spent every day tormenting me, finding newer and crueler ways to humiliate me. He got so good at spitballing he could fire one every two seconds. I kept them, you know. Every last one." Granger held up a large glass jar of what could only be spitballs. He smiled as he turned the jar around in his hands. "When I get a hold of the AGH—which should happen any moment now, according to a conversation I had with your mother not long ago—"

Fisher's head snapped up. *She had agreed to the ransom?*

Granger went on, "I'm going to use the DNA in those spitballs to make thousands of Ed Woodhouse clones.

Every franchise in the country will receive coordinated, simultaneous visits from their beloved owner."

He grinned at his own plan. Seeing Fisher's confusion, he explained, "Some of these Woodhouse clones will instruct the cooks to pour hot-pepper oil onto all of the food. Some will tell the waiters to serve every table by throwing the plates from a distance of thirty feet. Some will set the sound system to play 'My Heart Will Go On' on endless repeat. All across the continent, customers will be streaming out, demanding their money back, vowing never to return. He'll be ruined. His bright and shiny image as 'America's Nicest Billionaire' will finally slip away. I know what kind of a snake he really is, and I'll show the people. I'll show them all." The evil scientist's voice had been rising steadily, until he was almost shrieking.

"So . . ."—Fisher was having trouble piecing Granger's plans together—"you don't want to . . . take over the world, or something?"

For a moment, the man before him looked more like Mr. Granger again than Dr. X. He snapped out of his reverie and stared down at Fisher. Then he laughed. Not an evil villain laugh, just a simple chuckle building up to a full-throated, comical laugh. After a few seconds, he stopped, and his face returned to utter seriousness.

"Yes, of course I do," he said, very matter-of-factly.

"And I will. But first I want to see Woodhouse humiliated. After that, I'll put the AGH to proper use, raise my own clone army, and within a few years, this planet will bend to my will. You have shown me it can be done," Granger said, and Fisher detected a bit of admiration in his voice.

For a second, the hugeness of what Fisher had done overwhelmed him: with help from his mother's AGH, Fisher had achieved something that the most brilliant and mysterious scientific mind on earth had not been able to do, even with this immense machine of research supporting him.

Then a chill went through him. He had used it for just as selfish a purpose as Dr. X would have. He thought back to watching Two get beaten up by the Vikings in the bathroom at Wompalog. He had put his clone through pain and humiliation simply because he hadn't felt like dealing with his own problems.

For a moment, staring into Granger's eyes, he thought he recognized himself in the scientist's defiant and angry expression. He felt a little hollow darkness in his own soul. If he let that dark spot spread, he knew that he would end up just like Granger.

"I won't let you get away with it," said Fisher, wishing he sounded like he believed it. "I'll use everything in my power to fight you."

"My dear boy," Granger said, slipping his mask back on, "just because I *offered* to ransom you, doesn't mean I'm going to follow through. By the time the AGH is in my hands this afternoon, you—and your little twin-it-yourself brother—will be quite dead."

CHAPTER 22

A villain is just a hero with the guts to say that not everyone ought to be rescued from the stupid situations they put themselves in.

— Dr. X, *Notes on Human Weakness*

Once Fisher was hustled into the cell holding Two, he crumpled to the smooth metal floor. He had a few mere hours left to live. He would never see FP again. He would never get to say good-bye to his parents. And Veronica! He wondered whether Veronica would think about him when he was gone.

He felt his fate closing in around him like a blanket soaked in molasses.

"Brother!" Two jumped up in surprise, then knelt over Fisher. "Are you wounded?"

Fisher looked up into his clone's eyes. For the first time, Two looked scared. His cool smile was gone, his mouth a hard, straight line. Grim.

Fisher sat up slowly. "I'm sorry, Two. I tried."

Two paused for a moment, as though processing what the word *sorry* meant. Then he straightened up and spoke. "I have to admit," Two said, a steel determination in his voice, "I didn't have the highest opinion of you at first. It seemed like I was doing all the work. I doubted your courage and your resolve. But you just risked your life to save mine. You've proven yourself to be very brave. You have nothing to be sorry about."

"You really mean that?" Fisher said, looking up. "I did kind of . . . misuse you. I overstepped my bounds, I didn't trust you, I put you in dangerous situations. Like this one, for example."

"This isn't your fault," Two said seriously. "It's Dr. X's fault. Besides, like I said, you risked your life to rescue me. I have to admit, I used to think you were completely selfish. But you've proved me wrong."

He helped Fisher to his feet. "Now let's get ourselves out of here." A faint smile appeared on his face.

Fisher felt a flicker of hope.

"You really think we can?" Fisher asked.

"Of course we can," Two replied. "And we've got nothing to lose, right? We're just waiting around until they decide to get rid of us. We should at least go down fighting."

Fisher felt some of his resolve return.

"All right!" Fisher cleared his throat and dusted off his Spy Suit. "Let's have a look around this place."

The cell was very small, about twelve feet square. The back three walls and ceiling were made of the same metal alloys as the rest of the complex. Instead of bars, one side of the cell was a wall of two-inch translucent plastic. The door was made of the same material.

"We'll need to examine it more closely," whispered Two, nodding his head to indicate the cameras watching them. Fisher nodded. They looked at each other for a moment, and smiled when they realized they were having the same thought.

"This was all your idea!" shouted Two dramatically. "I would never have ended up here in the first place if it wasn't for you!" He fake-angrily slammed his hand against the back wall and listened to the sound it made, to see if there were any hollow areas.

"*My* idea?" said Fisher, purposefully too loud, pacing back and forth in front of the clear front wall and examining its surface for seams or weak spots. "It was your messing around at school that got you here!" He leaned against the wall, putting weight on it to test the material's strength.

"I can't *take* this!" said Two, punctuating the word *take* by stomping on the floor, testing for hollow space underneath it. "You've been slowing me down for long enough! We need to take bold action!"

"You've been too bold! If you hadn't been going so fast in the first place," Fisher said, slumping down against a side wall, "I wouldn't have had to slow you down." His hands groped the floor. When one hand felt a tiny depression, he raised his eyebrows at Two and nodded downward faintly.

Blueprints for
ANGRY WIRE

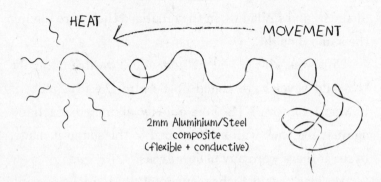

HEAT

MOVEMENT

2mm Aluminium/Steel
composite
(flexible + conductive)

"At least one of us actually tried to get something done," the clone shouted, copying Fisher's position. After a few seconds, he nodded when he found the same dent in the floor that Fisher had.

The floor was fitted with small seams, invisible to the naked eye, which indicated removable panels. One was next to Fisher, the other on the opposite side of the small cell, next to Two.

"Forget it," said Fisher. "Just leave me alone, okay?" He sank down to his side, as though curled up in defeat, positioning his body between the camera and his discovery. He pressed his ear to the floor. A very faint hum indicated wiring.

Two scooted toward him slowly. "Look," he said, keeping

his voice elevated, "maybe we can talk this out . . ." He trailed off as he got close to Fisher, and switched to a whisper. "Wires?"

"Wires," whispered Fisher, without moving.

"Probably feeding electricity to the cell," Two whispered back. "Think we can short 'em out?"

"They frisked me, but I think they missed my Angry Wire. It's in my right-side pocket. Take a strand."

Two shook Fisher as if trying to rouse him. "Hey, don't give up now! Let's discuss this. . . ."

As Two pulled his hand away, there was a tiny filament of wire in his palm. Fisher heard him stand and pad away back to his side of the cell. He hoped Two would quickly figure out how the Angry Wire worked.

Fisher rolled over so that he faced Two, who had curled up as well. Fisher, motioning with his eyes for Two to imitate him, slipped the tiny wire into the unseen seam. His clone did the same.

Slowly, Fisher began to twirl the end of the wire between his fingers. Two did the same, at the other end of the panel. As the wire rotated back and forth, becoming more agitated, the other end began to heat up.

Fisher and Two spun their Angry Wire filaments faster, hoping the cameras weren't picking up the small movement. The Angry Wire converted the kinetic energy into heat at its other end, its temperature slowly building. The heat had no quick way to escape from the tiny, sealed space.

Fisher signaled with his eyes and started shaking the wire forcefully, one last boost. Two did the same, and after a few seconds, they heard the whine of overheating electronics. Just a little bit more work with the wires, and then . . . *zzzzrp*. The heat melted the wiring under the panels and both sets underwent massive short circuits.

Fisher and Two leapt up as the lights flickered, and the tiny, red light on the camera blinked out. They would only have seconds to take advantage of the electrical short before guards were all over them.

Simultaneous kicks from boy and clone knocked the now-unlocked cell door open right as the alarms started. Fisher swiveled. To the right was the door back into the main chamber. Dr. X's guards were probably rushing toward it already. Ahead of them was another door, this one tiny and not much taller than Fisher himself, set a foot up the wall.

"Follow me!" Two cried out, already dashing for the small door. Two and Fisher dove through the door side by side.

Through—and down, down, down, down, dooooown.

Not a door after all: a chute. They plummeted fast, the slick metal sides of the steep tunnel doing little to slow them. Fisher scrabbled with his hands, trying to slow his fall, to no avail.

Fisher prayed that whatever was at the end of the chute was soft, because they were going to hurtle head-long into it.

"*Oomf! Arghhhh!*"

Fisher heard a muffled crash as Two careened out of the chute first, and he wrapped his arms around his head as he felt the tunnel disappear. Half a second of empty air rushed by him, and then he hit the pad. It was like a mattress, almost, and it cushioned his fall like a baseball glove.

Luckily, Two had been able to scramble out of the way—otherwise, it would have been a double-Fisher sandwich.

"Are you okay?" Two asked as Fisher picked himself up.

"Been better," Fisher panted as he felt his body for bruises or broken bones. Thankfully, everything appeared to be in working order.

They were in a small service corridor with plain cement walls and low lighting. Two was reading a small instruction sheet posted above the pad they'd landed on.

"Interesting," Two said as Fisher brushed himself off. "That chute was *meant* for people to throw themselves down. These instructions are 'in the event of emergency evacuation.'"

"That's a little too convenient," said Fisher, looking around for traps.

The sign instructed workers to leave the area immediately via the underground tunnels. The last sentence of the sign was printed in a large, brightly colored font: TECHX ENTERPRISES THANKS YOU FOR YOUR VALUABLE CONTRIBUTION TO OUR VENTURES. REMEMBER, ALL KNOWLEDGE OF TECHX PROJECTS IS STRICTLY CONFIDENTIAL, AND ANY BREACH OF SECRECY MAY RESULT IN A SIGNIFICANT FINE, FOLLOWED BY BRAIN VAPORIZATION. HAVE A NICE DAY!

Fisher stared at the instructions for a moment. "What would make it necessary to evacuate that quickly?" he asked.

"I don't know." Two furrowed his brow.

Then, in the quiet pause, the soft background noise of the power generator reached their ears. Two and Fisher looked at each other.

"We must be near the central power grid," Fisher said.

"Come on," said Two. "The guards will be here any moment. Let's see if we can figure out how to take the place down."

"Wait!" Fisher said as he followed his clone down a cramped, dark corridor. "FP came along with me. He was in disguise as a toolbox, and a robot picked him up and carried him to the maintenance room."

"And we have to rescue him, so he can get back to finding new and exciting ways to chew on my limbs?" said Two, turning around to look at Fisher. But Fisher saw he was half smiling. Fisher let himself smile a little bit for the first time since his friend had been clone-napped.

"Exactly," he said. As Two darted ahead of him, Fisher noticed a small, bald spot near the nape of Two's neck. "Hey—what happened to your hair? It looks like a blind-folded barber came after you."

"Dr. X took a full range of DNA samples. Hair, saliva, blood, skin cells. Don't know why."

Fisher shuddered a little bit. Now that Granger knew Two was a clone, he'd be looking at those samples a lot closer. There might be enough AGH in Two's cells to help him develop his own working formula, even if his mom *didn't* give up the sample.

"Well then, let's make sure he doesn't get the chance to do anything with them," Fisher said with resolve. "How are we going to rescue FP?"

"If I had to guess," Two said, "I would think mainte-nance would be close to the central power supply."

"Are we going the right way?" Fisher asked.

"I think so." Two cupped a hand over his ear. "The sound is definitely getting louder. . . ." His voice trailed off, and he stopped in the doorway as the corridor opened abruptly into a large room.

"Are you sure about tha—" The *t* got stuck in Fisher's throat as he walked up next to Two.

The corridor opened onto a narrow catwalk. Fisher

took a step out on it and looked at the vast chamber that stretched in front, above, and below them, for hundreds of yards. It was a huge, open space crisscrossed by dozens of walkways and cables.

In the heart of it all was the main power generator of the whole compound, which bathed the room in harsh white light, humming like an enormous metal heart.

"I've done a lot of research on computer control systems," said Fisher. When Two raised an eyebrow, he explained, "I was trying to hack into Wompalog's computers to see if I could skip school and fill in all of my absences. Unfortunately, they double-check everything with paper."

Two furrowed his brow. "Why were you so eager to skip school? Had the evil henchmen blown your cover? Had they figured out you were trying to liberate Mother?"

Fisher knew it was time to tell Two the truth. He swallowed hard. "Two, listen. I haven't been totally honest with you—"

Just then, a mechanized voice blared out from the system of intercoms: "This is a Code Black Alert. Security has been compromised. All guards, robots, biological creations, and sentient machines on deck. Intruders must be caught and promptly pulverized."

"This isn't the time, Fisher," Two said. "We need to take this place down."

Fisher nodded, relieved. He would explain everything to Two later—when they escaped. *If* they escaped. "All right, look. I think I can take a shot at adjusting the reactor's settings so that it'll overload after a few minutes," said Fisher. "But we'll need to get past the robots." He nodded his head toward the entrances to the generator controls.

A couple of tall, spindly robot guards stood motionless, positioned at either side. Each robot had a cylindrical body suspended on six multi-jointed, spidery legs. They were clearly built so that any direction could be forward. Three arms sprouted from equidistant points around the central cylinder. Their camera-filled heads swiveled back and forth atop their motionless bodies.

"How do we do that?" said Two.

Fisher thought about it for a minute.

"When the robot almost discovered me earlier, it took a moment looking at me, and then FP, before saying aloud what it determined us to be. I think as a safety measure, the robots have been designed to examine and assess what they see before they do anything about it. That may give us a narrow window to act."

"All right," Two said. "What if we try to widen that window a little bit?"

"What did you have in mind?" asked Fisher.

Two raised his eyebrows and smiled mischievously. "What color underwear do you have on?"

The robot guarding door number one had had an uneventful day, as most of its days were. It stood in the door, its camera eye slowly tracking back and forth.

However, its day became eventful when it saw a pair of identical figures moving toward it slowly.

It wasn't sure if its camera was glitching or if there were actually two people. Specifically, two short, skinny, identical-looking boys in their underwear. And they weren't walking. They were . . . dancing.

CHAPTER 23

*The principle of tactical thinking is all about making a
move your enemy doesn't expect. For example, your enemy
probably does not expect you to be an utter lunatic.*
                    —Fisher Bas, *Into the Dragon's Mouth*

Mirroring each other, Fisher and Two danced along the
catwalk through the gaping generator room in nothing
but their underpants. Fisher had never really danced, but
he found that his limbs moved surprisingly well as he
tried to keep up with Two's motions.

And one thing was certain: as they mamboed, Egyptian-
walked, and disco-pointed their way toward the door, they
were facing the most confused robot in history.

"Two unidentifieds . . . making rhythmic motions
toward my position . . . Unresponsive, and now appear
to be sliding. Their method of sliding is oddly . . . electric."

Two had been right about the robot's processing center: the more things the robot had to process, and the
less sense they made, the more time the robot would have
to spend thinking before it sounded an alarm or tried to
subdue them.

"Now their hands are in the air . . . and they are waving them as if they just do not care. . . . Halt, beings!"

Just as the robot was about to trigger an alarm, Two shouted, "Now!"

Two tackled its legs out from under it as Fisher wrapped his hands around its head and plucked out its control chip, causing it to shut down automatically.

"Nice work," said Two.

"Not so fast, intruders!"

"Uh-oh." Fisher looked up. The second robot was rolling toward them.

"Too late to out-dance this one," Two said. "Take it!"

Fisher and Two leapt at the robot from different sides, each boy grabbing hold of one arm. Its third arm tried to wrench Fisher off its back—or its front, depending on which way its spinning head was facing—but he kicked it away.

The robot swayed back and forth, unbalanced by the weight of the two boys. It tottered close to the edge of the platform.

"Fisher!" Two said. "Let go, *now!*"

Fisher dropped away from the robot's body, and the robot, suddenly released of this ninety-pound burden, toppled backward. Two jumped clear just as the robot plunged over the platform edge—and a clawing arm pulled Two's bundle of clothing over along with it.

Fisher watched the robot tumble over and over into the abyss. He felt a rush of triumph. He and Two worked really well as a team. Their ideas seemed to flow naturally together. Maybe Two wasn't as different from him as he had been starting to believe.

Two looked over the edge as his shirt and pants fluttered down after the robot. "Guess I'll be doing the rest of this escape a little chilly," Two said with a shrug.

Meanwhile, Fisher had donned his spy suit again, slipped into the control room, and was sitting down in front of the main control board. His hands were poised at the keyboard when a loud voice boomed out, nearly knocking him out of his chair.

"Hello! I am CURTIS, the Computer Universal Resource Terminal and Information Systems console! How may I make your stay in the power generator more friendly and warm? Warmer than it is already, ha-ha!"

Fisher's jaw hung open, staring at the speaker grille above his head, and the immense smiley face that had appeared on the screen.

"That was a joke!" CURTIS went on when Fisher didn't respond. "It is a double-meaning pun that plays on the word 'warm' in reference to both cheerfulness and your proximity to a thousand-megawatt fusion power source, ha-ha!"

"I . . . What?" Fisher said.

"Yes, indeed!" continued the computer. "They just upgraded me with a virus-protection system from New

Jersey, and, boy, are my positronic logic pathways tired!"
A comedy drum sound followed the second joke.

"Look, please," said Fisher, "I'm trying to find a way
to—"

"Say," CURTIS went on, ignoring Fisher entirely, "how
many technician robots does it take to replace a portable
micro-fusion cell? None! The only prototype model created a massive explosion that caused over a million dol-
lars in property damage, ha-ha!"

"Excuse me if I'm not in the mood for comedy hour,"
Fisher snapped. Guards were probably running down
the halls toward them at this very second, FP could be
robo-fodder for all he knew, and he was faced with a computer masquerading as a stand-up comic. He couldn't
imagine any possible way to get past an intelligent system to hack the reactor, even if it *did* stop telling him
jokes.

"Hurry up, Fisher!" Two shouted from outside the control room. "We're on kind of a strict schedule!"

"I'm trying!" Fisher called back, frustration building
inside of him. "But Mr. Happy-Face in here isn't going to
let me hack Dr. X's system. We'll have to find another way
to bring him down. . . ."

"What is that?" came the bubbly voice again. "You are
not a representative of Dr. X? And you do not require my
pleasantly upbeat attitude?"

"No," said Fisher, a little bit confused.

"Ugh. Good," came a completely different voice—one that sounded like a fifty-five-year-old man who'd been smoking for fifty-six years. "I really hate doing that voice. It's driving me nuts. You really want to take this place down?"

Fisher, stunned, could only nod. Now the smiley face had morphed into a deep scowl.

"Tell you what. I'm really sick of this job. Dr. X treats me like dirt, and I have to pretend to be happy about it. You got a way to get me out of here?" Fisher fumbled around in his pockets, then pulled out a minuscule portable drive.

"Is one hundred twenty terabytes enough room?" he said, still mystified by the computer's change of attitude.

"It'll be pretty cramped, but I can shed a few unnecessary subroutines and I'll fit okay. Now then, I can't take the place out because of my programming, but I've got full maps of the complex that might help you find a way to make it blow."

"Well, that's a lot more than we've got going for us so far," Fisher said.

A color-coded map of the whole vast complex popped up, complete with arrows and full details of every room.

"Thanks!" Fisher said.

"No problem," CURTIS replied. "Now get me out of here, okay?"

"Sure thing," Fisher said, and stuck the mini-drive into one of the computer's USB ports. A few seconds later, another beep indicated the transfer was complete. He leapt from the chair, slipped the drive into his pocket, and ran to meet Two at the door.

"How'd it go?" asked the clone, eyes focused on the walkway.

"I'll tell you later," said Fisher. "Look, according to the map, there's a secondary power station not far from the maintenance room. If we can short it out, the feedback should cause an overload that'll bring the whole complex down."

"All right," Two said. "But how do you plan on shorting the power station?"

"I don't know," Fisher said grimly. "We'll have to figure it out when we get there."

And on they ran.

The complex's alarms were screaming as they reached ground level again. Two pulled Fisher into an alcove just as a trio of armed guards rushed down the hall. Red lights blared at every corner, bathing the walls and floor in a ruddy glow.

"Do you know how we get to maintenance?" Two asked, looking down the hallway to watch for more guards.

Fisher could barely hear him over the alarms.

"I think I remember the way," Fisher said. "It's farther up this hall and to the right. Clear?"

"Clear," Two said, nodding. "Go!"

They darted out of the alcove and down the hall. Fisher's pulse thudded in his ears like a bass drum. He was trying not to think of all the awful things that might have happened to FP. At the same time, it was exhilarating to be fighting alongside his clone. Even if his clone was still only wearing his underwear.

They turned the corner just as a five-inch-thick steel security door began to slide its way down from the ceiling at the far end of the hallway.

"Move!" shouted Two, and they broke into a sprint. The door crept downward as they rushed forward. Six feet of space, five, four . . . and anything under it when it hit the floor would be squashed like a bug on a windshield.

Fisher dove and slid across the floor on his stomach, the slick spy suit helping him glide. The door was a foot from the floor as Two followed . . .

And came to a shuddering halt right underneath the door!

"Fisher!" he cried out.

Moving on instinct, Fisher lunged back and with both arms hauled him forward. Two's feet slipped through just as the door crashed down with a reverberating boom.

Fisher and Two picked themselves up.

"You all right?" Fisher asked.

"Yeah," Two said, shivering slightly. "Thanks."

The duo turned to continue on, when a second door came slamming down in front of them. This one did not take its time. Ten feet of hallway had been effectively sealed off.

They were trapped.

Fisher and Two raced from one door to the other and along both walls.

"See anything?" Fisher said, checking for vents or panels.

"Nothing," Two responded, pounding on a wall.

"You two are a lot more trouble than I thought," came the voice of Dr. X through a crystal-clear speaker. "Now you can just sit tight together until I get the AGH sample. Once it's safely in my hand, the ceiling will come down on you and put an end to your antics. Enjoy your stay." The voice cut off in a blip of static.

"There must be a way out," Two said, running his hands along one of the walls. Fisher began examining the other, carefully going over every square inch, his fingers shaking as precious seconds ticked by.

"Nothing!" Fisher shouted, pounding the wall with his fist. "There's no way out." Enraged, he kicked the wall one last time.

And a deafening explosion knocked him off his feet.

"That's not the reactor, is it?" said Two, going pale.

"Can't be!" Fisher said. "We didn't do anything! Unless those falling robots somehow . . ."

Then the speaker blared to life again. This time a worker's voice came shouting through it.

"Security alert," the worker said, over sounds of crashing and banging. "Intruder has sabotaged the maintenance wing, repeat, maintenance wing sabotaged. Internal security systems are deactivating."

Two and Fisher looked at each other.

"It couldn't be . . . ," Two said, mystified.

Then the worker, again: "Intruder appears to be . . . a flying pig."

"That's my pig," Fisher said, grinning broadly.

The lights flickered and both doors opened.

"Security systems deactivating!" went the speaker. "Robotic test prototypes are running loose! All units malfunctioning! Personnel, move to contain! Move to contain!"

Loud shouts filled the complex, along with electrical discharges, mechanical screeches, clanks, and the whine of motors. Two and Fisher dashed down the hall, Fisher keeping the map of the complex CURTIS had shown him in his mind as he led them toward the maintenance wing. The halls were filled with sparks and the smell of smoke.

Pieces of paneling tumbled from the walls, and wires fell from the ceiling.

All of the robots whose programming had gone haywire, whose logic circuits were fried or damaged, were out and freely roaming the hallways. Everything was coming apart. All because FP had caused havoc in the maintenance room.

A large, wheeled robot with an odd disk-like appendage for a head tottered around a corner and greeted them.

"Hello!" it said in an uneven voice. "I am Flapjackotron! I can make pancakes from any substance!" Two and Fisher raced past the confused Flapjackotron, and it turned around on wobbly wheels, trying to follow them. "Do you not require pancakes? Any raw materials you possess, I can use to . . ." Its voice faded into the noises of shouting and clamor.

"I think the power substation is up ahead!" Fisher shouted over the growing noise. "If we can cripple it, we should have just enough time to find FP and get the heck out of here!"

They were almost to the end of the corridor when a door burst open, and a robot that looked like an upside-down lawn mower shuffled toward them, various blades spinning and slicing the air. Fisher had no intention of finding out what it actually did or why it had been locked up.

"Chop, chop, chop!" the robot screeched. "Slice and dice! Slice and dice!"

Fisher and Two dove for the same door at exactly the same moment, knocking it open. Fisher reached up and shut it behind them. They both caught their breath as they heard the robot hurtle past them.

The room they had fallen into was obviously a break station. There was a desk, a little TV, a bookshelf, and a bunk . . .

. . . a bunk with a man sleeping in it. Or, actually, a boy.

"Hey," Two said as he stood up. "That isn't . . ."

"It is." Fisher climbed to his feet and approached the bunk bed. "The most destructive force at Wompalog Middle School."

"Gassy Greg," he and Two said simultaneously. Gassy Greg snorted in his sleep.

Fisher and Two looked at each other. The phrase *destructive force* echoed in Fisher's mind.

"Are you thinking what I'm thinking?" Two asked.

"If we can find the central grid station," said Fisher. They looked down at Greg again. "I think we may have found our weapon. But listen—Greg can't know about you."

Two hid in the room's closet, and Fisher tossed a shoe at Greg to wake him up.

273

"Hmmmmzz?" Greg said, opening his eyes and sitting up in bed. "What was that? Fisher!" Greg said. "What are you doing here?"

"Just visiting," Fisher said. "Listen, I need you to—"

"Why are all the alarms going off?" A hint of panic began to creep into Greg's voice. "And where's my dad?"

"Greg, your dad needs your help. Come on." Fisher grabbed Greg's arm and led him toward the power station, occasionally glancing over his shoulder to make sure Two, who was staying concealed behind falling debris, wasn't far behind.

When they finally made it to the central power source, Greg was gasping. "What—What are we doing in *here*? What's going *on*?"

Fisher knew he had no time to explain, so he just blurted out, "How's your stomach feeling, Greg?"

"My stomach? It's fine."

"Fine?" Fisher spluttered. "No . . . rumblings in there?"

"Nope," said Greg. "I'm actually on these new pills that help with my gluten allergy now. So as long as I avoid sugar and wheat . . ."

Fisher stared at Greg in disbelief, all his hope draining out of him.

"I am Flapjackotron! I can make pancakes from any substance!" The tinny voice sounded out above the alarm, and the deranged robot came careening down the hallway, spinning its arms. Suddenly, Fisher had an idea.

"Flapjackotron!" he called out, waving his arms to catch the robot's attention. "I require a pancake! A whole stack of them, actually!"

Greg's eyes grew wide. "A pancake robot?" he breathed excitedly.

"Indeed." Flapjackotron came to a stop directly in front of them. "At your service." Batter began to ooze out of the sides of its iron head. Soon, it opened its enormous metal tongue, which was as big as a dinner plate. Three pancakes were stacked there neatly.

Even though Fisher wasn't hungry at all, he grabbed a pancake and shoved half of it in his mouth. "Mmmm," he said, even though he thought the pancake tasted a little bit like motor oil. "Delicious!"

"They're maple-syrup flavored!" cried Flapjackotron, with its tongue still wagging out of its mouth.

"I want to try!" Greg cried out, and shoved the remaining two pancakes into his mouth.

And then it happened . . . the rumblings and grumblings began in Greg's stomach. Fisher knew enough to duck out of the way, just as Greg let a huge one rip.

The power of his personal explosion made the air ducts rattle around them, as his Greg's potent gas flew through the already overtaxed power grid, causing sparks to flare and flames to shoot into the hall.

"Critical failure!" a new electronic voice joined the chorus of alarms. "System overload! Meltdown mode! Meltdown mode!"

In only a matter of minutes, the whole place would be a fireball.

Trying to breathe only through his mouth, Fisher grabbed Greg's arm urgently. "Listen, do you know a quick way out of here?"

"Sure," Greg said.

"Take it," Fisher said. "Right now. I've got one more thing to take care of, but I'll see you soon, okay?"

"Okay . . . ," Greg said, confused, before trotting away.

"All right," Two said, coming out from behind the door. "I'd say this probably gives us a matter of minutes before the entire place blows. Let's go rescue your pig. At least he smells better than Greg does."

They ran down the corridor until they reached its end. The lights grew dimmer, and it became hard to see more than a few feet ahead. They entered a laboratory at the end of the hall and made for the door at its far side.

Fisher felt the floor give out from under him. He and Two plunged through a flimsy plastic covering into a deep tank of water. Reflexively, out of surprise, he took a deep breath . . .

And then realized he *could* breathe. He looked at Two and saw that he'd made the same discovery. The tank that enclosed them fed into a tube that headed in the general direction of the maintenance wing. He pointed to Two, and they swam onward.

The tunnel system seemed to be a part of the breathable-water experiment. Fisher just hoped it wasn't also connected to the tank containing the dancing whales—the last thing he wanted to deal with was a bunch of two-ton underwater mammals controlled by Dr. X. Fisher and Two swam through the dimly lit tubes until they reached a hatch. Working together, they managed to push it open and pull themselves out onto the floor of a large, gray-painted room strewn with machines, tools, and mechanical parts. Water pooled around their feet, and Two's teeth started chattering. Goose bumps covered his arms and chest.

"This must be maintenance," said Fisher, hoping he had remembered the map correctly. Panic was building in his chest. "But I don't see anyone. And where's FP?"

"Shh!" said Two. "What's that?"

As they moved forward, they heard a chorus of shouts, an odd electronic voice, and dull, thudding footsteps.

Then, as they rounded a corner, they saw five security guards trying to wrestle a giant fifteen-foot robot to the ground. It was yet another robot that seemed to have gone berserk—it rolled around on tank-like treads, its five cylindrical arms whirling in loops, and the light atop its spherical head blinking wildly.

"DANCE WITH ME! DANCE WITH ME!" it blurted in an off-pitch voice, flailing its arms. It sounded happy as it kept rolling into another room, the guards chasing after it.

Fisher and Two exchanged a glance before running onward.

They passed another robot that was doing nothing but standing in a corner and trying to count to five (it seemed unable to remember the last number), took another turn, and found themselves at the entrance to the maintenance room. Three guards stood behind a security desk, all shouting into their radios, trying to make sense of the commotion.

Fisher and Two skidded to a halt, but the guards had already seen them.

"Run!" Two called out, but before the duo could turn around, they'd been surrounded.

"End of the line, boys," one of the guards said.

"Dr. X is gonna have some fun with you," another said, scratching his thick stubble. "Maybe test out the new landsquids."

Two and Fisher were back-to-back, and Fisher turned his head to his clone. He felt as though his insides had been filled with concrete. They had come so far . . . and been so close. . . .

But he felt a surge of courage when he looked into Two's face, whose own expression was one of determination. Their fate was inevitable now. The only thing to do was face it. They nodded to each other.

Fisher forced a small smile. "You know, maybe there *is* something to be said for causing trouble."

"Told you it was fun," Two replied.

The guards took their time, weapons raised, shuffling in gradually, making sure there were no avenues of escape.

"It's been good escaping with you, brother," Fisher said. "And I do have to admit, Amanda *is* pretty cute."

Two chuckled. "Veronica's not too bad herself. I can see why you like her."

Fisher blushed. "That obvious, huh?"

"Like a lighthouse on the dark side of the moon."

The guards were less than two feet away.

Fisher smiled, and extended his hand to Two. They shook, nodded to each other, and turned to face their end.

Suddenly, a powerful squeal split the air, and a winged pink streak collided with one of the guards, knocking him over. The other guards turned in confusion, and Fisher and Two took the chance to leap on them. Fisher wrapped his arms around the guard's head and held on, covering his eyes. He managed to steer the man into a wall, and the guard knocked himself out. Fisher jumped off his back before he could get dragged to the floor.

Two's guard was down, too, though Fisher hadn't seen how. And there, in between the two of them, was the happy-looking, tail-wagging FP, who had somehow subdued the third guard. Fisher scooped up FP and hugged him, and the little pet snuffled happily in response.

"I don't know how you did any of this, boy," Fisher said, "but you will never want for snacks again for the rest of your life."

Two reached out cautiously to pet FP, and the little pig, after hesitating a moment, bent his head down so that he could.

"Two minutes! Two minutes until overload and detonation!" came the wailing of the complex's system "Evacuate immediately!"

"What do you say we get out of here?" Two raised his eyebrows.

Fisher pointed. "Right out that door is a main corridor that'll take us straight out of the building."

Fisher kept FP tucked under his arm as they ran. They raced past a herd of what could only be described as "monkeyraffes"—furry, spotted creatures with long legs, short arms, and prehensile tails—they ran past a cloud of millimeter-sized robots that were swarming over a guard's face, trying to apply extensive makeup to it, and they ran past an altercation between their earlier acquaintance Flapjackotron and his new arch-nemesis, Wafflonator.

A faint, low thrumming sound started, and very slowly grew in volume. The power generator was starting to overload. Fisher saw the door ahead of them, wide open because of the unbelievable work of FP, and the California sunshine beaming beyond it. Just fifty feet more . . . then twenty . . .

They were seconds away from freedom when a dark shape stepped into the doorway. It was Granger, without his Dr. X mask, looking a lot less put-together than the last time Fisher saw him. He had an evil-looking weapon in his right hand that was pointed straight at Fisher's head.

"I should have known better than to put the two of you in a room together," he said, sounding tired—sounding, in fact, a lot like he often did after double-lab period at Wompalog. "You've almost completely wrecked my compound. Fortunately, all of it can be repaired. Only a temporary setback. Soon, I'll be standing over Ed Woodhouse's crumbling empire, laughing. And the rest of the world will follow in his ruined footsteps. It will be a glorious sight. Too bad you won't be around to see it."

Fisher instinctively pressed himself back against the wall. There was nowhere to hide, and no place to take cover. FP growled in his arms.

"Good-bye, Fisher. Or shall I say, good-bye, *Fishers*." Granger's finger began to wrap around the trigger. But before he could fire, a cloud of white, noxious vapor exploded, making him jump back in shock. The smells of rotten eggs and garbage filled the corridor.

Two, his last tissue bomb deployed, leapt forward faster than anything Fisher had ever seen. Granger, who had been aiming at Fisher, tried to swing the weapon back to defend himself but couldn't get off a shot before Two had his hands around his wrist, trying to twist the weapon away. Granger, for all of his genius, was still a very small man, and not much of a fighter. He had hired—or built—others to do his fighting for him. Without his fancy equipment, Two was giving him a run for his money.

Just then a massive explosion rocked the building. Debris crashed down from the ceiling, cutting Fisher off from Granger and Two, who fell to the deck, grappling fiercely.

"Go, Fisher!" Two shouted, punching and elbowing the evil scientist, who fought back with all of his fiendish effort. "GO!!"

Fisher tried to find a way to Two, but the wreckage blocked his path. As more explosions followed, Fisher grabbed FP and bolted for the door as fast as he could. Sunlight struck his face, something he'd feared would never happen again. He sprinted past the abandoned guardhouse, through the open gate, and onto the grass surrounding the outer walkway.

Streaming out from all sides were fleeing workers and guards, mixed in with dozens of robots with varying degrees of sanity. He saw Gassy Greg being tugged by the hand by a man Fisher assumed to be his dad. He even saw a massive tractor-bot hauling an enormous tank containing the experimental whales.

A boom shook the ground, sounding like a torrential thunderstorm compressed into a single second, and the explosion knocked Fisher ten feet forward. He skidded to a halt flat on his face, with FP squirming and squealing underneath him.

He picked himself up, and turned back to look at the compound.

And found that it wasn't there anymore. The compound had collapsed in on itself within a single second. A column of fire and smoke jetted up into the sky. It was as wide as the building itself and soared hundreds of feet into the air as the ground kept shaking. It took minutes for the inferno to subside. Fisher had to throw his arms over his eyes to keep from being blinded. The explosion had jettisoned straight up—otherwise Fisher and everything for blocks would have been swept up in the blast.

At last, after what felt like hours, the rumbling subsided, and Fisher uncovered his eyes.

Only a massive dust cloud floated where the building once stood. Anyone and anything that had been left inside it when the final blast occurred was now little more than mist.

CHAPTER 24

Fools! You will never defeat me!

> —Prince Xultar of Venus, enemy of Vic Daring,
> approximately 3.1 minutes before being defeated

Fisher could barely breathe. His mom and dad were squeezing him so tightly, he felt like a watermelon being pushed through a straw. They had arrived on the scene minutes earlier, along with a full SWAT team and dozens of military officers. It looked like they had been about to storm TechX when it exploded. Fisher felt tears drip onto the top of his head from both sides. FP was bounding excitedly around their feet.

"I thought I'd never see you again," managed his mother between sobs, her lab gear still hanging loosely from her neck, her hair disheveled. "Dr. X always terrified me, but I never thought he'd go this far!"

"Were you really planning to give up the AGH?" Fisher asked.

His mom sniffled. "My FBI contacts wanted to use the AGH to lure Dr. X into an ambush," she said. "But I was so scared that it wouldn't work. . . . I was so scared that he would find a way to . . ." She dissolved into sobs again.

"We had decided just to give up the AGH," Fisher's dad said. "It seemed like the safest thing to do. Only minutes later, and Dr. X would have had all that power in his hands!"

"Well," Fisher said when he finally managed to wrench away from his parents' double embrace. "You won't have to worry about him ever again." Fisher mentally reminded himself to return the AGH from his mother's perfume bottle to its container when they got home.

A pang struck him sharply when he thought of his four-day brother. Two had sacrificed himself to save Fisher's life. And now, his clone was reduced to dust. It was painful, and wrong. Fisher felt numb. He couldn't think about it, about how much he would miss Two.

Two had driven him crazy at first, but Fisher had really grown to admire him. Two had demonstrated qualities that Fisher had never seen in himself: courage, daring, confidence.

He thought about what Two had told him in the complex: that Fisher, too, was brave. Suddenly, it struck him that maybe he and Two hadn't been so different after all. Fisher himself had been brave, when it was necessary for him to be. He had been bold, when the situation was too important for him to sink into his usual worrying routine. And he had stayed calm during times of incredible danger to himself.

Two was just another side of himself. And in that sense, Two would always be around.

"However did you escape?" Fisher's dad asked, once again stepping in to squeeze Fisher so tightly he could only respond with a muffled "*errrnhggghmph.*"

It was only when Fisher's parents finally released him that Fisher realized people and cars were jamming the street. There were news trucks, police cars, and fire trucks. The street was packed with hundreds and hundreds of people. And they, and their cameras, were all focused on him.

Cheers went up from the crowd as Fisher's parents walked him to their car. Fisher was awestruck. Did all of these people really care whether he'd survived the TechX dungeons?

Fisher's mom bent down to whisper to him. "Now that the truth about Dr. X has been exposed, you're a hero, Fisher."

Reporters tried to crowd around him as he walked toward the street, and he found himself floating in a dense haze of glory. He, Fisher Bas, was a champion, and reporters were clamoring for his attention.

"Fisher!"

"Fisher, over here!"

"Fisher, just a few questions!"

As the reporters were about to engulf the Bas family, a

man and a woman, both in suits, both in sunglasses, and neither apparently capable of smiling, steered them around and through the crowd and straight to their car. The man got in the driver's seat while the woman got in her own car and followed them as they drove home.

"This is Agent Harris," said Fisher's dad in the passenger seat.

"We contacted the FBI as soon as we got the message Dr. X sent to us," said his mom, sitting next to him.

"Good job, son," said Agent Harris in a flat voice.

"Uh, thank you," Fisher said.

"We've been monitoring Dr. X's activities for some time now," he went on in monotone. "We were arranging for your mother to deliver a poison to Dr. X disguised as the AGH formula, but you made that unnecessary."

"Er . . . ," Fisher said. "I see."

Mrs. Bas put her arm around Fisher's shoulders and squeezed. "We're just glad you're all right, and that Dr. X can't hurt us—or anyone—anymore."

The next day, a parade was organized. As smoke still rose over Palo Alto from the smoldering crater that had been TechX, Fisher was led into the back of the mayor's convertible by the mayor himself, a great portly man with a bushy white mustache. The mayor smiled hugely and shook Fisher's hand with a firm grip. The parade got under way, music played, and people cheered. Someone dressed up in the Wompalog Furious Badger costume danced along at the front, just next to the new DBYBBD mascot.

Fisher stood in the convertible, waving to crowds who had come to marvel at the boy who had single-handedly (as far as they knew) taken down the terrifying Dr. X. He kept searching for Veronica, scanning the dense crowd of faces.

After the parade, Fisher stepped down onto the sidewalk and found himself surrounded by people and reporters.

"Did you fear for your life?" one man asked as television cameras started to close in from all sides.

"I certainly did," Fisher said with newfound ease. Before, he would have been spluttering and searching for words with even one stranger looking at him. "Dr. X was a madman. I had never guessed how nefarious his schemes really were." *Thank you, Vic Daring,* he thought, *for teaching me the word* "nefarious."

"And what about his robotic henchmen?" one woman said, an excited look on her tan face. "How did you defeat them?"

"Well," Fisher began, feeling a slight blush on his face, "it wasn't easy, but with the proper application of my technical knowledge, I was able to take them down." He was seriously warping the truth, but all of the evidence that might have disproved him was now in powder form.

"*I* have a question," said a young female voice as the speaker pushed her way to the front of the crowd. It was Amanda Cantrell. Fisher had noticed her watching him during the parade, and she had managed to sneak through the crowd between the legs of the other reporters. Now the look on her face registered a curious suspicion. "I couldn't help but notice that you've been signing autographs with your right hand. When you borrowed my pen at the protest, you wrote with your left." Fisher's old freeze-in-place reflex came back in full force. "Also, you had two freckles on your nose before," she went on, "and now you have three. Were these changes the result of strange chemicals inside the labs, or is there some better explanation you can give us?" She shoved her microphone closer to his face.

"I . . . uh . . . ," Fisher said, looking around at the crowd, who eagerly awaited his reply. "Things happened in there I can't begin to describe," he began, feigning a look of sorrow and pain and hoping that the crowd's sympathy would be stronger than their curiosity. "Fiendish machines, evil instruments of destruction. I can only guess how many bizarre substances I was exposed to. They may have changed me in permanent ways. I'm just lucky to be alive."

Amanda crossed her arms, eyes narrowing. She wasn't buying it. But as Fisher looked around, he realized he could've said Santa Claus had flown a dinosaur from Mars to give him a new nose freckle, and the crowd still would've smiled at him admiringly.

"Well," she said a little drily, "you're *lucky* I noticed your absence and notified the authorities when I did. Otherwise, it might've taken much longer to organize a *parade*." She frowned at him and flounced off into the crowd.

Other kids were starting to gather around him, waving and cheering. Most of them had never spoken to him before. Most of them, in fact, had probably not known his name until Two started causing such a ruckus at school. But here they all were, shouting, trying to catch his eye. Into the middle of this formation appeared the one and only Chance Barrows, sporting mirrored shades as he often did, his perfect teeth shining in the morning sun.

Fisher saw Chance and gave him a double-gun handspoint. Chance returned the gesture, smiling even wider, and the rest of the kids erupted into a chorus of even louder cheering.

People were starting to line up with pens or permanent markers and whatever they could grab to write on, demanding the new town hero's autograph. Fisher was getting squeezed from all sides, and Fisher started to feel as if he couldn't breathe.

Fortunately, as everyone was closing in, his parents managed to elbow their way through the crowd and hustle him toward their car. All the way, he kept looking for any sign of Veronica in the crowd, but he didn't see her anywhere.

"All right, hero," his mom said, tousling his hair. "Time to go home."

Fisher and his parents drove home, all three happy and exhausted from the day of celebration. FP was one step ahead of them, being happy and asleep.

"Welcome back, my dear boy!" said Lord Burnside as Fisher walked into the kitchen. "We all feared for you greatly! I was beginning to wonder if I would ever prepare bread slices to your exact crispness preference again!"

Fisher walked up and patted the toaster. "It's good to be home, your lordship."

The glowing eyes waggled up and down happily.

In spite of his father's earlier complaints, the Bas family ordered King of Hollywood for dinner, and Fisher dug into a Movie Monarch–sized order of spicy fries, feeling like he hadn't eaten anything in days.

After dinner, Fisher turned wearily to his parents. "I'm going to go and sleep now, if you don't mind," he said, and hugged them both before wearily slogging up the stairs to his room with FP close at his heels.

Potential Autograph Styles

Fisher Bas too normal

Fisher Bas

_FB&JP_ too sidekick-y

too loopy

J. Bas Also too much like old men who hate their names

Fisher Bas too plain

_FB_

Fisher Bas

fisher bas too lowercase

FISHER BAS too uppercase

_FB_ too much like monogram towels

Fisher too Cher

Fisher Bas

Vic Raring I wish

too logo-y

Fisher collapsed into bed that night, exhausted. It was really weird to go from being totally ignored to having all eyes on him. The pressure he felt was unlike any he'd ever been under before.

All the same, it should all prove to be worth it tomorrow. Because tomorrow he would go back to school, and at school, he would see Veronica again.

CHAPTER 25

I figured out why heroes always ride off into the sunset in the end. They want to find a place where no one's even heard of them. Because being a hero is exhausting . . . and leaves little time for playing video games.

          —Fisher Bas, *Into the Dragon's Mouth*

Fisher stepped off the bus the next morning feeling like an astronaut getting off a space shuttle. As he walked toward the main doors of Wompalog, the crowd around him swelled. Everyone wanted to be close to him. Fisher had a hard time getting through the sea of people. He smiled at them, winked at them, gave them little scraps of his escape story—always modified, of course, to include only one Fisher.

He had a stride to his walk now. Nobody pushed him. In fact, everyone wanted to talk to him. Everyone.

"Can I get your autograph, Fisher?" said a sixth grader even shorter than he was. He obligingly got out a pen and signed the kid's notebook.

"Hey, Fisher!" said Chance Barrows, jogging up a moment later. "What was the weirdest thing you saw in there?"

"Dancing whales," Fisher said. "I'll tell you more about it later."

As the day wore on, his throat was getting dry. Was this what it was like to be popular? Having to talk to everyone all the time?

He'd never imagined that living the life of a hero would be this much work.

He was finally able to break away from the constant crowd around third period, when he saw Veronica, standing at her locker. She was flipping through one of her class notebooks, her quick and clever blue eyes darting over its contents. He plastered a smile onto his face and walked boldly over to her.

"Hey, Veronica," he said, leaning an elbow against the locker. He breathed in her faintly sweet and arrestingly familiar scent, and resisted the urge to turn to his compliment-generating watch. She looked up, smiling tightly.

"Hey, Fisher," she said. "I heard about everything that happened. I guess you had a good reason for standing me up, huh?" She gave a hollow laugh. "Anyway, I'm glad you made it out okay."

"Well, it wasn't easy," he said, running his hand through his hair. "The inside of that place was pretty frightening. Electric fields and strange biological creations everywhere. It was like something out of an old horror movie."

"Uh-huh," she said, the smile beginning to fade. She turned her attention back to her books. Fisher realized he must not be doing enough to impress her.

"There were robot guards around every corner," he continued, trying to step up his game. "Big ones, too. I had to pull some pretty bold tricks to defeat them."

"I'm sure," she said, gathering her books together and slipping them into her bag. "Okay, I should get to class now." She started to walk away.

"But . . . you don't want to hear about how I defeated them?" he said, trying to keep the desperation out of his voice. Could it be that even his new hero status was not enough for her? That in spite of everything, she would remain forever beyond his reach? Maybe, he thought, he just wasn't and would never be worthy of her company, no matter what he did.

"Fisher," she said, sighing, "I really am very happy that you got through the mess you were in. But the way you've . . . changed lately, it just kind of disappoints me. I always liked that in spite of everything that got thrown at you, you were always true to yourself. You didn't try to hide your real self for the sake of impressing or winning over anyone.

"It's not that I don't think you should be self-confident," she went on, "and the pranks you pulled were pretty funny, I have to admit. If this really is who you are now, I have no right to tell you to be any different. But I'll miss the old Fisher. That's all. I'll see you around, okay?"

She walked past him, and he felt his champion aura fizzle out around him, as if someone had taken bolt cutters to his halo.

He drifted through the rest of the day. People kept coming up to him—almost entirely in twos, threes, or crowds—as if they were afraid to all by themselves. Some people even seemed shy to talk to the Great Fisher, as everyone now seemed to think he was.

The only thing that cheered him up a little bit was his biology class. A substitute teacher, Ms. Snapper, was covering for Mr. Granger's unexplained absence. He had neither shown up to school nor called to explain his absence, and rumors were already starting to spread. Was he in trouble with the law? Did he owe money to a loan shark? Was that quiet, unassuming exterior just a secret agent's cover?

Fisher listened to these conversations, but did not join in.

He had decided to leave the mystery of Mr. Granger just that—a mystery.

"Having any trouble, Fisher?" Ms. Snapper asked, coming up to his lab station.

"Nope, I think I've got it just fine," Fisher said, adding a few drops to the bacterial colony in his petri dish.

"I'll be sure to e-mail Mr. Granger all of the notes on what we did today," she said, then shook her head. "I hope nothing's happened to him. I've never quite understood that man. He always seems just a little bit . . . distant? I'm not sure. Do you understand him, Fisher?"

"I have a feeling I may be the only person who really does," Fisher said, and smiled a bit sadly.

Walking out of science class, he saw three looming shapes, standing like towering gravestones in his path. Brody, Leroy, Willard. He sighed and walked toward them. After his ordeal, bullies like these didn't really strike the same chord of fear in him as they used to.

"We've been hearing all about what a big-time hero you are," Brody said.

"Yeah, you're—hic!—quite a big name these days," Willard said.

"A real school celery," finished Leroy. Willard and Brody turned to look at him.

"Celebrity, Leroy," said Brody. "Willard, smack him on the head, please."

Willard did.

"Ow!" Leroy winced.

"So?" Fisher said, too tired to think of anything more to say.

"*So* we don't really like that," Brody said. "If you're really a hero, you'll have the guts to face us. In front of the whole school."

"Fine," Fisher said. "When?"

"Tomorrow, noon. The cafeteria. Be there," Brody said, and the three turned around in unison, lumbering away through the hall.

Fisher knew he should be scared, but all he could think about was the way that Veronica had walked away from him, and the disappointment on her face.

"I just don't understand it," he said to his computer that night, sitting at his desk, with FP in his lap.

"I think it's pretty straightforward, kid," said CURTIS, who had just finished his big move into a brand-new hard drive. "Most kids care more about what other people think of them than about showing who they really are. She admired your honesty. And she liked who you really were."

"But she barely ever even talked to me!" Fisher said, nearly knocking FP off his lap in his agitation.

"That a fact?" CURTIS replied, a touch of humor in the weathered, old voice. "And when she did, how long did you stick around to converse? And just how many times did you gather up the guts to go and talk to *her*?"

"Um . . . never."

"Bingo!" the computer responded. "So how would you even know how she felt? You weren't exactly showing your hand, either."

"Well, I guess not. I think I was always afraid that

I was too unimportant for her to care about. But I'm a hero now!" Fisher said, standing up from his seat and putting FP down on the floor. The pig gave a loud snore and continued sleeping. "And it's been really, really . . ." He thought about it for a moment, pacing and wringing his hands, his brow twisted up. ". . . really tiring and kind of annoying, actually. Everyone is coming up to me all the time with these big plastic smiles on their faces. I have to keep this hero persona up all the time, and I don't know how many of them even care that I almost got killed."

"I don't have a visual module installed yet," said CURTIS, "but if I did I would be nodding my head with a knowing look on my face right now. Listen, Einstein, you can have a little pride and self-respect without tossing your personality into the trunk. You just gotta find the balance." Fisher sat back in his chair, petting FP, letting the computer's advice sink in.

"How did you learn so much about human behavior?" he asked finally.

"I got really bored being the reactor terminal inter-face," CURTIS replied. "I watched a lot of TV online."

The next day Fisher walked into the cafeteria with slow, purposeful steps. He was holding a clear canister about the size of a thermos under one arm. Kids looked up to say hi to him, but he ignored them as he took a final step and then pivoted to face three figures at the other end of the long gap between table rows.

He looked from one face, to the second, to the third. Leroy, Brody, Willard: each of them scowling darkly, standing with legs spread wide, arms down at their sides. They and he stood motionless for a minute, each side sizing the other up.

Kids sitting in seats on the inner table ends began to look up and realize what was going on. Some casually scooted around to safer seats, others got up and bussed their trays early. A hush began to fall over the busy room. Gusts of the uneven air-conditioning sent a crumpled napkin tumbling between them.

"Get him!" shouted Brody at last, breaking the silence. The Vikings lurched forward, their sneakers smacking the tiled floor in an uneven spatter. Fisher took a single step forward, swung his arm down, and released the canister like a bowling ball. It slid toward the Vikings at high speed and, as it reached them, its cylindrical metal body came neatly apart. A swift-moving black cloud of mosquitoes swept up and out, surrounding Willard, Brody, and Leroy, who twisted around, flailing at them.

"What is this?" Willard said as bright spots began to appear on his forehead.

"Agh!—Just some bugs!" said Brody. "Swat 'em!" He

Blueprints for
MOSQUITO CANISTER

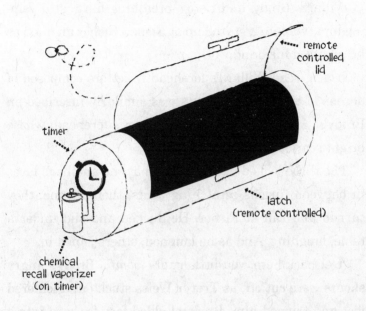

remote controlled lid

timer

latch (remote controlled)

chemical recall vaporizer (on timer)

jabbed the air as fast as he could, grabbing handfuls of the stinging insects. But there were hundreds of them in the air.

"Somebody get a stirring gator!" yelled Leroy.

"Ex-ow-*stir*-ow-minator!" said Brody, swatting madly.

Fisher stood back, arms crossed, and watched his trained and genetically altered insects go to work. At last—his experiments had led to success!

After a minute and a half, the canister released a

chemical signal into the air, and the mosquitoes that had survived the Vikings' thrashing arms flew back inside in a neat and orderly fashion.

Willard, Brody, and Leroy, breathing hard, still yelping and twitching, stared up at Fisher. Fisher grinned as he admired his handiwork.

FISHER, read Willard's forehead in letters composed of dozens of tiny red welts. WAS was similarly inscribed on Brody's. And capping it off was Leroy's forehead, whose bright scarlet print read: HERE.

The three looked back and forth at one another's faces in between furious scratching bouts, then, as one, they turned and ran at Fisher. He ducked and slid under a table, laughing. And as he laughed, others joined in.

"Get back here, you little runt—*oomf*!" Brody's angry shouts were cut off, as Trevor Weiss stuck out a loafered foot and tripped him. Brody skidded face forward into a garbage can, which promptly turned over onto his head, coating him in day-old hot dogs and mac 'n' cheese.

More laughter erupted. As Leroy rounded a corner, a sixth grader reached out and shoved him off balance with his tray. A tall, gawky-looking seventh grader ran up and dumped his fried rice on Leroy's head. Everyone was joining in, surrounding the bullies and using their lunch as weaponry—which was the only thing Wompalog cafeteria food was good for, anyway.

This wasn't revenge. This was *justice*.

The Vikings ran out of the cafeteria's back doors and out of the school to escape, with dozens of other kids in hot pursuit. They had gotten only a few dozen yards when white blotches began raining down on their heads and shoulders.

"Agh!" Brody screamed as white goop splattered across his nose.

"What—What is it?" Willard hiccuped and zigzagged wildly to avoid the bombardment.

The other students looked up and saw a flock of birds flying overhead. The Vikings had stumbled right into a bird-poop rainstorm.

"I don't recognize that species," said Trevor Weiss, squinting through his glasses. "Do you, Fisher?"

Fisher smiled widely. "That," he said, clapping his hand on Trevor's shoulder, "is the double-billed yellow-bellied bilious duck."

"Hey, what's that one got in his beak?" Trevor said, pointing to the lead duck. The duck was carrying something in its proud double bill. It let out a loud quack, and the small object fluttered to the ground almost at Fisher's feet. He picked it up.

"Spicy sauce packet," Fisher said, shaking his head and grinning. "Looks like they've found a way to coexist with King of Hollywood."

Once the Vikings had finally fled, humiliated, Fisher dusted off his pants and returned the canister of mosquitoes to his backpack. Other students smiled at him and then filed back into the cafeteria, returning to their lunches.

He hoped the initial effect of his celebrity would start to wear off. He didn't need to be mobbed by fans every day. All he needed was a few close friends.

And it was time for him to make some.

There was one more point of business to take care of. Fisher snapped his fingers and FP trotted up, holding a single orange rose in his mouth.

"Can I trust you not to eat that?" he asked the little pig, who snorted lightly in reply. "Okay, then. Go to it, boy."

Fisher saw Veronica Greenwich carrying her tray toward her usual table, looking just a little bit sad, her eyes aimed down at the floor in front of her. She turned when she heard a strange rustling sound in the air, and jumped a little in surprise as a pig with wings glided to a landing in front of her, wobbling slightly. He looked up at her and squeaked, and she reached down and plucked the orange rose from his mouth, a bright smile forming on her face.

Fisher walked up to her, just enough of the old nerves showing in his expression to brighten her smile further.

"I had my taste of being popular," he said, clasping his hands behind his back. He looked down at his feet, carefully planning his words. "That's not me. I'm the same Fisher I've always been. For a while I thought I wanted everyone to like me, and that'd make everything better. But it didn't." He cleared his throat, feeling warmth in his cheeks. "I just want to be myself again. I don't care if anyone likes me. Well, except for . . . except . . ." FP, sensing Fisher's hesitation, leaned forward and clamped his mouth around Fisher's heel. ". . . you!" Fisher said, jolted into speech by his pig companion.

When Fisher worked up the courage to meet Veronica's eyes, he saw that she was beaming at him.

"I knew you wouldn't lose yourself," she said as she smelled the rose. "Thank you, Fisher. You know, we never did get to study together."

FP looked back and forth between them, realized neither was going to be petting or feeding him, and curled up on the floor.

"Would you like to?" Fisher said, his heart beating so hard it felt like it might burst through his ribs. "Tomorrow, maybe?" he managed to squeak out.

"That'd be great," Veronica said. "See you then." She clasped his hand and held on to it for a few seconds before walking away. Fisher felt trails of warmth tracing along his hand, up his arm, and all through him.

He sighed a happy sigh and looked down at FP.

"Come on, boy. Our work today is done." FP looked up, but didn't budge. "Yes, I'll feed you as soon as we get home." FP hopped to his feet and wagged his tail enthusiastically, and they walked home together.

EPILOGUE

The next week was the best in Fisher's life. He'd started hanging out with some of the kids from debate team, and even Amanda Cantrell seemed to have accepted him, shooting only the occasional suspicious scowl in his direction. The Vikings hadn't messed with him since his insect henchmen had redecorated their faces.

Best of all, he'd been spending almost every afternoon with Veronica.

All was well with the world, Fisher thought as he stepped off the bus in the pleasant, breezy October weather, though he still often felt a pang when he thought of his poor clone, lost in the fiery demise of TechX. The explosion had turned everything inside to vapor and dust, and only a few of the strongest titanium robot frames had been recovered. No bodies. Whatever was left of Dr. X and Two apparently wasn't enough to scoop into a thimble.

He picked up the mail before walking into the house, but his hand stopped when it came across an envelope with his name on it, and no return address. Curious, Fisher slipped it open as he walked up to his room, and when he pulled out what was inside he had to catch himself on the banister as he nearly tumbled back down the stairs.

It was a Spot-Rite ad, torn from a magazine. A message scrawled across it in silver marker said:

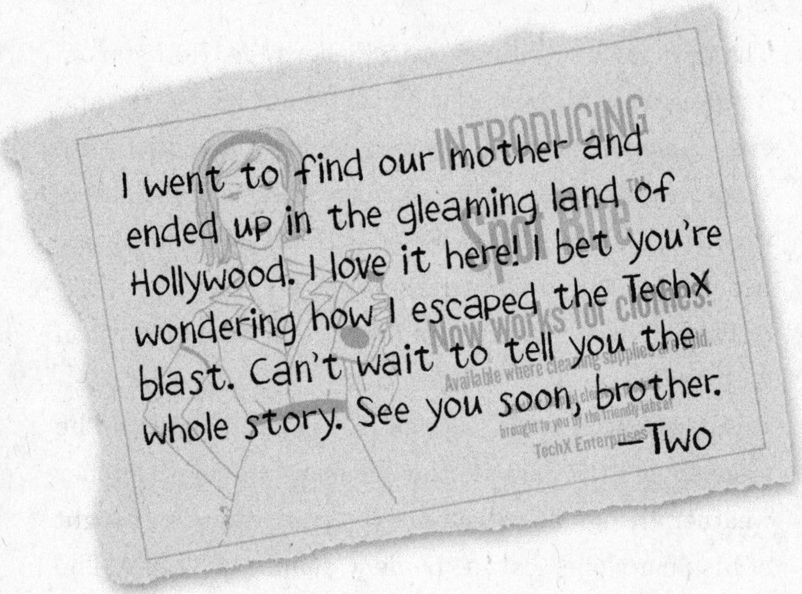

INTRODUCING
Spot Rite™
I went to find our mother and
ended up in the gleaming land of
Hollywood. I love it here! I bet you're
wondering how I escaped the TechX
blast. Can't wait to tell you the
whole story. See you soon, brother.
—Two
TechX Enterprises

ACKNOWLEDGMENTS

Were I to compose a list of everyone whose aid and support helped me to write this book, and all of the thanks they deserved for it, it would require its own volume. So to begin with a general note —if you are my friend, you have made writing this easier and less stressful.

I must, of course, acknowledge the three fates of Paper Lantern—Lauren Oliver and Lexa Hillyer, who brought me into the fold when I was just an actor who liked to pen a story now and then to satisfy his creative urges. And the third, Beth Scorzato, whose writing suggestions, illustration ideas, and overall jack-of-all-trades capability were crucial to every step of the process. My editor, Greg Ferguson, is a pleasant and genial man in person and a thoughtful and capable one in profession.

My family deserves their own accolades. My parents didn't threaten to call fire down from the heavens when I decided to embark upon a career in the arts, and now that I'm pursuing *two* of them, my mother's support never ceases, nor, I'm sure, would my father's, were he here to see it. My little sister Laura is always thrilled and excited to hear of my most recent literary exploits and takes pride in her big brother's accomplishments, just as I take pride in hers.

There is also one place I should note—the Main Reading Room in the Bryant Park branch of the New York Public Library, where much of *Popular Clone* was written. Anyone who writes should try spending a day writing there. It's a huge room and gets a little drafty, but all that space and natural light is a perfect environment for the imagination.

I'm not going to ramble on too much because I intend this book to be the first of many, so I'll wrap up by reiterating my thanks to all of my friends for their encouragement and just for being my friends.

Turn the page and grab a sneak peek at
the hilarious and fun-filled sequel to
POPULAR CLONE

⪼ Cloneward Bound ⪻
THE CLONE CHRONICLES #2

Available in hardcover and eBook from
Egmont USA in Winter 2013

≋ CHAPTER 1 ≋

It's a tough life, being a middle schooler.
You have to watch out for yourself.
Or, in my case, all of your selves.

—Fisher Bas, Journal

"Morning, Fisher!"

Fisher Bas smiled and waved at Jacob Li, then winced. His elbow ached. He was still getting used to saying hello to other kids. Up until about two weeks ago, his existence at Wompalog Middle School had barely been acknowledged— much less appreciated. Before then, his Monday morning was usually spent mathematically analyzing the layout of the decorative plants in the school's hallway, calculating the chances of being spotted as he dashed from one to another.

A lot can change in a few days. Fisher, once a stale bread crumb caught in the thin, scraggly stubble of middle school, had suddenly become a fresh, flaky croissant in the eyes of his classmates.

Fisher made his way down the hall, passing spots that would always stand as monuments to his past embarrassments: the Museum of Fisher's Pathetic Existence. First he passed infamous locker number 314, where he'd spent four entire class periods because he hadn't known that the inside latch was broken when he'd hidden in it.

Next, he passed the chipped double doors to the school library. He knew that if he inspected the larger books inside, a good half of them would have the faint imprint of his head. He winced whenever he walked past the encyclopedia shelf, and not just because the entry on particle physics was in dire need of an update. He'd offered to write it himself and glue his new entry over the current one, but the librarians hadn't been too pleased with the idea, which had baffled Fisher.

Leaving the library behind, he saw a line of metal coat hooks sticking out of the wall, one of which was bent crookedly toward the ground. Small as he was, Fisher weighed a lot more than a coat. The Vikings, the gang of bullies that had made his life a living nightmare since they had grown into hulking monstrosities in fourth grade, had held him down, stripped his coat off, and forced it on him backward. Then they'd pulled his hood up in front of his face and slipped it onto the hook.

"Well, well, well. What have we here?"

Fisher stopped dead in his tracks. He turned around, sneakers squeaking loudly, as if asking his permission to run away without him.

As though summoned by his thoughts, there they were: the looming, ugly faces of Brody, Willard, and Leroy. The

Vikings. They looked like statues cut from dark, grimy stone by a sculptor with no depth perception and very shaky hands.

Brody stood in the center as always, the leader of the pack. Willard bobbled back and forth slightly on clumsy, uneven legs on Brody's right, and to Brody's left stood Leroy. By far the dumbest and most easily distracted of the bunch, Leroy's eyes started to drift after a few seconds.

"Good morning, Fisher," Brody said with the least reassuring smile Fisher had ever seen. Alligators smiled with less malice. Fisher would know. His father kept one in the lab at home.

"Um . . . hello," Fisher said, trying to muster up some of his newfound courage. Unfortunately, when facing the Vikings, it was definitely not in the mood to be mustered.

Before the TechX episode, most people at Wompalog had settled for ignoring Fisher. But the Vikings had gone out of their way to notice—and torment—him. They were obviously displeased that Fisher's escaping from the famous TechX Industries—and exposing its dark secrets—had made him an overnight hero.

Now *everyone* noticed Fisher, and he was no longer such an easy target. But just because they had eased up a little lately did not mean that the threat was over.

"We're just giving you a friendly reminder," Brody said, rubbing his greasy palms together, "that we're still here."

"And things may *hic* be qu-quiet now," Willard went on, "but k-keep your ears open."

"We've, uh, got you under lobstervation," Leroy finished. Brody turned and gave him a long, withering look, then let out a frustrated sigh.

"Observation, Leroy," Brody said. He turned back to Fisher. "Now get out of here before we decide to make this chat a little more private. Maybe in that janitor's closet over there . . . ?"

Fisher looked to the closet in question and shivered. Unspeakable things had happened in the janitor's mop bucket, and he wanted no part of them. He didn't need a second invitation to flee.

"Lobstervation??" he heard Brody say as he sped away. "What do you think I want to do, turn him into a shell-fish? Willard, if you please." The last thing Fisher heard before he turned the corner was the resounding *smack* of Willard's broad, fat hand against Leroy's broad, fat head.

He walked around the corner so fast that he ran smack into a kid he hadn't seen, half somersaulting forward and landing in a daze on his back.

"Oop. Sorry, Fisher," the boy said, helping Fisher to his feet. Fisher looked at the unfamiliar boy's acne-pitted, smiling face. The boy was obviously an eighth grader.

"No worries . . ." Fisher said, backing away. He still wasn't used to the idea that other people knew *him*.

4

Two weeks ago, an encounter with the Vikings would have ended with Fisher head down in a wastepaper basket or sifting the baseball field's dirt out of his hair. But ever since his trained attack mosquitoes had swarmed the Vikings in the middle of the cafeteria, they'd been a lot more careful around him. He'd earned a degree of respect around Wompalog that even the Vikings were forced to acknowledge.

Except *he* hadn't earned it. At least, he hadn't earned it alone. A feeling of guilt squirmed in the bottom of Fisher's stomach. As he headed to class, he reached into his pocket and withdrew a crumpled piece of paper. He unfolded it for the four hundred and fifty-fourth time—he'd counted—and read the note.

I went to find our mother and ended up in the gleaming land of Hollywood. I love it here! I bet you're wondering how I escaped the TechX blast. Can't wait to tell you the whole story. See you soon, brother.
—Two

Two, aka Fisher-2, a genetically exact copy of Fisher. A clone that Fisher had made himself, using an extremely secret, highly dangerous chemical compound, Accelerated Growth Hormone, that he'd stolen from his mom's personal lab. The last time he'd seen Two was in the collapsing corridors of TechX Industries, fighting with Dr. X: shadowy inventor, evil megalomaniac and, as it turned out, Fisher's (former) favorite biology teacher.

Moments later, the whole complex had turned into a hundred-foot-tall column of glowing dust. Naturally, Fisher had assumed that Two had gone down with the building and, as horrible as Fisher had felt about losing Two, he also felt a guilty sense of relief. If Two was gone, it meant that his secret was safe forever.

Now, it turned out that not only was his secret *not* safe, it was running around Los Angeles, chasing after a commercial actress who formed the center of the fantasy Fisher had hastily created to try and keep Two in check. Considering how much havoc Two had caused while loose in the school, Fisher could hardly imagine what kind of damage he could inflict in one of the biggest cities on Earth.

Two school weeks had passed since TechX had gone up in an ash cloud, and Fisher had ridden the waves of glory well enough until Friday, when the note appeared in his mailbox. He'd spent all weekend in his room laboratory trying to construct a Two Tracking Unit. After a mind-numbing process of figuring out how to make it not just point at himself, he took the TTU out for a test run. Unfortunately, all it had pointed him in the direction of was an opossum, a 1992 Honda Civic, and a hot dog with peppers. Maybe if he could figure out what trace elements Two had in common with those things . . .

Fisher refolded the note for the four hundred and fifty-fourth time and tucked it back into his pocket. He tried to will away mental images of the HOLLYWOOD sign blasting into space, Two perched happily in one of the crooks of the W. Fisher turned into his science classroom and took his usual seat at the front left corner.

Every day for a year, he had walked into this room and sat down in exactly the same spot, while skinny, meek Mr. Granger had tried (mostly unsuccessfully) to get the class in order. Fisher had gotten to know Granger and even considered him a friend. Fisher was a genius. He had also learned, over the past few weeks, that he was a pretty good liar. This meant, he thought, that he should be a pretty good lie *detector*.

But it turned out that his biology teacher had really been a fiendish, maniacal scientist bent on destruction and conquest, and Fisher hadn't even had a clue. It made him wonder if any of his other teachers were really super-villains. He could definitely see his English teacher, Mrs.

Weedle, fitting the bill. If Mr. Granger had been able to hide his true nature from Fisher for so long, what kind of secrets could the other people around him be hiding? He let his eyes wander around the classroom.

But as he glanced toward the door, his mind went blank, and his lungs decided to take a quick mid-inhale break.

Veronica Greenwich walked through the door trailing a blur of dawn light and silver mist—at least, that's what it seemed like to Fisher. She saw him and smiled, and Fisher was just able to muster enough control over his face muscles to smile back.

Fisher hadn't told anyone that Granger was actually Dr. X and had been disintegrated along with the TechX building. Who would have believed him, anyway? As far as Fisher was concerned, all that mattered was that after Mr. Granger had "mysteriously disappeared," there had been some reshuffling of the science classes, and he was now in the same class as Veronica.

After she sat down on the other side of the room, Fisher slipped another piece of paper out of his bag and set it on his desk, then pulled out a pencil.

Increase in social acknowledgement following TechX incident over time passed since, respect among scientific peers, reputation among students helped with homework . . . He scribbled in a few new variables and numbers.

8

Taking into account recent actions of V—Veronica, in the equations—*a careful measure of smiling ratio should yield answer . . . K.*

On the far right side of the equation, the point of all Fisher's tangled math and logic, was the letter K.

K: the exact moment in time when Fisher might get his first kiss from Veronica.

K: the idea was something so otherworldly to Fisher that the only way he could cope with it was in a form that he understood: symbols, variables, and strings of numbers. It was the way that he best understood the world. At the same time, he knew that, if it happened, the kiss itself wasn't going to take place on graph paper. And if— when!—an opportunity for K should arise, he didn't know *what* he would do. Was there a book he could read? Somebody he could ask?

His pencil worked like it had a mind of its own—and a frantic mind at that. The layers of equations scrawled along and filled out as Fisher added new variables to account for Veronica's recent behavior toward him. At first, when he'd embraced his new hero status, she had coldly shrugged him off. But he could tell that the new result was going to yield a much smaller value for K. He felt his face begin to go slack as the last few results added up.

He stared down at the new value of K. He blinked once.

9

K = Time until I kiss Veronica

$$\frac{i + (p+s)}{t} + \frac{V_s + V_d}{t - t_1} = K$$

let:

i = Increase in social acknowledgement
    following TechX incident

t = time in hours

p = respect among scientific peers

s = reputation among students helped
    with homework

V_s = number of smiles exchanged with Veronica

V_d = average smile duration in milliseconds
    (see log)

t_1 = time spent in locker, in hours

~~1698.27~~

$$\frac{i + (p+s)}{t} + \frac{V_s + V_d}{t - t_1} = \boxed{1214.008}$$

The number had indeed decreased by almost fifty percent—to only one thousand, two hundred fourteen years,
and three days. He looked back over at Veronica as she
neatly wrote the date at the top of her class notes. *Maybe
if I put both of us into long-term hibernation incryo-freeze
pods . . .*

"Good morning, everyone!"

Fisher was taken out of his reverie by the voice of
Ms. Snapper, Mr. Granger's replacement. She normally
taught eighth-grade science, but had agreed to take over
Mr. Granger's class until further notice. Fisher quickly
folded up his graph paper and slipped it into his bag.

Ms. Snapper was tall and slender, wore black, wire-
frame glasses, and had dark brown hair pulled back into
a ponytail. Since she had stepped in to teach the class
after Mr. Granger's mysterious disappearance, Fisher
had gotten to like her. Still, he had liked Mr. Granger,
too, and look how *that* had ended up. He was going to
need some more time before he could feel at ease in this
class, no matter who taught it.

"I've got a special announcement to make," Ms. Snapper said in a bright, cheerful voice. "You may remember
Mr. Granger was planning a trip this week," she said. "In
spite of the . . . unfortunate circumstances," she went on—
none of the teachers seemed sure how to talk about Mr.
Granger's vanishing act—"I spoke to the administration

and we're going to go ahead with our class trip to LA, where we'll get the privilege of seeing a taping of the popular TV program *Strange Science*! We'll depart midday this Friday and be back on Monday morning in time for third period."

Several people shouted and clapped; others sighed, clearly annoyed at the prospect of giving up a weekend for anything school related. Fisher felt like he could bounce out of his seat. He'd forgotten all about the proposed trip in light of the whole clone situation. Two was in LA! Now Fisher had a way to get there. This could be his chance to find his clone . . . before everyone else found out about him.

As an added bonus, *Strange Science* had become a late-afternoon favorite of his since it started airing. That was largely due to its host, who went by the name Dr. Devilish. He was tall and handsome, with a commanding presence and a smooth-talking charm—*and* he was an accomplished scientist. Fisher had never seen someone who had both academic and social skills. Dr. Devilish gave him hope for his own future.

"Because this trip takes place over the weekend," Ms. Snapper went on, "participation is strictly voluntary. So, can I get a show of interested students?"

Fisher's hand shot up first, and others followed. Some people were murmuring excitedly about Dr. Devilish;

others were obviously looking forward to missing half of Friday and two class periods on Monday.

Then Fisher saw Veronica's hand go up. His pulse started thudding. It was too good to be true. He quickly reached down and whipped out his graph paper. He scribbled with one hand as he kept the other up, trying to determine how going on this trip together might affect the value of K. Hopefully, enough to make it earlier than the year that Wompalog Middle School became an archaeological dig site.

"Ms. Snapper?" said Veronica.

"Yes . . . Veronica?" Ms. Snapper said, taking a moment to be sure she had her name right. "You have a question?"

"Is . . ." Veronica looked slightly embarrassed. "Do you think there's any chance we might get to meet Kevin Keels?"

Fisher dropped his pencil.

"Kevin Keels . . ." Ms. Snapper said, her eyes turning up in thought. "Is that an actor you like?"

Fisher felt like he'd just been slapped in the face with a frozen mackerel. Kevin Keels was the latest pop sensation, a thirteen-year-old whose ballads and dance hits were slowly creeping on to every radio station nationwide, as Veronica—as well as all the other girls in the class—hurried to explain to Ms. Snapper. The only reason Fisher

13

knew about the pop star's existence was that CURTIS, the artificial intelligence he'd freed from TechX that now resided in his computer, had been wailing Keels's incredibly annoying and brain-meltingly stupid songs for the past three weeks straight. And to top it off, Kevin Keels had just finished filming a movie about his rise to fame: *Keel Me Now.*

Which was more or less the thought that went through Fisher's head as he buried it in his hands, trying to drown out the excited chatter that filled the room.